THE BEST, MOST ADVENTUROUS WORK OF TODAY'S RISING NEW PLAYWRIGHTS

Actors at all levels of training and interest will find that this collection gives them stimulating, challenging material to use to hone their craft or as audition pieces. Here is bold, muscular, distinctively American theater, reflecting every region of the country. From the broad farce of Bruce and Charlotte's scene in Christopher Durang's BEYOND THERAPY to the terrifying power of Weston's monologue in Sam Shepard's CURSE OF THE STARVING CLASS, this innovative anthology offers a broad spectrum of the exciting new drama being produced on Broadway, Off-Broadway, Off-Off Broadway, and in regional and university theaters.

FRANK PIKE is a playwright and teacher whose work has been produced in New York and Los Angeles, among other U.S. cities. He has been a faculty member at the University of Minnesota and Middlebury College, and has received grants from the Mellon Foundation, the Bush Foundation, and the Jerome Foundation.

THOMAS G. DUNN is the Director of New Dramatists, the New York–based national organization. He is the founder of The Playwright's Center, a major Midwest playwriting organization, and the author of plays for both children and adults.

Pike and Dunn are co-authors of *The Playwright's Handbook* (Plume).

Scenes and Monologues from the New American Theater

EDITED BY
Frank Pike
and
Thomas G. Dunn

A MENTOR BOOK

MENTOR
Published by the Penguin Group
Penguin Books USA Inc., 375 Hudson Street,
New York, New York 10014, U.S.A.
Penguin Books Ltd, 27 Wrights Lane,
London W8 5TZ, England
Penguin Books Australia Ltd, Ringwood,
Victoria, Australia
Penguin Books Canada Ltd, 10 Alcorn Avenue,
Toronto, Ontario, Canada M4V 3B2
Penguin Books (N.Z.) Ltd, 182–190 Wairau Road,
Auckland 10, New Zealand

Penguin Books Ltd, Registered Offices:
Harmondsworth, Middlesex, England

Published by Mentor, an imprint of New American Library,
a division of Penguin Books USA Inc.

First Printing, March, 1988
11 10 9 8 7 6 5 4 3

 REGISTERED TRADEMARK—MARCA REGISTRADA

Library of Congress Catalog Card Number: 87-61677

Printed in the United States of America

To all of the playwrights who allowed us
to use their material in putting together
this book and to all the playwrights who
submitted material for consideration.

ACKNOWLEDGMENTS

To Spencer Beckwith, Claudia Reilly, Heidi Jo Edwards, and Eileen Fallon.

And especially to all of the agents who helped to get the permission forms that made this book possible, including Helen Merrill, Lois Berman, Luis Sanjurjo, Gil Parker, Howard Rosenstone, Lucy Kroll, Susan Schulman, Esther Sherman, Biff Liff, Sam Lockwood, Milton Goldman, Bret Adams, and Mary Harden.

And last but not least, Abbot Van Nostrand at Samuel French and Andrew Leslie at Dramatists' Play Service.

Contents

3. Scenes for Two Men

4. Monologues for Women

5. Monologues for Men

Foreword

Just when everyone was saying there were no more good American playwrights, enter Christopher Durang, Charles Fuller, Beth Henley, David Mamet, Marsha Norman, Sam Shepard, Wendy Wasserstein, August Wilson, Lanford Wilson, and many other exciting new writers, whose plays have won critical acclaim and audience support all over the country. And with good reason: the last decade or so has produced such beautifully crafted and absorbing plays as *Sister Mary Ignatius Explains It All for You, A Soldier's Play, Crimes of the Heart, Curse of the Starving Class, Isn't It Romantic, Ma Rainey's Black Bottom, Talley's Folly* . . . the list goes on and on.

This new breed of playwright, the product of a renaissance in theater, not only in New York, but in theaters across the country, has created a new kind of playwriting: muscular, bold, distinctively American, with fresh and idiosyncratic points of view reflecting every region of the country. In putting together *Scenes and Monologues from the New American Theater*, we have tried to include the best, the most adventurous work of today's rising new playwrights, material that actors at all levels of training and interest will find stimulating, challenging, and fun.

Many people will use this book for scene study and auditioning. Professional, amateur, and college acting classes encourage realistic, slice-of-life scenes and monologues that an actor-in-training can easily identify with. When talking about acting, realism is a relative term.

What was realistic in the thirties, forties, and fifties is a "style" now. Yet most collections cull their material from "realistic" American plays of the thirties, forties, and fifties—material that has little relevance to today's actor, except as an exercise in style. With the emphasis on the latest plays the American theater has to offer, written by up-and-coming playwrights from all backgrounds, from all parts of the country, the scenes and monologues in this book are realistic *and* relevant.

Sections One through Three are made up almost entirely of two-character scenes—for man/woman, woman/woman, and man/man teams. The scenes range from light comedy to domestic drama to broad farce to witty repartee to high tragedy, embracing the entire spectrum of modern theatrical styles, literally "something for everyone."

Sections Four and Five contain monologues for women and for men, respectively. An actor uses monologues for two purposes: as exercises in acting classes and, even more important, as audition pieces. As casting directors stress to their students time and time again in How to Audition classes, with only two or three minutes in an audition to win over a director, an interesting, unhackneyed audition piece is critical to survival. We have tried to provide the actor with winning monologues, from the down-to-earth to the outlandish, from simple and subtle dramatic monologues to bravura comedy.

In all five chapters, each selection is preceded by a brief description of the scene or monologue in the context of the play. When describing the piece, we've tried hard not to color the actor's interpretation of a particular character or moment in the play, but instead to provide the actor with the essentials, a starting point for imagination, exploration, and realization.

At the end of the book are two appendices that should prove helpful in finding yet more new material for scene study and auditions. The first appendix, "The Playwrights," provides a brief resume of each playwright whose work is included in the book. A listing of the playwright's representative work is part of this resume. If a particular playwright—especially a playwright who is unfamiliar to you—interests you, you can look at his or her other plays for more material to work with. The second appendix, "Where to Find New Plays," provides a guide for obtaining relatively unknown new plays—what agents, theater organizations, and specialty publishers to contact.

We hope you enjoy using *Scenes and Monologues from the New American Theater* as much as we enjoyed putting it together.

> —Frank Pike and Thomas G. Dunn
> *New York City*

1.

Scenes for A Man and A Woman

BEYOND THERAPY
by Christopher Durang

Beyond Therapy was written on a commission from the Phoenix Theatre in New York City and was produced by the Phoenix with Stephen Collins and Sigourney Weaver heading the cast. The play opened on Broadway at the Brooks Atkinson Theater the following year with John Lithgow and Dianne Wiest.

A farcical send-up of modern psychology and sexuality, *Beyond Therapy* traces the bizarre, on-again, off-again romance of a couple who meet through the personals column of *The New York Review of Books*. Prudence works at *People* magazine; Bruce is a bisexual, with a demanding lover. Things aren't strange enough, but the couple have to be coached by their lunatic psychiatrists, who have more than enough adjustment problems of their own. For instance, in the following scene between Bruce and his shrink, Charlotte Wallace . . .

The office of CHARLOTTE WALLACE. *Probably reddish hair, bright clothing; a Snoopy dog on her desk. If there are walls in the set around her, they have drawings done by children.*

CHARLOTTE [*into intercom*]: You may send the next patient in, Marcia. [*She arranges herself at her desk, smiles in anticipation. Enter* BRUCE. *He sits.*] Hello.

BRUCE: Hello. [*Pause*] Should I just begin?

CHARLOTTE: Would you like to begin?

BRUCE: I threw a glass of water at someone in a restaurant.

CHARLOTTE: Did you?

BRUCE: Yes.

CHARLOTTE: Did they get all wet?

BRUCE: Yes. [*Silence*]

CHARLOTTE [*points to child's drawing*]: Did I show you this drawing?

BRUCE: I don't remember. They all look alike.

CHARLOTTE: It was drawn by an emotionally disturbed three-year-old. His parents beat him every morning after breakfast. Orange juice, toast, Special K.

BRUCE: Uh huh.

CHARLOTTE: Do you see the point I'm making?

BRUCE: Yes, I do, sort of. [*Pause*] What point are you making?

CHARLOTTE: Well, the point is that when a porpoise first comes to me, it is often immediately clear . . . did I say porpoise? What word do I want? Porpoise. Pompous. Pom Pom. Paparazzi. Polyester. Pollywog. Olley olley oxen free. Patient. I'm sorry, I mean patient. Now what was I saying?

BRUCE: Something about when a patient comes to you.

CHARLOTTE [*slightly irritated*]: Well, give me more of a clue.

BRUCE: Something about the child's drawing and when a patient comes to you?

CHARLOTTE: Yes. No, I need more. Give me more of a hint.

BRUCE: I don't know.

CHARLOTTE: Oh I hate this, when I forget what I'm saying. Oh, damn. Oh, damn, damn, damn. Well, we'll just have to forge on. You say something for a while, and I'll keep trying to remember what I was saying. [*She moves her lips.*]

BRUCE [*after a bit*]: Do you want me to talk?

CHARLOTTE: Would you like to talk?

BRUCE: I had an answer to the ad I put in.

CHARLOTTE: Ad?

BRUCE: Personal ad.

CHARLOTTE [*remembering, happy*]: Oh, yes. Personal ad. I told you that was how the first Mr. Wallace and I met. Oh yes. I love personal ads. They're so basic. Did it work out for you?

BRUCE: Well, I liked her, and I tried to be emotionally open with her. I even let myself cry.

CHARLOTTE: Good for you!

BRUCE: But she didn't like me. And then she threw water in my face.

CHARLOTTE: Oh, dear. I'm so sorry. One has to be so brave to be emotionally open and vulnerable. Oh, you poor thing. I'm going to give you a hug. [*She hugs him.*] What did you do when she threw water in your face?

BRUCE: I threw it back in her face.

CHARLOTTE: Oh good for you! Bravo! [*She barks for Snoopy and bounces him up and down.*] Ruff, ruff, ruff! Oh, I feel you getting so much more emotionally expressive since you've been in therapy, I'm proud of you.

BRUCE: Maybe it was my fault. I probably came on too strong.

CHARLOTTE: Uh, life is so difficult. I know when I met the second Mr. Wallace . . . you know, it's so strange, all my husbands have had the same surname of Wallace, this has been a theme in my own analysis . . . Well, when I met the second Mr. Wallace, I got a filing cabinet caught in my throat . . . I don't mean a filing cabinet. What do I mean? Filing cabinet, frying pan, frog's eggs, faculty wives, frankincense, fornication, Folies Bergère, falling, falling, fork, fish fork, fish bone. I got a fish bone caught in my throat. [*Smiles. Long silence*]

BRUCE: And did you get it out?

CHARLOTTE: Oh yes. Then we got married, and we had quite a wonderful relationship for a while, but then he started to see this fishwife and we broke up. I don't mean fishwife, I mean waitress. Is that a word, waitress?

BRUCE: Yes. Woman who works in a restaurant.

CHARLOTTE: No, she didn't work in a restaurant, she worked in a department store. Sales . . . lady. That's what she was.

BRUCE: That's too bad.

CHARLOTTE: He was buying a gift for me, and then he ran off with the saleslady. He never even gave me the gift, he just left me a note. And then I was so very alone for a while. [*Cries. After a bit, he gives her a hug and a few kisses from the Snoopy doll. She is suitably grateful.*] I'm afraid I'm taking up too much of your session. I'll knock a few dollars off the bill. You talk for a while, I'm getting tired anyway.

BRUCE: Well, so I'm sort of afraid to put another ad in the paper since seeing how this one worked out.

CHARLOTTE: Oh, don't be afraid! Never be afraid to risk, to risk! I've told you about *Equus*, haven't I? That doctor, Doctor Dysart, with whom I greatly identify, saw that it was better to risk madness and to blind horses with a metal spike, than to be safe and conventional and dull. Ecc, ecc, equus! Naaaaaaay! [*For Snoopy*] Ruff ruff ruff!

BRUCE: So you think I should put in another ad?

CHARLOTTE: Yes I do. But this time, we need an ad that will get someone exceptional, someone who can appreciate your uniqueness.

BRUCE: In what ways am I unique? [*Sort of pleased*]

CHARLOTTE: Oh I don't know, the usual ways. Now let's see. [*Writing on pad*] White male, 30 to 35, 6'2", no—6'5", green eyes, Pulitzer Prize–winning author, into Kierkegaard, Mahler, Joan Didion and sex, seeks similar-minded attractive female for unique encounters. Sense of humor a must. Write box whatever whatever. There, that should catch you someone excellent. Why don't you take this out to the office, and my dirigible will type it up for you. I don't mean dirigible, I mean Saskatchewan.

BRUCE: Secretary.

CHARLOTTE: Yes, that's what I mean.

BRUCE: You know we haven't mentioned how my putting these ads in the paper for women is making Bob feel. He's real hostile about it.

CHARLOTTE: Who's Bob?

BRUCE: He's the guy I've been living with for a year.

CHARLOTTE: Bob. Oh dear. I'm sorry. I thought you were someone else for this whole session. You're not Thomas Norton?

BRUCE: No, I'm Bruce Lathrop.

CHARLOTTE: Oh, yes. Bruce and Bob. It all comes back now. Well I'm very sorry. But this is a good ad anyway, I think, so just bring it out to my dirigible, and then come on back in and we'll talk about something else for a while. I know, I mean secretary. Sometimes I think I should get my blood sugar checked.

BRUCE: Alright, thank you, Mrs. Wallace.

CHARLOTTE: See you next week.

BRUCE: I thought you wanted me to come right back to finish the session.

CHARLOTTE: Oh yes, see you in a few minutes. [*He exits.* CHARLOTTE *speaks into intercom.*] Marcia, dear, send in the next porpoise please. Wait, I don't mean porpoise, I mean . . . pony, Pekinese, parka, penis, no not that. I'm sorry, Marcia, I'll buzz back when I think of it. [*She moves her lips, trying to remember.*]

FENCES
by August Wilson

Originally performed in workshop at the Eugene O'Neill Theater Center's National Playwrights Conference, *Fences* was first presented by the Yale Repertory Theater in a production directed by Lloyd Richards, starring James Earl Jones.

It is the late fifties; the hot winds of change that would make the sixties a turbulent, racing, dangerous and provocative decade are beginning to blow. Troy Maxon, a fifty-three-year-old garbageman, was a brilliant young ball player, but he was not allowed to play in the major leagues because of his color. And he was too old to play when Jackie Robinson finally broke the color barrier. Stymied, bitter with the knowledge of what he could have been, Troy turns his bottled-up rage on his wife and children, destroying their chances for any real happiness, any real future.

Troy has been having an affair with a woman named Alberta. In the following scene, on the porch of their house, Troy and Rose learn that Alberta has died in childbirth.

TROY: What you want from me, Rose?
ROSE: I want you to act like my husband.
TROY: You ain't wanted me to act like your husband last night. You ain't wanted no part of me.
ROSE: You going down there to see her ain't you. You

going down there to be with her and then wanna come crawl in my bed.

TROY: I ain't gonna see nobody. I told you what I was gonna do.

ROSE: I ain't gonna stand for this too much longer. You living on borrowed time with me.

TROY: My whole life I been living on borrowed time.

ROSE: Troy, I want you to come home tomorrow after work.

TROY: Rose . . . I don't mess up my pay. You know that now. I takes my pay and I gives it to you. I don't have no money but what you give me back. I just want to have a little time to myself . . . a little time to enjoy life.

ROSE: Troy, I am you wife! What about me? When's my time to enjoy life?

TROY: I don't know what to tell you, Rose. I just don't know what to tell you. [*The telephone is heard ringing inside the house.* ROSE *exits into the house.* TROY *sits down on the steps of the porch. Presently* ROSE *returns.*]

ROSE: Troy. . . . There somebody on the phone from the hospital. They want to talk to you. They say it's about Alberta. [TROY *exits into the house.* ROSE *stands apprehensive, waiting, preparing herself for any possible scenario.* TROY *enters, pained and downcast.*]

ROSE: Troy, what is it? What's the matter?

TROY: Alberta died having the baby.

ROSE: No! . . . She's too young to die, Troy.

TROY: Death don't know nobody's age. Sometimes I don't even think he knows their name. The Bible say he comes like a thief in the night. You don't know how many times he comes before he finds you home.

ROSE: What about the baby? Is the baby alright?

TROY: Baby's alright. It's a girl. They say it's healthy.

ROSE: I'm sorry, Troy.

TROY: Yeah, so am I. Sorry ain't gonna do nothing.

ROSE: I ain't said it was gonna do nothing. [*Pause*] Who's gonna bury her.

TROY: She had family, Rose! She wasn't living in the world by herself!

ROSE [*With an edge*]: I know she wasn't living in the world by herself. I just asked who was gonna bury her.

TROY: What you care about who's gonna bury the woman? Next you gonna ask me if she had any insurance.

ROSE: I know you hurt, Troy . . . but you ain't got to act like that. That was a nasty thing to say.

TROY: That's the first thing that jumped out your mouth . . . "Who's gonna bury her?" Like I'm fixing to take on that task by myself.

ROSE: Troy, I ain't said that.

TROY: You may as well, that's what you thinking.

ROSE: I see I can't get no sense out of you. I'm going on back in the house. [ROSE *exits into the house.* TROY *walks to the edge of the yard and looks up at the sky.*]

TROY [*with a quiet rage that threatens to consume him*]: Alright. I been wading in the water. Yessir! I been walking all over the river Jordan. But what it get me, huh? What it get me? I done been baptized in the blood of the lamb and the fire of the Holy Ghost. But what I got, huh? Salvation? I got salvation? My enemies all around me picking the flesh from my bones. I'm choking on my own blood. And all you got to give me is salvation?

You done raised up the dry bones from the desert . . . you done parted the Red Sea . . . you done tumbled the walls of Jericho . . . you done taken Abraham and Jacob and fixed them in a high place . . . and you can't give Troy Maxon his due? Something wrong here. The Lord is my refuge and strength . . . that's what the Bible say. And every time I weaken in the face of adversity . . . every time I stretch out my hand toward you

. . . you reach out and slap me! Every time my enemies throw me down . . . you kick me! Now why's that? You can't stand the sight of an honest man? You don't recognize the face of the just? You wanna help give over my blood to my enemies?

I done give you everything you asked for. I don't have no other gods before you . . . I don't lie . . . I don't steal . . . I keep hold the sabbath . . . I don't covet my neighbors goods . . . I done give you everything! Every single day do I not say: Forgive me father my trespasses as I forgive those who trespass against me? Well, where's all this forgiveness of the Lord? You done visited trials and tribulations on me like falling rain and I answered every one! You done cast me down in the den of thieves and I walked through it like Daniel in the lion's den! You done burdened my heart with pain and I found a song to soothe it! The Bible say the Lord giveth. Well, where's my givings? Where's my milk and honey? I done paid up on the dues . . . but where's my benefits? Where's the salvation I can see? The Bible say "Thou shalt be with me this day in Paradise." This day! Not tomorrow! Well, where's my paradise? Where's my room in this mansion you talking about? Where's all these givings of the Lord? You ain't never done nothing but take from me! Now it's my turn! I'm asking for my givings. I ain't strode through the waters of Jordan for nothing! I ain't walked through the valley of the shadow of death to find nothing on the other side! I ain't turned my cheek to the hands of my enemies to be struck down! I'm asking for my givings! I'm standing here ready to collect. I'm standing here full lit by the fire of the Holy Ghost and I ain't fearing nothing! The Bible say it takes a mighty army to defeat the just! I'm asking for my givings. I want the salvation that belongs to me. I don't want nobody else's. I want what's mine. Then we be alright. In Jesus name. Amen.

SERENADING LOUIE
by Lanford Wilson

Serenading Louie was first performed at the Washington Theater Club in Washington, D.C. The play was reworked and subsequently performed by the Circle Repertory Company. A very successful revival was produced by Second Stage at the Public Theater in New York City.

The crises of being in your thirties—the careers on hold, the suffocating blandness of suburbia, the marriages that fall short of their expectations, the yearning for youth, for emotional connection—is the subject matter of *Serenading Louie*. The play is a portrait of two couples: Alex and Gabby, and Carl and Mary. Carl is a former athlete, a man who sits on his anger, who is willing to let things slide. For example, he cannot confront his wife, Mary, about the affair she is having with his accountant. He secretly hopes it will burn out, and Mary will come back to him. The following scene is a marvelous exercise in subtext—exploring the meaning beneath the words being spoken. Carl has stayed home from work, so he's there as Mary is dressing for her rendezvous with their accountant. Mary, of course, doesn't let on where she's going. What's more, Carl doesn't let on he knows about the whole affair. What the characters say, floating on top of what they want to say, mean to say, but avoid saying, makes the scene both poignant and funny.

Early evening. CARL *is standing in the middle of the room.* MARY *enters from the bedroom, carrying her shoes. She is getting dressed, will put on the shoes, belt, scarf, etc. during the scene.*

MARY: Gabby scares me. I don't know if she scares me or if she's freaking out and imagining it: someone keeps following her.

CARL: Man or woman?

MARY: Oh, she's a very sweet girl. You should indulge her sometimes. She's scared.

CARL: I just asked if it was a man or woman. [CARL *crosses to* MARY *to zip her dress.*]

MARY: A man but not like that. Oldish, very distinguished, she thought. Very unlike a rapist. [CARL *has slipped his arms around her.*] Is your watch right? I've got to split. Hat, gloves, purse, shoes, what?

CARL: Keys, list . . .

MARY: What list?

CARL: Did you have a list?

MARY: No list.

CARL: Umbrella?

MARY: It wouldn't dare. Purse, scarf, shoes, gloves, keys, no list . . . [CARL *crosses to the closet and gets* MARY'S *coat.*]

CARL: I thought it was a party for someone's birth . . .

MARY [*crosses to the desk.*]: Right! Right . . . present! Thank God, that's all I'd need. [MARY *takes it from the desk, putting it into her purse.* CARL *follows to the desk.*] Present. Keys in purse. Pencil for bridge scores . . . Anyone else we'd make it during the week, but Sue works. If you'd let me know you weren't going in today. Now, you're not going to forget to pick up Ellie at five-forty. She hates walking home carrying her ballet slippers.

CARL: Check.

MARY: She loves the class; she just doesn't like the school. Take her night bag, drop her at Bunny's,

I've got her PJ's and all her paraphernalia already in it.

CARL: I know, I know.

MARY: And you'll remember to turn off the oven when the bell rings.

CARL [*in a thicker mood than she*]: I'll not forget.

MARY: Chicken pot pie; it's no good burned. You're going to forget, aren't you?

CARL [*smiling*]: No, no, what's to forget. The bell rings, turn off the oven.

MARY: There's bologna and cheese in the fridge if you forget. It should be time by now.

CARL: You're going to pick up Sue?

MARY: Sue and Alice; I'm late, you're right. [MARY *crosses to the front door.*]

CARL [*frowning, reluctantly*]: Honey, I'd like to . . . [CARL *halts, looking at her. She looks to him. All movement and sound are arrested for a count of fifteen.*]

MARY: [*A rapid, overlapping exchange now*] What, doll?

CARL: Talk, you know.

MARY: I know . . . we will. Nothing's wrong is there? [MARY *crosses to the living room.*]

CARL: No, no.

MARY: With that Atlanta business?

CARL: No, no.

MARY [*still lightly*]: What is it?

CARL: No, no, it's nothing.

MARY: We're running all over, we're never home together, I know . . .

CARL: It's nothing, Mary, I just get . . . edgy . . . it'll pass.

MARY [*She crosses to CARL, maneuvering him to the sofa.*] I know, baby. It'll pass. [*She sits, smiling.*] Sit a second.

CARL: It's OK, no, it'll . . .

MARY: Sit a second. [*She pulls him down to sit beside her, relaxes.*]

CARL: No, I never know when I'm going to be here; even Ellie, with her new schedule . . .

MARY: Oh, but she loves it . . .

CARL: No, no, I think it's great. She's a little lady . . . a little goddess.

MARY: I don't think Ellie would respond well to being worshipped. I know I wouldn't.

CARL: Sure you do.

MARY: Do you like the shadow puppet?

CARL: Yeah. He's cute; it's cute.

MARY: A little fierce, but I thought he was amusing. He's about a thousand years old . . . well, old in any case, they said. He's parchment.

CARL: They had puppet shows back then? And we think we're so advanced.

MARY: I wouldn't think they'd be much like ours. I mean it's not Punch and Judy. I think it's more closely related to religious stories, like for children, but not just . . .

CARL: Bible school.

MARY: Well, it wouldn't be "Bible." Their equivalent . . . "Bhagavad-Gita Illustrated" or whatever. *Bible school?* Did you do that?

CARL [*laughing*]: No, I don't think I managed . . . that was summertime; would have interfered with softball practice, but Sunday School . . . I went to that every Sunday, bright and early. Well, nine o'clock.

MARY: I can't imagine. What did you do?

CARL: What did . . .

MARY: What was it like? Did you like it?

CARL: Oh, yeah . . . I liked . . . Well, there wasn't any question of not liking . . . it was this thing you did. We, ah . . . what was it . . . ? We all had these . . . our own . . . like pulp-paper quarterlies— thin little magazines that we were taught from— with orange and black illustrations of young Jesus, aged eleven, in the temple astonishing the . . .

MARY: Whoever. Right . . .

CARL: And we were taught by the judge's daughter or his son or some such, and they were seventeen, probably, and knew all the psalms by heart. Especially the twenty-third. "Valley of the shadow of death, I will fear no evil for Thou art with me. Thy rod and Thy staff, they comfort me . . ." [*He sighs.* MARY *is polite attention personified.*] Oh, God . . . and uh . . . when it was someone's birthday . . . their ninth or tenth, we sang: "Ebert's had a birthday, we're so glad. Let us see how many he has had." [MARY, *charmed, has been laughing at this.*]

MARY: Oh, that's wonderful. *Ebert?*

CARL: Well, I just picked Ebert at random, there were some pretty incredible names. We had a boy named Dillard and twin girls called Ima Daisy and Ura Pansy . . .

MARY: Ura Pansy . . . no . . . nobody would saddle a kid with . . .

CARL: Swear to God. Ima Daisy and Ura Pansy Maggard. That kinda ruins it, doesn't it?

MARY: How can you remember that? How do you remember that tune?

CARL: How do you forget it? I learned it before "Happy Birthday to You." And Ebert had brought pennies and he dropped them into his round cardboard Quaker Oats box with that very severe Quaker in this flat hat . . . and the pennies hit the bottom and bounced like dropping on a drum. Or it might have been—that's funny—a milk bottle with tin foil over the cap—I remember them both—and in that case they jingled around in the glass. [*Beat*] I can hear them both. Anyway, as Ebert . . .

MARY: [*laughing*]: Ebert.

CARL: Well, or Dillard. We sang, "How old are you?" and Dillard dropped his pennies and we all counted. One. Two. Three. Four. Five. Up to eight or nine, or sometimes very dramatically, "Ten!" and we all . . . you know, the boys . . . watched those nine years go into the bottle and longed to be twenty-one and have a draft card . . .

MARY: I can't imagine . . .

CARL: Or at least sixteen and have our driver's license, and my Aunt Grace used to say, "Don't wish your life away." Then when the teacher, the mayor's daughter, or sheriff's son, had a birthday, he played too and . . .

MARY: Of course.

CARL: . . . and that was an Event that lasted forever because he had to drop eighteen drumming pennies into that—

MARY: Or the other . . . the milk bottle.

CARL: Right. And it seemed to last half the Sunday School period.

MARY: I'm sure.

CARL: That was an Event . . . kids came from the other classrooms to watch. Everything was an Event then. The smallest thing that happened was an Event.

MARY: Of course.

CARL: And we don't have those anymore. Why is that? What's happened? [*He slides from his mood, back closer to his first one.*]

MARY [*still quizzical*]: What?

CARL: I don't know. That wars and deaths, birthdays, Easter, even Christmas. Nothing gets to me like that now. [*A slight pause*] Things go by and nothing reaches us, does it? Nothing's an Event anymore.

MARY: Ummm. [*Pause. She jingles the keys.*]

CARL [*more or less coming out of it for her benefit*]: You've got to go.

MARY: Oh, I know. [*Getting up*] Now, I'm not going to tell you about the pie again—if it burns, there's bologna and cheese.

CARL: Turn off the oven; pick up Ellie at five-forty. Take her overnight bag . . . Drop her at Bunny's.

MARY: You'll be all right. Can we go out tomorrow

night? Would you like that? I think I would. Just us?

CARL: Great. Saturday night . . .

MARY: Dinner and maybe a movie . . . I'd like that . . . we can call Betty to stay with Ellen. OK? I'd love that.

CARL: It's a deal.

MARY: OK, now, I've got to run. If the girls call, tell them I've left. [*She kisses him on the top of the head.*] OK?

CARL: OK. Right.

MARY [*opening the door*]: Bye-bye, sweetheart.

CARL: Bye-bye. [*MARY leaves. CARL crosses to the sofa, his smile fades, he looks down to the floor with a worried look; after a count of ten, he looks up to the audience with a sense of urgency. The buzzer sounds in the kitchen, offstage. CARL turns his head to the sound.*]

TWO MASTERS
by Frank Manley

The Rain of Terror was produced at the Actors Theater of Louisville, as part of the Humana Festival of New American Plays. The play, one of two short plays under the umbrella title, *Two Masters,* had previously been produced by Theater Emory in conjunction with the Atlanta New Play Project.

Oletta Crews and James Terry Crews live in a house trailer somewhere in Georgia. They tell the story of how Q. B. Ferris, who murdered two men when he escaped from a nearby prison work camp, came to their house on a stormy evening, and why, despite

Ferris's seemingly real affection for them, they decided to kill him. In the following scene, Oletta and James describe the murder. They talk directly to the audience, addressing them as if it was a third character in the play.

JAMES TERRY CREWS [*prompting*]: You were afraid.

OLETTA CREWS: Yes.

JAMES TERRY CREWS: You killed him because you were afraid.

OLETTA CREWS: Yes. [*And then*] I didn't kill him.

JAMES TERRY CREWS: I killed him.

OLETTA CREWS [*shouting*]: Don't listen to him. Listen to me. He don't know nothing.

JAMES TERRY CREWS [*explaining to the audience*]: I don't know nothing.

OLETTA CREWS: He just did it. I heard the voice.

JAMES TERRY CREWS [*explaining*]: She heard the voice. I'm the one murdered him.

OLETTA CREWS [*shouting*]: It wasn't a murder. The police said that. They say, "You shoot whoever you want to, lady, breaks in your house and keeps you hostage."

JAMES TERRY CREWS: Damn right, wouldn't you? [*Explaining*] She was afraid he might kill her.

OLETTA CREWS: Yes, and I was afraid he might kill him too [*indicating her husband*]. I need him to help me. Besides, I heard the voice. It spoke in my heart. [*And then she stops, as though reflecting.*] You can't serve two masters. That's what it said. "No man can serve two masters: for either he will hate the one, and love the other; or else he will hold to the one and despise the other." I thought how to do it.

JAMES TERRY CREWS: How to kill him.

OLETTA CREWS: I thought of ways how to do it. Like roach tablets, putting them in his grits at breakfast, and then I thought: What if they don't work? What if they just work on roaches? Then I thought

of rat poison. But what if it tastes funny? Draino.
That's too strong. Lysol and Clorox. He might
have to drink a gallon. Poison is out.

JAMES TERRY CREWS: I told her about the nail.

OLETTA CREWS: That was later, when he went to bed.

JAMES TERRY CREWS [*begins*]: In the ear . . .

OLETTA CREWS [*shouting*]: It was all over by then. I
already figured it out. He said, "What about a
nail?" And I said "A nail?" And he said, "I read
about it in the paper."

JAMES TERRY CREWS: No, I didn't. It was in the *Police
Gazette*, in the Charlotte, North Carolina, bus
station. I was there waiting, and I went to the
newsstand and picked up the magazines like you
do, looking for pictures . . .

OLETTA CREWS: They got pictures of half-naked women
where they been raped in the *Police Gazette*. That's
what he was looking at.

JAMES TERRY CREWS: No, I wasn't. I was just looking,
waiting for the time to pass till I got my bus, and I
picked up the *Police Gazette*, and the first thing I
turned to, that was it. Nail Murder. All about
how this farmer in Kansas and this girlfriend he
got killed her husband by driving a thirty penny
nail in his ear. [JAMES TERRY CREWS *glances about*.]
They killed him by driving a nail in his ear.
[*Leaning forward*] You know why they did that?

OLETTA CREWS [*breaking in, shouting*]: So it wouldn't
be a wound. They know that. That nail went in,
and they wiped up the blood and burned the rag
and called the doctor and said, "He rose up in the
bed and shouted and fell over dead." And the
doctor didn't even look in the ear. Said, "Must
have been a heart attack." And they almost got
away with it except for the farmer. He went crazy
and confessed it all. Otherwise they'd have joined
the farms, his and the one she got from the murder, and made a million dollars by now selling it
off for shopping centers.

JAMES TERRY CREWS: You ever hear anything like that?

That's what you call a perfect crime, except he went crazy.

OLETTA CREWS: That's where he went wrong. That's why it ain't perfect. So I told him the nail was out. [*Intimately to the audience*] I even thought of cutting his throat. Waiting till he was asleep and then creep in the light at the end of the hall shining in so we could see the vein in his neck beating and then pull the razor across it. But what if the gristle was too hard to cut through? I ain't that strong, and I knew he couldn't do it [*indicating her husband*]. He can talk about nails all he wants to, but he couldn't even hold it still. He's too soft. He might look at him and feel sorry for him. I couldn't chance it. I didn't want Duke getting up, throat flapping open from ear to ear where I cut at it and him not dead. Ain't no telling what he might do, bleeding like that, bubbling and shouting. He'd kill me for sure. That's when I knew James Terry have to shoot him.

JAMES TERRY CREWS: I had to. You heard her.

OLETTA CREWS [*shouting*]: Hold on. Don't rush ahead. They ain't finished the dishes yet. I got out of the bathroom and they came in and sat down, and James Terry said, "Duke's been telling me about all the good times they had in the work camp. He liked it there." And I said, "If he liked it so much, why didn't he stay? Why come around here bothering us?" And then he says, "What's on TV?" And I said, "Nothing." And he says, "They got 'Monday Night Football'?" And I said, "I don't watch it. I don't know the rules." And he said, "What about you, old dad?"—meaning my husband, James Terry Crews.

JAMES TERRY CREWS: I said I don't watch it either. It's too rough.

OLETTA CREWS: That's right. I told him, "That game's all right for the work camp," I said. "Rough men done worse than that to each other every day of their lives, but it ain't all right for women and children. It's too rough. Besides which," I told him, "it ain't Monday night." And he said, "Not Monday?" And I said, "That's right. Yesterday was Monday. This is Tuesday." And he laughed at that and said, "Lord God," and grinned like he just ate something he shouldn't.

JAMES TERRY CREWS: He had this kind of shit-eating grin.

OLETTA CREWS: It was attractive. I don't mean that. He said, "I can keep up with it in the work camp. It's when I get out. That's when I lose track." And I said, "How many times you get out?" And he said every chance he got. That and Monday Night Football's his only pleasure, he said, that and beating up on folks to get in the work camp in the first place. "And grinning," I said. "You left out grinning." And he laughed and said, "That's right, momma. That's the only pleasure I got, that and being here with you. What about going to bed?" And I thought this is when the raping commences. And I said, "Not me. I don't go to bed and get raped." And you know what he did? [*Pause*] He laughed. [*Indignantly*] He fell on the floor like he couldn't stand up and kicked his feet in the air, pretending. Looked like the devil come up through the floor from hell. And he said, "Momma, you ever think you gonna get raped, you know what I'd do?" But I didn't answer. I was too ashamed, and he laughed and said, "I'd stay up instead. I'd stay up all night before I'd go to bed and get raped." And so on like that. But I didn't look at him. I heard him scrabbling around down there at my feet, but I didn't dare cast my eyes on him to see what nasty things he was doing.

JAMES TERRY CREWS: He was getting up.

OLETTA CREWS: I didn't want to see what it was for fear it might be something I didn't want to. That's how he was. He didn't care. Then I felt him lean over me grinning and mocking, and say what he meant was for me to go to one bed and him to another and sleep this time, if that was all right with me. And that's when I knew there wasn't no way. Even if I could have saved him before, I knew I couldn't after that. [*Pause*] I was a prisoner in my own house.

JAMES TERRY CREWS [*intimately to the audience*]: He trusted us. He said, "I sleep light, but I trust you anyway, old dad. I know you don't want me to go back to the work camp for nine more years." And he said to Mrs. Crews, "Wake me for breakfast you hear me, momma? Don't let me oversleep my welcome. I'm just going to rest a minute. Then I'm going to have to leave you, much as you hate to see me go."

OLETTA CREWS [*shouting*]: And I thought then, to California. He's going to California without me and leave me alone and take all the money. And that's when I told James Terry to kill him. I said, "Go get your gun."

SCENES AND REVELATIONS
by Elan Garonzik

Scenes and Revelations had its world premiere at Chicago's Goodman Theater. It was produced Off-Broadway at The Production Company and on Broadway at Circle in the Square. The play has received numerous regional theater playwriting awards, including the Mark Klein Award, the Audrey Wood National Playwriting Award, and the Los Angeles Drama-Logue Award.

A bittersweet tale of first love, *Scenes and Revelations* focuses on the lives of four sisters living in rural Pennsylvania at the turn of the century. The following scene is between the eldest sister, Helena, and Samuel, the man she has hired to manage the family's farm. Samuel is a New Englander, bent on a life in California, and he has only stopped in Lancaster County to earn a little money before continuing his journey west. Helena's parents have been dead for many years, but she has successfully managed to raise and educate her younger sisters. Now that the youngest sister is married and off living in Nebraska, Helena can finally pay some attention to her own dreams and desires, even though she is unsure of exactly what they are. She is attracted to Samuel's poetic spirit, and to discover the extent of her feelings she has plotted a little time alone with him; she has asked him to come down to this corner of the farm to go over the ledger and accounts when normally this task would have been done up in the house.

It is summer—one of those late June days in Pennsylvania when the sudden heat and humidity take you by surprise, marking the sure end of Spring. We are at the raspberry patch, imagined. HELENA *stands downright; she has a flirtatious and expectant look on her face; she's opened her blouse a bit and has a handkerchief in her sleeve—during the scene she'll dab her forehead and neck with it. The bushes run downstage along the apron.* SAMUEL *stands a few feet back, center stage, where he has placed a wooden bucket with a ladle in it. He has unbuttoned his collar a bit, and also has a handkerchief to wipe his face. Though they've known each other for weeks, this is a first date.*

SAMUEL: [*He holds a rather large black ledger; they are going over the farm's receipts.*] And we spent seven dollars on new planking for the barn. The fence on the north acres needs some more wire. I ordered it, but until it comes, I've asked the men not to use it.

HELENA [*not terribly concerned*]: Did you pay them?

SAMUEL: Gave Jake and Scottie twenty extra. For the work they did last April. Think I should've given them more?

HELENA [*dabs her neck and smiles*]: Did you have it? [*Turns her back to him, facing the audience. She opens her collar flirtatiously.*]

SAMUEL: No. Not really. But they're good boys, and this way they won't mind some extra work. Scottie's getting married, you know. And we went through the supplies last week.

HELENA [*laughs*]: You always say "we."

SAMUEL: I beg your pardon.

HELENA: You always say "we." We did this. We did that. Isn't there just one of you?

SAMUEL: It's just an expression. Do you want me to go on with this? [*She smiles and shakes her head.*]

HELENA: Scottie's getting married. Does that mean we'll have to look for someone else then?

SAMUEL: Oh, I think he's happy.

HELENA: And yourself?

SAMUEL: Oh I'm very happy.

HELENA: No, I mean California. I just want to be— well, you know—*prepared* for when you leave. Do you know?

SAMUEL [*plays with her*]: Well . . . *we* looked at *our* savings last week—

HELENA [*mock admonition*]: You. Singular, Samuel. *You* looked at *your* savings last week. [*They both smile.*]

SAMUEL: It's the heat.

HELENA: I know. June twenty-first, the first day of summer, and just look at these raspberries. Already rotting on the vine. If this is June, good god I don't want to even think about July. Or August.

SAMUEL [*who has moved to get a drink of water from the bucket*]: Sun should go down in a few minutes. Then it should cool off some. Water?

HELENA [*turns her back to him again*]: I'll go up to the house soon and make some tea. [SAMUEL *looks at her back, then decides to take off his shirt, and does so while she's talking.*] My father planted these raspberries. I've always been surprised that something so good can come from so little labor. So. You didn't answer me. [*Stoops*] If you're going to California, I'd just like to know [*stands up*] —when you think you'll be [*turns to face him*] leaving. Oh.

SAMUEL: You don't mind, do you? [*Turns to pick up the ledger from the ground—she doesn't take her eyes off him.*] Listen. Maybe we should just go back to the ledger.

HELENA [*turning away*]: May I say something? I mean would you be awfully insulted if—

SAMUEL: Helena, no please, go right ahead.

HELENA: I know everyone's moving west. There's this great wave across the continent right now. But surely you're a little bit more objective. Surely you can't believe San Francisco's paved with gold, no matter what they say. You understand, do as you please. I just don't want you to go off to California. And then be surprised.

SAMUEL: I won't be.

HELENA: That's all I wanted.

SAMUEL: And I'm not going to California to be rich.

HELENA [*realizing things got a bit testy*]: Really. This is most unfortunate. I only meant—

SAMUEL: Haven't you ever thought to go west, Helena? Just to forget about the farm, wave goodbye to your sisters . . . And head out west past the Rockies?

HELENA: Well, I imagine, at one time or another . . . But you must understand, Samuel. I've obligations. And responsibilities.

SAMUEL: Well so have I. But to myself. I count myself first.

HELENA: That's where we—[*catches her frank tone, but not in time to change it*]—differ then. Really. I shouldn't have asked you down here. We could've gone over the ledger up in the house. Where it's cooler.

SAMUEL: Haven't you ever looked over that hill where the sun's setting right now? Haven't you ever thought life's just got to be, it just has to be better than *what is?* I'm going to California, Helena, because I'm awful tired of the East Coast. I'm tired of the milkman and the doctor and the paper everyday. Everyone's always coming at you, telling you what to do, what to think. Well, I've had enough. And as soon as I've saved up enough money, I'm getting out. And if you'd any sense about you, you'd want to get out also. You'd kiss Millie and Charlotte goodbye, sell this place, and— [*Stops himself.*]

HELENA: And what?

SAMUEL: And nothing.

HELENA: But you must have meant something?

SAMUEL: You sit here—I've seen you—on the back porch—late at night. You want something. When are you going to say: Me. It's my chance. What I want. Me! [*Offers her water.*]

HELENA [*moves to take it from him; he moves away*]: I said that once. I did. But it was a very long time ago. And no one listened anyway.

SAMUEL: Why didn't you sell the farm when your father died? [HELENA *makes a motion with her hand, as if to say something, but doesn't.*] I'm sorry.

HELENA [*still caught up in this, she moves downleft*]: There's no need to be sorry.

SAMUEL: You don't have to answer. I mean you don't even have to answer yourself. Oh—there it goes! —Just a thin slip of red left . . . there, on the bottom of the sky. [*She faces him.*] And now! . . . [*moves to downright*] And now!—gone. Forever. All the light of June twenty-first, the first day of summer, eighteen ninety-four: gone forever. And we'll never see it again. [*Pause*] Listen. You can just begin to hear the crickets.

HELENA [*after a moment*]: There are some things in life, Samuel, that are so private. Things that should . . . shouldn't be said to just anyone. After mother died and father was so sick—I was very young: very young and very pretty and very smart. My goodness, Spring slides into your life. And suddenly you're a young woman instead of a girl. Suddenly the idea of sharing your life with someone: that doesn't seem like such a silly notion anymore. There was one young man in particular: Jason Armstrong. The son of Mr. Armstrong of the bank in town. I think you know him. [*Repeats the name to herself, smiling.*] Jason Armstrong. It was the summer right after my commencement. Every day had a breeze and—my god, there are times in life when everything's so perfect. Every day you wake up to sun on your lace curtains—And the whole house smells of lilacs. You want to hang onto it, clutch it, bag it up for those not so perfect days that lie ahead. We spent much of that summer together, Jason and I. Yet father was so sick. Spitting up blood. Passing water on his bedsheets so I had to change them every day. When August came, I said to myself: god, father dies and this family's going to fall apart like pick up sticks. However, Jason had just finished college and was going to New York to work for his uncle. One day, in late August, a day like today when the heat really did come upon us, I said to Jason: Please! Take me away. I don't want to live here anymore. Please, marry me! And that was it . . . Jason said I didn't love him—all I really wanted was escape. And that was it . . . Like some train stopped and I was asked to disembark at this station. Where I still am. Where I've proved with utter vengeance how very little I wanted escape. And am as you find me today: Sitting on the back porch. Pulling stems off blades of grass. [*They look at one another a moment.*] Really. I should've kept this to the ledger.

SAMUEL: Come with me.

HELENA: What?

SAMUEL: I said come with me. To California. With me. [*Moves to her.*]

HELENA: I can't.

SAMUEL: Yes you can, Helena. It's not—

HELENA: No, Samuel, I can't. It's unthinkable. [*She turns to go, he grabs her hand and forces her to face him.*]

SAMUEL: Helena, I've been looking at you. Night after night. Seeing that you want—

HELENA: Samuel, please, let go of me!

SAMUEL: You've been here all these years. Waiting for something. Looking out, asking for so much to come to you.

HELENA: Samuel, please!

SAMUEL: Wanting so much. Desiring so much. [*She struggles a moment to be free. He pulls her towards him and kisses her with strength.*]

OPEN ADMISSIONS
by Shirley Lauro

Open Admissions was first performed by the Ensemble Studio Theater as part of their annual one-act festival. The play was named one of the ten best plays of 1981 by *The New York Times* and won the Dramatists' Guild Award for "outstanding play of the year on a controversial theme" and the Samuel French Playwriting Award. A full-length version of the play opened the next year at the Long Wharf Theater in New Haven, Connecticut; another production of the full-length version subsequently opened on Broadway.

Calvin Jefferson, a disadvantaged black student, attends a city college in New York under an open admissions policy. The system pushes him towards graduation despite his fifth grade reading level. For instance, his speech professor, Alice Miller, gives him a B on every assignment, no matter how poor the presentation. Frustrated and angry at the whole sham of his "education," Calvin approaches his professor in her office, demanding to actually be taught. Alice, a Shakespearean scholar relegated to teaching entry-level speech courses to uninterested undergraduates, is every bit as bitter with anger, every bit as disappointed over a promise unfulfilled as Calvin.

ALICE: Oh, Calvin, what are you arguing about? You did a good job!
CALVIN: "B" job, right?

ALICE: Yes.

CALVIN [*crosses to* ALICE]: Well, what's that "B" standin for? Cause I'll tell you somethin you wanna know the truth: I stood up there didn' hardly know the sense a anythin I read, couldn't hardly even read it at all. Only you didn't notice. Wasn't even listenin, sittin there back a the room jiss thumbin through your book. [ALICE *crosses to desk*.] So you know what I done? Skip one whole paragraph, tess you out—you jiss kep thumbin through your book! An then you give me a "B"! [*He has followed* ALICE *to desk*.]

ALICE [*puts papers in box and throws out old coffee cup*]: Well that just shows how well you did the part!

CALVIN: You wanna give me somethin I could "identify" with, how come you ain' let me do that other dude in the play . . .

ALICE: Iago?

CALVIN: Yeah. What is it they calls him? Othello's . . .

ALICE: Subordinate.

CALVIN: Go right along there with my speech syndrome, wouldn' it now? See, Iago has to work for the Man. I identifies with him! He gits jealous man. Know what I mean? Or that Gravedigger? Shovelin dirt for his day's work! How come you wouldn't let me do him? Thass the question I wanna ax you!

ALICE [*turns to* CALVIN]: "Ask" me, Calvin, "Ask" me!

CALVIN [*steps SR*]: "Ax" you? Okay, man. [*Turns to* ALICE] Miss Shakespeare, Speech Communications 1! [*Crosses US of* ALICE] Know what I'll "ax" you right here in this room, this day, at this here desk right now? I'll "ax" you how come I have been in this here college three months on this here Open Admissions an I don't know nothin more than when I came in here? You know what

I mean? This supposed to be some big break for me. This here is where all them smart Jewish boys has gone from the Bronx Science and went an become some Big Time Doctors at Bellvue. An some Big Time Judges in the Family Court an like that there. And now it's supposed to be my turn. [ALICE *looks away and* CALVIN *crosses R of* ALICE.] You know what I mean? [*He crosses UR.*] An my sister Jonelle took me out of foster care where I been in six homes and five schools to give me my chance. [*He crosses DR.*] Livin with her an she workin three shifts in some "Ladies Restroom" give me my opportunity. An she say she gonna buss her ass git me this education I don't end up on the streets! [*Crosses on a diagonal to* ALICE] Cause I have got *brains*! [ALICE *sits in student chair.* CALVIN *crosses in back, to her left.*] You understand what I am Communicatin to you? My high school has tole me I got brains an can make somethin outta my life if I gits me the chance! And now this here's supposed to be my chance! High school says you folks gonna bring me up to date on my education and git me even. Only nothin is happenin to me in my head except I am gettin more and more confused about what I knows and what I don't know! [*He sits in swivel chair.*] So what I wanna "ax" you is: How come you don't sit down with me and teach me which way to git my ideas down instead of givin me a "B". [ALICE *rises and crosses UR.*] I don't even turn no outline in? Jiss give me a "B". [*He rises and crosses R of* ALICE.] An Lester a "B"! An Melba a "B"! An Sam a "B"! What's that "B" standin for anyhow? Cause it surely ain't standin for no piece of work!

ALICE: Calvin don't blame me! [CALVIN *crosses DR.*] I'm trying! God knows I'm trying! The times are rough for everyone. I'm a Shakespearean scholar, and they have me teaching beginning Speech. I was supposed to have 12 graduate students a class, 9 classes a week, and they gave me 35 Freshmen a class, 20 classes a week. I hear 157 speeches a week! You know what that's like? And I go home late on the subway scared to death! In graduate school they told me I'd have a first rate career. Then I started here and they said: "Hang on! Things will improve!" But they only got worse . . . and worse! Now I've been here for twelve years and I haven't written one word in my field! I haven't read five research books! I'm exhausted . . . and I'm finished! We all have to bend. I'm just hanging on now . . . supporting my little girl . . . earning a living . . . and that's all . . . [*She crosses to desk.*]

CALVIN [*faces* ALICE]: What I'm supposed to do, feel sorry for you? Least you can *earn* a livin! Clean office, private phone, name on the door with all them B.A.'s, M.A.'s, Ph.D.'s.

ALICE: You can have those too. [*She crosses DR to* CALVIN.] Look, last year we got 10 black students into Ivy League Graduate Programs. And they were no better than you. They were just *perceived* [*points to blackboard*] as better. Now that's the whole key for you . . . to be perceived as better! So you can get good recommendations and do well on interviews. You're good looking and ambitious and you have a fine native intelligence. You can make it, Calvin. All we have to do is work on improving your Positive Communicator's Image . . . by getting rid of that Street Speech. Don't you see?

CALVIN: See what? What you axin *me* to see?

ALICE: "Asking" me to see, Calvin. "Asking" me to see!

CALVIN [*starts out of control at this, enraged, crosses UC and bangs on file cabinet*]: Ooooeee! Ooooeee! You wanna *see*? You wanna *see*? Ooooeee!

ALICE: Calvin stop it! STOP IT!

CALVIN: "Calvin stop it?" "Stop it?" [*Picks up school books from desk.*] There any black professors here?

ALICE [*crosses UR*]: No! They got cut . . . the budget's low . . . they got . . .

CALVIN [*interrupting*]: *Cut? They* got CUT? [*Crosses to* ALICE *and backs her to the DS edge of desk.*] Gonna *cut you,* lady! Gonna cut you, throw you out the fuckin window, throw the fuckin books out the fuckin window, burn it all mother fuckin down, FUCKIN DOWN!!!

ALICE: Calvin! Stop it! STOP IT! YOU HEAR ME?

CALVIN [*turns away, center stage*]: I CAN'T!! *YOU* HEAR *ME*? I CAN'T! *YOU* HEAR *ME*! I CAN'T! YOU GOTTA GIVE ME MY EDUCATION! GOTTA TEACH ME! GIVE ME SOMETHING NOW! GIVE ME NOW! NOW! NOW! NOW! NOW! NOW!

LEVITATION
by Timothy Mason

Since *Levitation* was first presented by the Circle Repertory Company, the play has proved popular with regional and community theaters across the country.

Joe, an aspiring playwright, presently writing headlines for a New York tabloid, returns to his childhood home in Minneapolis to find sanctuary from the disappointments of a career going nowhere and a love life going sour. During the early morning hours of an August night full of shooting stars, he confronts his rather dotty parents, his sister, his lover . . . his past. As the play progresses, the audience begins to realize that none of the people Joe sees are actually present on the front porch of his childhood home; rather, they are ghosts, the conjurings of a homesick young man who cannot cope with his parents' mortality. In the following scene, Joe and his mother, Ada, talk about their relationship and Joe's part genius, part oddball father.

ADA: He doesn't need to see any shooting *stars*, for goodness sake. At something o'clock in the *morning*.

JOE: Can't you just let things happen for once? It's important to him.

ADA [*irritated*]: Just let things happen? For once?

JOE: Just . . . let it happen.

ADA: What is that, some *phrase*? I don't know why you're picking on me . . .

JOE: I'm *not*. I mean, it's not going to kill any of us to sit on the porch at . . . [*checks watch*] . . . two-thirty and look at the sky, is it?

ADA: Just let it happen, *man*.

JOE: All right, all right, I'm sorry, I give up . . .

ADA: No, no, I'm going to sit here and be spontaneous. [ADA *sits on the swing. Long pause*] Well. Do you notice anything different?

JOE: Uh . . . Your hair?

ADA: Oh, no, it just gets more and more gray in it, no surprises there. Something here *is* different, though . . .

JOE: I give up.

ADA: Go ahead—guess.

JOE: No . . .

ADA: Do you want me to tell you if you're getting warmer?

JOE: No!

ADA: Do you mean you give up?

JOE: Yes, yes!

ADA: Dad lowered the porch swing.

JOE: Wow. [JOE *looks at her blankly*.]

ADA: My feet can finally touch the floor! [JOE *laughs and puts his arm around* ADA's *shoulder*.] For *years* I have hated this swing. My entire life I've been sitting in chairs that made me feel . . . insignificant. Go on, you're all sweaty.

JOE: Keep Feet on Floor Says Midwestern Matron. [JOE *withdraws his arm and kisses* ADA's *cheek; she is delighted*.]

ADA: Whew! You smell like potatoes.

JOE: Thanks, my aftershave. You feeling more significant now?

ADA: Not really. When I was a child my teachers would say, "We'll let the littlest girl in the class answer that one." Can you imagine how that made me feel? No, your father is really very thoughtful, even when he has to be reminded to be. After twenty-six years living in this house, my feet dangling in the air every summer, one day he just up and lowers the swing. A remarkably *kind* man. You're thin. Do you know how thin you are?

JOE: Dad says I look good.

ADA: He would, he's not an observant person.

JOE: I'm not thin.

ADA: You're *terribly* thin.

JOE: Mom! I'm gross!

ADA: You're *gaunt*. You can see the bones in your face. You look like your Great Uncle Bredahl looked just before he started eating wood.

JOE: Well, maybe it runs in the family: a long line of unrequited *hunger*.

ADA: You look like a skeleton. Is that a beer? Is that a can of beer?

JOE: No. It's a medieval wind instrument.

ADA: No it's not, it's a can of beer you're drinking!

JOE: I thought it would fatten me up.

ADA: A steady diet of cigarettes and beer, oh, *yes*! Did he have one, too? Boy, oh, boy!

JOE: Would you like one?

ADA: No, I would *not* like one. [*Small pause*] Out here where everyone can see me.

JOE: Everyone! Mom, it's two-thirty, there's nobody going to see you.

ADA [*significantly*]: They're out there. [*They both look out into the night.*] Perhaps just a little of yours, I'm so dry. [JOE *hands her his beer.* ADA *demurely takes a sip and grimaces.*] Augh! Awful. Tastes like potatoes. What on earth is keeping Dad?

JOE: How is he? I mean, how's his health?

ADA: Oh, he's fine.

JOE: No, I mean it: how are *you*?

ADA: Old.

JOE: Aw, Mom, don't say that.

ADA: Why not?

JOE: I don't know, I just can't stand to hear you say it, that's all.

ADA: All right, I'll say something else. [*Pause*] Except I don't quite know how else to put it. Oh, I don't mean that I feel different than I ever did, except for in my body, of course. It's funny, the voice in my head is the same as when I was eighteen, or twelve, or sixty. I'm the same person, I keep waiting for that to change, but it doesn't, I keep waiting for some of that wisdom that's supposed to come with age, but I have a feeling it's just not coming. When I was a young woman, when I was having the first of the children, I remember pitying people who were forty. Poor things, I thought, forty years old. Well, that's forty years ago, now. Where did you eat supper?

JOE: That new French restaurant that opened up in St. Paul.

ADA: With whom?

JOE: A couple of friends from the *Dispatch*. I miss you, Mom. I miss Dad.

ADA: Well, we miss you, too. What did you have? You smell like garlic.

JOE [*opening another beer*]: I woke up in New York this morning and realized how much I miss you.

ADA: Don't have another . . .

JOE: I . . . worry about you. [*Small pause*]

ADA: What have you heard about me? Is Dad keeping something from me?

JOE: No! No, no, no . . . Dad's not *keeping* anything from you, you're fine.

ADA: Of course I'm not fine! My arthritis is a constant torment . . .

JOE [*exasperated*]: Oh, geez. [*Snaps fingers*] Like *that* it's out of control.

ADA: [*quietly*]: It's . . . out of control?

JOE: Oh, my God.

ADA: Don't take the name of the Lord in vain. Did Dad call secretly and tell you to come?

JOE: No! I'm as fearful for him as I am for you.

ADA: You mean . . . he has it, too?

JOE: Mom! Nobody has anything! I'm sorry I brought it up! Whatever it was! [*Pause*]

ADA: I wish you wouldn't frighten me like that.

JOE: I guess I'm just . . . missing the two of you, that's all.

ADA: Well, if you miss us so much, don't you think you could have eaten with us your first night home?

JOE: Oh, maybe we *should* turn in.

ADA: I'll never get to sleep now. [*Pause*] Last night Dad and I were sitting here and a family of ducks waddled out from that clump of pines, crossed the road and disappeared, down over the river bank. She reminded me of me.

JOE: Who?

ADA: The mother duck, she looked so ragged.

JOE: You're too much, Mom.

ADA: She looked completely beat.

JOE: Domestic Abuse Among the Ducks! It Could Happen In Your Own Backyard.

ADA: Dad said he'd invited them.

JOE: The ducks?

ADA: He's forever inviting. I don't know, Joe. He's fine, but . . .

JOE: But what?

ADA: Just promise me one thing.

JOE: Sure.

ADA: Whatever you do, don't get your father going on levitation.

LIFE AND LIMB
by Keith Reddin

Life and Limb was first presented as a staged reading at the National Playwrights Conference of the Eugene O'Neill Theater Center. The South Coast Repertory in California premiered the play. The play was subsequently presented at Playwrights Horizons in New York City in a production directed by Thomas Babe, starring Robert Joy and Elizabeth Perkins.

Life and Limb, a dark comedy, traces the 1950s American dream going dry. Franklin Clagg returns home from the Korean conflict, his right arm lost in battle, his hopes dashed. Unable to find work, he sinks fast, plagued by a succession of catastrophes. The ultimate blow: His wife, Effie, who retreats from life by spending all her time at the movies, dies when the balcony of the Fox Theater collapses while she is watching Barbara Stanwyck's *Cattle Queen of Montana*. She ends up in hell—a middle-class hell, where the women spend all their time doing laundry, going shopping, making pot holders. In the following scene, Effie has been granted a temporary reprieve from hell;

she comes back to her apartment in Morristown, New Jersey, to talk things over with a rather surprised Franklin.

FRANKLIN *sits on couch, reading paper.* EFFIE *enters.*

FRANKLIN: Effie, is that you?

EFFIE: Yeah, it's me Franklin.

FRANKLIN: But honey you're dead.

EFFIE: I still am.

FRANKLIN: My God, what are you doing here?

EFFIE: I wanted to see how you were getting on.

FRANKLIN: But how did . . . ? I mean you're dead. Deceased.

EFFIE: You know I had to sign up for this trip months ago. They weren't sure whether I could get off or not. But I really nagged at them and so here I am.

FRANKLIN: This is incredible.

EFFIE: So you look good Franklin. You got a moustache.

FRANKLIN: Yeah. You look the same.

EFFIE: Jeez, I looked the same since I was fifteen. Of course, I started putting on weight, but after you're dead, you stop worrying about your figure.

FRANKLIN: Where have you been all these years?

EFFIE: Jeez, Franklin, this'll hand you a laugh. I was, well, I still am in hell.

FRANKLIN: You went to hell?

EFFIE: Go figure it, huh? Straight into the fiery pit.

FRANKLIN: But you were such a good Catholic, you always went to confession. I figured if anybody was, you were a shoo-in for heaven. Is there a heaven?

EFFIE: I don't know about that, but as far as I can see everybody goes to hell, most of all good Catholics.

FRANKLIN: I'm sorry Effie, but this is tough for me to register all this I mean I buried you and all.

EFFIE: I understand.

FRANKLIN: So how'd you get here?

EFFIE: I took a cab.

FRANKLIN: You took a cab from hell?

EFFIE: No, I caught one at Newark.

FRANKLIN: How was the ride?

EFFIE: From Newark?

FRANKLIN: Yeah, I guess.

EFFIE: Oh, it was okay. A lot of us there took off today. Is this a holiday or something I don't know about? Is it some saint's day I've forgotten?

FRANKLIN: Effie, you make it sound like a charter trip to Bear Mountain. You just came back from the dead.

EFFIE: I almost got off a month earlier, but it didn't work out. Plus I'm not in so good with my supervisors.

FRANKLIN: They have supervisors?

EFFIE: I got upset at first, and thought I'd never get off, but Doina she talked to me and I decided to try again.

FRANKLIN: You still see Doina, huh?

EFFIE: Yeah, she's the only person I could really talk to.

FRANKLIN: It doesn't make sense, you in hell.

EFFIE: Well, this is something I gotta confess, Franklin. I did transgress in the realm of the living.

FRANKLIN: Whattya mean transgress?

EFFIE: I sinned a little.

FRANKLIN: You sinned? You?

EFFIE: Some afternoon sins.

FRANKLIN: What are you getting at?

EFFIE: Like I had an affair while I was alive. I believe this has a great deal to do with me being in hell.

FRANKLIN: When did you have an affair? When was this? Did I know you at this time? When was this?

EFFIE: Around Christmas, 1954.

FRANKLIN: Wow.

EFFIE: Yeah.

FRANKLIN: This is incredible.

EFFIE: I'm sorry.

FRANKLIN: I'm very upset, I hope you know.

EFFIE: I thought you might be, that's why I figure had to tell you in person.

FRANKLIN: How could you do this Effie? How coul you commit adultery without me?

EFFIE: I was unhappy. My life was going nowhere You were out of work. I prayed a lot. Doina talked to me.

FRANKLIN: Sure, she talked you into having an affair.

EFFIE: That's not it, no.

FRANKLIN: Doina puts these crazy ideas in your head. You start acting crazy. I never knew, I'm going crazy. You're dead, you come back and tell me you had an affair, and I should be happy to see you?

EFFIE: Look, I'm sorry you're upset, but being in hell is not a lot of fun either, you know. Boy, I found that out quick. You know what they got me doing? All the time? Doina and me, they put us to work making potholders. We gotta make potholders for all eternity. Nice, job, huh? Jeez, you think we should be working like the retarded people making potholders and ashtrays and whisk brooms and things, that doesn't seem fair, but you forget about fair and unfair, you forget about all that quick. You just try to exist. You look pretty good with a moustache, like a movie actor.

FRANKLIN: Which one?

EFFIE: Not any particular one, just like what a movie star should.

FRANKLIN: You liked the movies so much.

EFFIE: They are the best thing. Especially 3-D. They still got 3-D?

FRANKLIN: It kinda faded.

EFFIE: That's too bad. I thought 3-D was very exciting at the time. I brung you back a pair of those glasses when you came back from Korea, remember?

FRANKLIN: Sure.

EFFIE: You could be nice to me. You could be sweet.

FRANKLIN: Sometimes.

EFFIE: You could sing with the radio.

FRANKLIN: Yeah, I did that.

EFFIE: You had a beautiful voice.

FRANKLIN: No.

EFFIE: You did. Doina thought so. Many people commented on this.

FRANKLIN: I could carry a tune.

EFFIE: Sing my favorite.

FRANKLIN: Come on.

EFFIE: Sing the one you used to sing when I used to come out of the bathroom with a towel on my head.

FRANKLIN: It's stupid.

EFFIE: Please. [EFFIE *goes to* FRANKLIN. *He holds her. He sings a melancholy song of the period, "Are You Lonesome Tonight?" They dance a bit as* FRANKLIN *hums. They break off.* EFFIE *moves away.*] I oughta get back.

FRANKLIN: Already?

EFFIE: Yeah?

FRANKLIN: Oh.

EFFIE: I'm sorry again about . . . you know.

FRANKLIN: Yeah . . .

EFFIE: I always loved you Franklin, that other thing didn't count.

FRANKLIN: Don't say that. I was a jerk a lot of the time.

EFFIE: You were upset about your arm.

FRANKLIN: I forgot about that . . . Just now, while you were here, I forgot about my arm. It wasn't on my mind.

EFFIE: I'm glad.

FRANKLIN: I'm sorry you're going away again. This is very serious. This is the most serious I've ever been with you Effie, I don't know what to do without you.

EFFIE: Yes you do. You know what to do and you do
    it. You do what you know is right. Franklin Roo
    sevelt Clagg.

FRANKLIN: Named after the 32nd president.

EFFIE: Yeah.

FRANKLIN: He was the only president I knew for a long
    time.

EFFIE: Is Eisenhower still president now?

FRANKLIN: Yes, he is.

EFFIE: Okay. Goodbye, Franklin.

FRANKLIN: Goodbye, Effie.

EFFIE: I miss you. I miss you and the movies. [EFFIE
    exits. FRANKLIN *stands, watches after her. Phone
    rings three times.* FRANKLIN *does not move.*]

THE DAY THEY
SHOT JOHN LENNON
by James McLure

The Day They Shot John Lennon was first presented by
the McCarter Theater Company in Princeton, New
Jersey. Berkshire Theater Festival also produced the
play.

It is December 9, 1980, the morning after John
Lennon was slain on his way home from an evening
out. Three teenagers, a couple of Vietnam vets, two
East Side singles-bar habituees, a young black, and an
elderly Jew are part of the crowd gathered outside the
Dakota building in New York where Lennon shared
an apartment with Yoko Ono. The play explores the
effect the death of Lennon had on people, especially
those who had a connection to the music and spirit of

the sixties. In the following scene, Fran Lowenstein and Brian Murphy, the singles-bar habituees, two lonely, unfulfilled people in their thirties who have just met, talk about the changes and the inertia in their lives since their youth at Woodstock.

BRIAN: Unbelievable.

FRAN: Disgusting.

BRIAN: Can you believe this?

FRAN: It's unbelievable.

BRIAN: I can't believe it.

FRAN: What has our society come to? Now we're shooting our artists. People we need. Our brightest talents. I mean, if someone's going to change the world, it's going to be an artist, not a politician. I mean, the man's only fault was to tell us about love. Is love that dangerous? The man wrote songs, for God's sake. He was trying to live a decent life. I mean the Beatles *were* the sixties! They changed the world! They taught us love—"Love is all you need."

BRIAN: Say, were you at Woodstock?

FRAN: Yeah. How'd you know?

BRIAN: I was a Woodstock too!

FRAN: Were you?

BRIAN: Yeah! Isn't that incredible.

FRAN: What a coincidence.

BRIAN: It's incredible! What a coincidence?

FRAN: I mean, how many people were at Woodstock?

BRIAN: Oh, about five hundred thousand. [*Pause*] Cigarette?

FRAN: I gave it up.

BRIAN: Good for you.

FRAN: It's a disgusting habit.

BRIAN: I know.

FRAN: It gives you cancer.

BRIAN: I know.

FRAN: I mean, how long does it take for people to wake up?

BRIAN: I know. How long's it been since you quit?

FRAN: Yesterday.

BRIAN: Well, still it's good that you stuck with it.

FRAN: Aw, what the hell. Gimme one. [*They smoke.*] Thanks.

BRIAN: I mean, in my opinion, there's no other composer of the twentieth century that can compare with Lennon. No way. [*Pause*] Name me one. [*Pause*]

FRAN: Well, Gershwin was good.

BRIAN: Sure he was. Sure he was. But he didn't have the effect that Lennon did.

FRAN: Well, of course not. You couldn't be more correct. But Gershwin wrote a lot of great tunes.

BRIAN: Well. Goes without saying. But that's not my point.

FRAN: "A Foggy Day in London Town" is one of my favorite songs.

BRIAN: O yeah, sure, terrific tune. I got an Ella Fitzgerald Album that's got a terrific rendition of "Foggy Day."

FRAN: I love Ella. She's the best.

BRIAN: But my point about the Beatles is that nobody, no group, no individual, no artist of any kind has ever created that kind of phenomenon before, or affected society in such a massive way. [*Pause*] That's my point about the Beatles.

FRAN [*slightly irked*]: I got your point. Right away I got your point.

BRIAN: Good. [*Pause*] I just didn't want you to miss my point.

FRAN: Unbelievable.

BRIAN: Yeah. I couldn't go to work today.

FRAN: Me either. I said to hell with it and walked right through the park.

BRIAN: Oh, you live on the east side?

FRAN: Yeah. I couldn't face work.

BRIAN: Where do you work?

FRAN: In a law firm.

BRIAN: You're a lawyer? That's fantastic.

FRAN: Not really. I'm a secretary.

BRIAN: Well, that's nice too.

FRAN: Yeah, but it's not fantastic. I have a B.F.A.

BRIAN: Me, I'm in advertising.

FRAN: Are you?

BRIAN: Yeah . . . uh, Brian Murphy.

FRAN: Uh, Fran Lowenstein. [*They shake.*] Hmpf.

BRIAN: What?

FRAN: You're in advertising and I'm a secretary on Madison Avenue.

BRIAN: So?

FRAN: We were both at Woodstock.

BRIAN: . . . Yeah. [They face forward.] It's unbelievable.

FRAN: It's disgusting.

TERRA NOVA
by Ted Tally

The Yale Repertory Theater first produced *Terra Nova*, Tally's MFA thesis production at the Yale School of Drama. The play went on to over seventy productions in ten nations, including an Off-Broadway production at the American Place Theater.

In the winter of 1911–12, Robert Falcon Scott and four Englishmen raced the Norwegian Roald Amundsen to the South Pole. Scott and his party not only lost the race, but perished from starvation and exposure, mere miles from a safe haven. *Terra Nova*'s cinematic structure moves fluidly back and forth in time and place between Scott's expedition fighting the Antarctic and a genteel Edwardian England hungry for heroes, ill-prepared for failure. In one of the flashback scenes, set in a garden in the Belgravia section of London, Scott's wife Kathleen confronts him on his yearning to leave for the Antarctic, his obsession to be a hero in the eyes of his countrymen.

———————

KATHLEEN *appears. She carried a small wrapped gift in one hand.*

KATHLEEN: Con. You said you were going upstairs to rest.

SCOTT: I—couldn't sleep. [*Pause*] I dreamt of Amundsen again.

KATHLEEN: Was he very frightening?

SCOTT: Frightening enough. I came down here. I wanted—I don't know what I wanted.

KATHLEEN: Why don't you come in now? [*Pause*] They've all gone.

SCOTT: A moment more, that's all.

KATHLEEN: You'll get a chill.

SCOTT: No. No, I won't.

KATHLEEN: I brought this. [*He turns and sees the gift.*] I thought, as he won't take notice inside, I shall simply have to tackle him in the garden. [*She tosses it to him.*]

SCOTT: What is it?

KATHLEEN: Haven't the foggiest. [*Scott opens the package and removes a knitted scarf.*]

SCOTT: Kath, it's lovely.

KATHLEEN: And you thought I'd never prove domestic. Well, you see? I've made a birthday party, and I've knitted a scarf.

SCOTT: Will you put it round me?

KATHLEEN: I'll do better. I'll tie you up in it. [*She wraps the scarf round his shoulders, draws him*

*close, kisses him fiercely. He breaks the embrace;
a moment of silence.*]

SCOTT: Peter asleep?

KATHLEEN: Tucked in ages ago. Not before insisting
on three stories. He was very cross because you
didn't kiss him good night. You'll get a severe
dressing-down in the A.M., I should think.

SCOTT: I'll look in on him later. You're not angry with
me?

KATHLEEN: No. I made your apologies for you. Everyone quite understood how preoccupied you must
be.

SCOTT: Did they. [*Pause*] I've spoiled it for you. I've
embarrassed you in front of your friends, haven't
I?

KATHLEEN: Con, it was for you. I wanted you to enjoy
your birthday. I wanted a big occasion.

SCOTT: Yes, well I like your artistic friends—really,
very much—only I just don't have much patience
for that society chatter. [*They laugh.*] 'Fraid I'll
never make a go of it as a celebrity.

KATHLEEN: Oh nonsense, people are charmed by you.
They all think it's terribly proper for an "explorer
chappie" to be enigmatic and withdrawn.

SCOTT: Rude.

KATHLEEN: Withdrawn. [*Pause*] It's lovely out. The air
is so still. [*She sits, takes a breath.*] What's that
smell, do you notice?

SCOTT: Lilacs. The whole place reeks of them, I can
barely breathe.

KATHLEEN: Don't be so sentimental.

SCOTT [*sitting beside her*]: Look at it all, Kath. The
goldfish pool, your sculptures, these bizarre flowers. It's the gaudiest terrace in Belgravia.

KATHLEEN: It is not gaudy. It's Italianate. [*He smiles,
takes out a pipe and lights it.*] Are the stars as nice
in the southern hemisphere? I suppose they're not
the same ones at all. [*Pause*] Is it really so different,

looking at them with the world turned wrongside-up?

SCOTT: The air is so much cleaner. Makes them look larger, brighter somehow. Sometimes they actually sparkle, with those little points on them, like a drawing in one of Peter's books. Still. [*Pause*] I've been happier here, I think, in this garden—than anywhere else in my life. Every flower in its place, I suppose.

KATHLEEN: But you will go back, and very soon. Won't you?

SCOTT [*after a pause*]: Am I as obvious as that?

KATHLEEN: Obvious! When you can't eat, can't sleep—when you curse yourself a hundred times a day for some half-imagined clumsiness and won't look your own son in the eye, obvious, yes, I should say so! You've never had a thought that could keep itself from your face, Con.

SCOTT: Tell me you want me to throw it over and I shall. I promise you have only to say it, even now.

KATHLEEN: Yes, that would certainly make it easier. That would give you what you've been searching for. A reason not to go.

SCOTT [*after a pause*]: We've only been married two years . . .

KATHLEEN: Yes.

SCOTT: And there's Peter—they can't expect . . .

KATHLEEN: No, of course not.

SCOTT: Well surely the press can see that, and the blessed British public. What in God's name do they want from me? I've been there already!

KATHLEEN: Halfway, yes. [*Pause*] It isn't the press, Con. There are a thousand excuses sufficient for them. But not one sufficient for you.

SCOTT: You. [*Pause*] You are sufficient for me.

KATHLEEN [*gently*]: No. You'd always measure me against what might have been. I'd always come out wanting. [*Pause*] Well you're going back, of course you are. You're the best man for the job, anyone can see that. "Scott of the Antarctic!" But I wonder—is there a single person in this country who can guess how you actually despise that place?

SCOTT: Kath, I don't . . .

KATHLEEN [*angrily*]: Despise it, yes, and yourself, until you have it! Well, go back and take it! Go, or stay, Con, I don't care, I don't care, so long as you'll only be happy again. It's that I can't bear. You walk through your days like a man in a dream. I talk to you but you hear nothing. I look in your eyes and see nothing. I wonder who you are. [*Pause*] And I am very much afraid I shall stop caring.

SCOTT [*after a pause*]: Inside tonight at the party—it was full of ghosts, Kath. They all looked like me, but their faces were younger. [*He knocks the ash from his pipe and puts it away.*] When you lit the candles on the cake, I cringed with every flame. Forty-one charges. Forty-one counts of guilt by mediocrity. [*Pause*] I ought to be in the Admiralty, Kath, a man my age, twenty-eight years of service—or at the very least a commodore on active duty. Duncan was a commodore at thirty-two! I'm not so certain any more they'd be willing to give me a flagship even if war came. Sometimes I think, what's the bloody use, I'll retire my commission, a captain's pension is not so bad. They think there's only one thing I'm good for, a damned half-pay land sailor, and getting a bit ragged even at that. [*In a bitter rush*] Do you know what Bridgeman said to me the other day? He told me if I were applying for the first expedition nowadays, I'd be rejected for reason of age. Me! He meant it as a joke. "Younger men, plenty in line, awfully rigorous don't you know." I was *seething*—I told him the damned scheme would never have *existed* if it hadn't been for me, and he said yes, of course you *formed* it, old man— why your very name is synonymous with polar exploration, and they'll always remember you for that, and because after all you did get *so* close, what *was* it, only a few hundred miles out, topping good show *that* was, old sport, and I said yes, old sport, they'll remember me all right, for about two years, my name on some bloody little plaque in the fifth-floor lavatory at the Admiralty! [*He rushes to a halt, out of breath, lost in himself. After a long moment he looks up at her and takes her in.*] You're shivering.

KATHLEEN: It's terribly cold.

SCOTT: Take the scarf.

KATHLEEN: No, you keep it.

SCOTT: I don't need it. Here.

KATHLEEN: I said keep it.

SCOTT [*angrily*]: Will you just take the damned thing? [*She looks at him, miserable.*] Oh Christ, Kath. Oh Christ I'm sorry . . .

KATHLEEN: I'm going back inside now, Con. Come inside. Come to bed.

SCOTT [*confused*]: In—a bit.

KATHLEEN: Will you be all right out here?

SCOTT: Yes—if I could just—have some time.

KATHLEEN: Good night. [*She turns to go.*]

SCOTT: Kath!

KATHLEEN [*stopping*]: Perhaps we shouldn't talk any more.

SCOTT: It isn't here for me, my love. I wish to God it were. I can't explain it or defend it. I can only beg you to think kindly of me.

KATHLEEN: I'm thinking more kindly of you than anyone ever has at any instant of your life. And the price is not small.

SCOTT: How? By letting me run on like a fool?

KATHLEEN: By letting you free. [*She goes to* SCOTT, *straightens the scarf around his neck.*] You'll look in on Peter, won't you?

SCOTT: Yes, of course.

KATHLEEN: Oh, we shall form a brave company of

two, Master Pedro and I. There's the whole mystery of nighttime to unravel, and journeys to the park. When I was young—I always wanted so very desperately to have a little boy to play with—if only I could be spared the nuisance of having a husband as well. Well, now you see I shall have my—now I shall have— [*He moves to comfort her, but she pushes him fiercely away.*] No! I will *not* be a silly woman, I *will* not. Now or ever. That much I promise you.

SCOTT [*softly*]: I'll come in soon. Just now I have to fix this garden in my mind, every twig, every blade of grass. Just now I have to be alone, love.

KATHLEEN: My poor Con. Will you ever be anything else? [SCOTT *and* KATHLEEN *look at one another in silence.*]

THE TERRORISTS
by Dallas Murphy

The Terrorists was first produced by Playwrights Horizons in New York City. Regional productions of the play include the Bay Area Playwrights Festival in California and the Williamstown Theater Festival in Massachusetts.

The Terrorists, a farcical meditation on the seduction of violence, focuses on a group of misfits who have gathered at the Everglades home of the Counselor, a man who has helped each of them in various ways to survive a harsh and violent world. Instead of giving them the sanctuary he promised, he molds them into an unlikely commando unit and manipulates them into

blowing up a bakery—for purposes that remain un-
clear. The following scene is the meeting of the gentle,
bungling Jules and the tough Queeny, two people who
by the end of the play have fallen in love.

QUEENY *lets herself in the front door. She sees* JULES,
stops and glowers at him.

QUEENY: Beat it. [*Pause*] This is my morning. What
the hell are you doing here on my morning.
JULES: He's out.
QUEENY: *Out?*
JULES: He just called from someplace.
QUEENY: Damn!
JULES: My name is Jules.
QUEENY: So?
JULES: Nothing.
QUEENY: Hey, what is this? Some kind of test to see
how I relate to strangers?
JULES: Pardon?
QUEENY: He probably thinks I alienate strangers on
sight. He probably thinks I bring it all on myself.
JULES: I came to see him too.
QUEENY: You'd have to say that.
JULES: Pardon?
QUEENY: You couldn't ever admit you're a test and
still be effective as one. I see right through that
stuff.
JULES: I'm sure he was just trying to help.
QUEENY: So this *is* a test.
JULES: No, I was just saying.
QUEENY: Well, it's true. I don't relate so well to stran-
gers. He knows that. We've discussed it. But why
do they always inflict themselves on me. How can
you relate to somebody who's getting ready to
jump on your back? Look, most people are self-
interested barbarians, but he says I can't live like

that—scared and suspicious of everybody. It's a big drag, he's right. You've got to live in the world.

JULES: I think most people are helpless and pathetic. [*Pause*]

QUEENY: Yeah, then why do they act like that?

JULES: Because they're frightened?

QUEENY: That's what he thinks I am. Frightened. He's right, but I have good reason. Like today. I go to the mall to see about this advertised special on coulottes. That was a big scam. They didn't have a single coulotte. Out in the parking lot, there's this clot of drunken chiropodists with plastic name tags from the convention over at the Doral. One little round guy asks me how to get to the Atlantic Ocean. I tell him five miles east, you can't miss it. I mean, I was relating. I even felt a little warm toward them they seemed so silly. Then this other one with that white stuff smeared on his nose asks if I can give them a lift. I say no, I have this MG with only two seats. Then White Nose says, "Never mind your car, *you* give us a lift." And he jumps on my back. Jumps on my back! You know, like horsey. Then the others dive on top of him and we go down in the azaleas. Did I bring that on myself or what?

JULES: What did you do?

QUEENY: What could I do? A ton of chiropodists on me. I screamed into the mulch. They ran off whooping and giggling. I tell you what I'd like to've done. Kicked them each in the crotch.

JULES: I think that's what they deserved.

QUEENY: You do? . . . I don't mean it's just men. It's a generally high level of humiliation all the time. Hell, you can't even shop.

JULES: Do you like Charlie Chaplin?

QUEENY: Charlie Chaplin?

JULES: The comedian.

QUEENY: I know who he is.

JULES: I think he understood that humiliation thing. . . . The tramp.

QUEENY: Charlie Chaplin, huh? [*Still trying to pinpoint* JULES, *she takes a cigarette from her purse.*] Cigarette?

JULES: No thank you.

QUEENY: Do you have a light? [JULES *takes a lighter from his pocket. Snaps it. Again. It doesn't work. He digs around in his duffle.*] Don't go to a lot of trouble. I shouldn't smoke anyway. [JULES *comes up with an ugly old blowtorch and* QUEENY *backs away.* JULES *continues to dig. He comes up with two sticks and starts rubbing them together vigorously.*]

JULES [*deadpan*]: Won't be long now. [QUEENY *giggles.*] It's a Harpo Marx gag. I modified it some. . . . It's incongruity that counts. And build.

QUEENY: You're a comic?

JULES: Just a beginner. . . . I started too late.

QUEENY: You from around here?

JULES: No, I just got here.

QUEENY: That's true of everybody down here. They just got here. I was born here, but I've been away.

JULES: I've never seen real coconut trees before, just plastic ones.

QUEENY: Oh yeah?

JULES: I like fish too.

QUEENY: Where do you know him from?

JULES: New York. I'm the one who started calling him Counselor.

QUEENY: Really? That was you? . . . Look, if you like fish, you should try the Seaquarium. I went last with my then-husband. He ruined it, but it's worth the trip.

JULES [*his face suddenly lights*]: Wow! Weren't you Queeny-in-Distress from the old cigarette commercial?

QUEENY [*a snarl*]: Yeah, what's it to you?

JULES: Oh. . . . Nothing. I didn't mean—

QUEENY: Yeah, I can see you didn't. I'm just not very proud of it, that's all. Look, I spent two years of my life tied to a tree or railroad track going, "Oh, oh, oh, please help me! Is no one man enough to help me!" That's humiliation like you read about.

JULES: I liked you. I used to watch a lot of television, and I liked you.

QUEENY: Sure. It was all sexual, the freaks. Everyone *liked* me—helpless, twisting against the ropes, then freed by the Low Tar & Nicotine Man with that thing stuck down his jumpsuit. I wanted to be a real actress, but I ended up in some ad man's sick fantasy. Look, my name's Dorothy.

JULES: I think you relate very well to strangers, Dorothy.

QUEENY: Well, you're different from most of the people the Counselor has down.

JULES: What sort of people?

QUEENY: Wasted.

JULES: He's trying to help them.

QUEENY: They lurk around for a while, then move on somewhere. I don't blame them—who wants to live in a swamp?

JULES: Would you like something to drink?

QUEENY: Some juice maybe.

[*Upstage there is a makeshift table with fruit juice and a bottle of rum.* JULES *pours a glass of orange juice.*]

JULES: Why did your husband ruin it? The Seaquarium.

QUEENY: My *then*-husband. He's no longer my husband. He's no longer alive. We were divorced already when he died. I'm not a widow. He was nuts, that's why.

[JULES *turns with the glass. He strides toward* QUEENY—*he trips and falls flat.* QUEENY *jumps, realizes it's a gag, and giggles.* JULES *hands her up a full glass of juice.*]

QUEENY: Wow! How'd you do that?

JULES: I don't do it all the time. Just for those who might think it's funny. Not everyone does.

QUEENY: I do. . . . It looks like you hurt your knee doing it.

JULES: I don't hurt myself falling anymore. No, as I was getting off the bus somebody pushed me from behind.

QUEENY: There! See, that's what I'm talking about.

JULES: I thought maybe it was the heat. You know, stepping out of the cool bus into the heat. Maybe it gets them crazy.

QUEENY: They were crazy to begin with, and they're coming down here by the busload. Crazies everywhere. Look, I'll get something for your knee. [*She goes off down the hall. A big, bright smile slowly envelops JULES' face. This is the first time his deadpan has given way to a smile. QUEENY returns with a damp washcloth. She sits beside him and dabs tenderly at his knee.*]

QUEENY: How's that?

JULES: Great, Dorothy.

QUEENY: Just a minor laceration.

JULES: Dorothy?

QUEENY: What?

JULES: Is there anyone out there?

QUEENY: Where?

JULES: I don't know. In the swamp?

QUEENY: Why? Did you see something?

JULES: Wild Bill took me for an intruder.

QUEENY: Him. He's nuts.

JULES: He seemed a little impetuous. . . .

QUEENY: Are you staying out here, with the Counselor?

JULES: I'm sort of up in the air.

QUEENY: I see. Look, not that it wasn't nice to meet you and all, but I drove two hours out here for nothing. Now I got to drive back. Tell him I was here, where was he? And keep that on your knee for a while. Infection. Wounds never really heal in this climate. [*She abruptly exits center.*]

JULES: Bye, . . . Dorothy.

THE DINING ROOM
by A. R. Gurney, Jr.

A phenomenally popular play in regional and community theaters, *The Dining Room* was first produced in the Studio Theater at Playwrights Horizons in New York City in a critically acclaimed production that moved to an extended run Off-Broadway at the Astor Place Theater.

True to its title, the play takes place in a dining room, or rather, one dining room representing many dining rooms. A small ensemble of actors acts out a variety of related stories about WASP culture, all set around a lovely, burnished, old-fashioned dining room table. The tasteful, comfortable setting provides a perfect medium for the squabbles, rifts, and clashes of an upper middle-class world caught between traditional values and modern expectations. In the following scene, for instance, Meg, a woman in her thirties, tells her rather old-fashioned father the rather unusual reasons behind the collapse of her marriage.

JIM *comes in from the hall, followed by his daughter,* MEG. *He is in his late sixties; she is about thirty.*

MEG: Where are you going now, Daddy?
JIM: I think your mother might want a drink.
MEG: She's reading to the children.
JIM: That's why she might want one.
MEG: She wants no such thing, Dad.

JIM: Then I want one.

MEG: Now? It's not even five.

JIM: Well then let's go see how the Red Sox are doing. [*He starts back out.*]

MEG: Daddy, *stop!*

JIM: Stop what?

MEG: Avoiding me. Ever since I arrived, we haven't been able to talk.

JIM: Good Lord, what do you mean? Seems to me everybody's been talking continuously and simultaneously from the moment you got off the plane.

MEG: *Alone,* Daddy. I mean *alone.* And you *know* I mean alone.

JIM: All right. We'll talk. [*Sits down*] Right here in the dining room. Good place to talk. Why not? Matter of fact, I'm kind of tired. It's been a long day.

MEG: I love this room. I've always loved it. Always.

JIM: Your mother and I still use it. Now and then. Once a week. Mrs. Robinson still comes in and cooks us a nice dinner and we have it in here. Still. Lamb chops. Broilers—

MEG [*suddenly*]: I've left him, Daddy. [*Pause*]

JIM: Oh, well now, a litle vacation. . . .

MEG: I've left him permanently. [*Pause*]

JIM: Yes, well, permanently is a very long word. . . .

MEG: I can't live with him, Dad. We don't get along at all. [*Pause*]

JIM: Oh, well, you may think that now. . . .

MEG: Could we live here, Dad? [*Pause*]

JIM: Here?

MEG: For a few months.

JIM: With three small children?

MEG: While I work out my life. [*Pause.* JIM *takes out a pocket watch and looks at it.*]

JIM: What time is it? A little after five. I think the sun is over the yardarm, don't you? Or if it isn't, it should be. I think it's almost permissible for you and I to have a little drink, Meg.

MEG: Can we stay here, Dad?

JIM: Make us a drink, Meggie.

MEG: All right. [*She goes into the kitchen; the door, of course, remains open.*]

JIM: [*calling to her*]: I'd like Scotch, sweetheart. Make it reasonably strong. You'll find the silver measuring gizmo in the drawer by the trays. I want two shots and a splash of water. And I like to use that big glass with the pheasants on it. And not too much ice. [*He gets up and moves around the table.*]

MEG'S VOICE [*within*]: All right.

JIM: I saw Mimi Mott the other day. . . . Can you hear me?

MEG'S VOICE [*within*]: I can hear you, Dad.

JIM: There she was, being a very good sport with her third husband. Her third. Who's deaf as a post and extremely disagreeable. So I took her aside— can you hear me?

MEG'S VOICE [*within*]: I'm listening, Dad.

JIM: I took her aside, and I said, "Now, Mimi, tell me the truth. If you had made half as much effort with your first husband as you've made with the last two, don't you think you'd still be married to him?" I asked her that. Point blank. And you know what Mimi said? She said, "Maybe." That's exactly what she said. "Maybe." If she had made the effort. [MEG *returns with two glasses. She gives one to* JIM.]

MEG: That's your generation, Dad.

JIM: That's every generation.

MEG: It's not mine.

JIM: Every generation has to make an effort.

MEG: I won't go back to him, Dad, I want to be here.

JIM [*looking at his glass*]: I wanted the glass with the pheasants on it.

MEG: I think the kids used it.

JIM: Oh. [*Pause. He drinks, moves away from her.*]

MEG: So can we stay, Dad?

JIM: I sleep in your room now. Your mother kicked

me out because I snore. And we use the boys'
room now to watch TV.

MEG: I'll use the guest room.

JIM: And the children?

MEG: They can sleep on the third floor. In the maids'
rooms.

JIM: We closed them off. Because of the oil bills.

MEG: I don't care, Dad. We'll work it out. Please.
[*Pause. He sits down at the other end of the table.*]

JIM: Give it another try first.

MEG: No.

JIM: Another try.

MEG: He's got someone else now, Dad. She's living
there right now. She's moved in.

JIM: Then fly back and kick her out.

MEG: Oh, Dad. . . .

JIM: I'm serious. You don't know this, but that's what
your mother did. One time I became romantically
involved with Mrs. Shoemaker. We took a little
trip together. To Sea Island. Your mother got
wind of it, and came right down, and told Betty
Shoemaker to get on the next train. That's all
there was to it. Now why don't you do that? Go
tell this woman to peddle her papers elsewhere.
We'll sit with the children while you do.

MEG: I've got someone too, Dad. [*Pause*]

JIM: You mean you've had a little fling.

MEG: I've been going with someone.

JIM: A little fling.

MEG: I've been living with him.

JIM: Where was your husband?

MEG: He stayed with his girl.

JIM: And your children?

MEG: Oh, they . . . came and went.

JIM: It sounds a little . . . complicated.

MEG: It is, Dad. That's why I needed to come home.
[*Pause. He drinks.*]

JIM: Now let's review the bidding, may we? Do you
plan to marry this new man?

MEG: No.

JIM: You're not in love with him?

MEG: No. He's already married, anyway.

JIM: And he's decided he loves his wife.

MEG: No.

JIM: But you've decided you don't love him.

MEG: Yes.

JIM: Or your husband.

MEG: Yes.

JIM: And your husband's fallen in love with someone else.

MEG: He lives with someone else.

JIM: And your children . . . my grandchildren . . . come and go among these various households.

MEG: Yes. Sort of. Yes.

JIM: Sounds extremely complicated.

MEG: It is, Dad. It really is. [*Pause. He drinks, thinks, gets up, paces.*]

JIM: Well then it seems to me the first thing you do is simplify things. That's the first thing. You ask the man you're living with to leave, you sue your husband for divorce, you hold onto your house, you keep the children in their present schools, you—

MEG: There's someone else, Dad. [*Pause*]

JIM: Someone else?

MEG: Someone else entirely.

JIM: A third person.

MEG: Yes.

JIM: What was that movie your mother and I liked so much? *The Third Man?* [*He sits, downstage left.*]

MEG: It's not a man, Dad. [*Pause*]

JIM: Not a man.

MEG: It's a woman.

JIM: A woman.

MEG: I've been involved with a woman, Dad, but it's not working, and I don't know who I am, and I've got to touch *base*, Daddy. I want to be here. [*She kneels at his feet. Pause.* JIM *gets slowly to his feet. He points to his glass.*]

JIM: I think I'll get a repair. Would you like a repair? I'll take your glass. I'll get us both repairs. [*He takes her glass and goes out to the kitchen, leaving the door open.*]

MEG [*moving around the dining room*]: I'm all mixed up, Dad. I'm all over the ball park. I've been seeing a crisis counselor, and I've taken a part-time job, and I've been jogging two miles a day, and none of it's working, Dad. I want to come home. I want to take my children to the zoo, and the park lake, and the art gallery, and do all those things you and mother used to do with all of us. I want to start again, Dad. I want to start all over again. [JIM *comes out from the kitchen, now carrying three glasses.*]

JIM: I made one for your mother. And I found the glass with the pheasants on it. In the trash. Somebody broke it. [*He crosses for the doorway.*] So let's have a nice cocktail with your mother, and see if we can get the children to sit quietly while we do.

MEG: You don't want us here, do you, Dad?

JIM [*stopping*]: Of course we do, darling. A week, ten days. You're most welcome.

MEG [*desperately*]: I can't go back, Dad!

JIM [*quietly*]: Neither can I, sweetheart. Neither can I. [*He shuffles on out.* MEG *stands for a moment in the dining room, then hurries out after him.*

WHY THE LORD CAME TO SAND MOUNTAIN
by Romulus Linney

Why the Lord Came to Sand Mountain was presented at the Philadelphia Festival for New Plays and Olympia Dukakis's Whole Theater in Montclair, New Jersey.

Why the Lord Came to Sand Mountain is the umbrella title for two short plays: *Sand Mountain Matchmaking* and *Why the Lord Came to Sand Mountain*. In the first play, a well-off young widow, Rebecca Tull, the daughter of a famous preacher, is pursued by several of the men of Sand Mountain—such "eligible" beaux as Clink Williams, Slate Foley, and, in the following scene, the Bible-thumping Radley Nollins.

RADLEY: So.

REBECCA: So.

RADLEY: I do comprehend how you must feel. A woman new here, with sensitive complexions and dainty ways. You let me see that in you, how fine you are. Not many here much prize sech qualities, but I do. I'm not afraid to say so, neither.

REBECCA: I will confess it is good to hear a man admit it.

RADLEY: A bull goose gits ramptious. Fractious. Not ever man rides a woman that hard, though some, telling the Lord's flat truth, get that way. They don't have no reliable guide. They burn and then marry, marry and then burn. I am protected agin sech fritter-minded misery.

REBECCA: By what?

RADLEY: By that there. [*He goes to the bureau, holds up its Bible.*] "And from the rib, which the Lord God had taken from man, made He a woman, and brought her unto the man." Genesis Chapter Two, Verse Two. [*Pause*]

REBECCA: Oh.

RADLEY: There is no doubt with me. A man of God I have always been and always will be, any wife I have can take refuge in that. "For Adam was first formed, and then Eve." Timothy Two, Verse Thirteen.

REBECCA: What a comfort.

RADLEY: "A virtuous woman is a crown to her husband, but she that maketh him ashamed is a rottenness in his bones." Proverbs, Twelve and Four.

REBECCA: You've been married before.

RADLEY: I have. Satan called my wife. She ran off with him, in the shape of a scoundrel called Buzzmore. "But she that liveth in pleasure is dead while she liveth." First Timothy Five, Verse Six.

REBECCA [*closes her eyes*]: "And men shall be lovers of their own selves, covetous, boasters, proud, blasphemers, unthankful, unholy, truce breakers, false accusers, incontinent, heady, high-minded and lovers of pleasure. From such turn away, for they creep into houses and lead captive silly women." Second Timothy Three, Verses Two through Six.

RADLEY: You know yore Bible, too.

REBECCA: A tad, yes. I would make you a misery of a wife.

RADLEY: Why?

REBECCA: Because I quote scripture good as you and better!

RADLEY: "Temper in a woman is like—"

REBECCA: Shut up, Radley! Just go home!

RADLEY: You are mocking me.

REBECCA: I'm not mocking you, I just do not want you!

RADLEY: "Favor is deceitful and beauty is vain, but a woman that feareth the Lord, she shall be praised." Proverbs Thirty-one and Thirty.

REBECCA: Radley? You know what that is. That is a great heavy hunk of last month's lard is what that is, and in her bones, Radley, a woman knows it, and you know it and I know it. Favor is good, Radley, and beauty is jest plain sun-ball wonderful, and the woman what goes about eternally a-fearing the Lord is scared of her own husband and I ain't going to live thataway, so go home! [*Pause.* RADLEY *gets up.*]

RADLEY: Then why play the pore soulful widderwoman hyar? Not jest to me, neither, but to any man come near you, and you not so picky and choosy you don't bat eyes at all of 'em! Amen! I understand Clink Williams and Slate Foley have been here courting you. Along with me, they're all you can expect herabouts. Tother men who'd have you, compared to us, are razorback hogs. Don't be a fool. Praise God, pick a man and live with him. I'll be back to find out which. [*Exit* RADLEY. *Music. It ends. Pause. No one else comes. Music. It ends. Pause.* REBECCA *shakes her head, clenches her fists, beats her knees, then bows her head.*]

REBECCA [*praying*]: Lord Jesus Christ. I am in the wilderness, here on this dreadful mountain. Forgive me, Lord, but I can't abide these people. I know I'm yet willful and too frisky for a decent widow like my Momma and Daddy say, but dear Lord, must I live in ignorant meanness and hateful contention like this? Help me, Lord. Deliver me from this place. Or if you won't, give me some sign, it ain't crazy I'll be on Sand Mountain. In Jesus name. Amen.

KID PURPLE
by Donald Wollner

A madcap comedy, *Kid Purple* was workshopped at the Aspen Playwrights Conference in Colorado and New Dramatists in New York City. The play was first produced at the Pheasant Run Theater in St. Charles, Illinois. Manhattan Punch Line Theater subsequently mounted the play, in a production directed by Don Scardino.

Benjamin "Kid Purple" Schwartz, born purple from the neck up, becomes the heavyweight champion of the world. When we first meet Kid Purple he's a five-year-old, ostracized by the other children in his neighborhood. They'll play Hide 'n Seek with him, but only if he's permanent "It." Kid's older sister, Michelle, offers him some advice.

KID: The guys in my neighborhood wouldn't play with me on account of the purple thing. I'd ask if I could play, but they'd run away from me. Sometimes they'd let me play Hide 'n Seek, but only on the condition that I was permanent It. [KID *hides his eyes and starts counting*.] One-one thousand, two-one thousand, three-one thousand, four—

[MICHELLE, BEN's *sister, enters. She is three years older than her brother and a good deal more confident.*]

MICHELLE: Permanent It, eh?

KID: Yeah.

MICHELLE: God, Benny are you dumb!

KID: That's easy for you to say, Michelle. You can play with anyone you want. I can't *buy* a game in this town. [*Looks out at audience*] I'm only five years old, but I gotta sound grown up. Who's gonna buy a book with baby talk in it?

MICHELLE: If they know you want to be it—

KID [*suddenly furious*]: What do you think I am, Michelle? Some kind of cluck?! I'd rather be hiding any day of the week. I have dreams about running into the woods and hiding under a leaf. Everybody can see me, but nobody knows what I am. They think I'm a lizard or a rock with strange moss on it or— [*Sees that Michelle isn't very interested.*] You know what I was thinking?

MICHELLE: What?

KID: I got an idea, Okay? I'm just going to say it and you tell me what you think.

MICHELLE: I am waiting with baited breath.

KID: Suppose I take a scissors, okay? Like you use for paper dolls—only ten times as big. I take the scissors and I cut off my head.

MICHELLE: What!!!?

KID: Let me anticipate some of your problems. A headless kid is going to be called a lot of names—especially when I start school—

MICHELLE: You like to eat, Ben!? You like to breathe!!?

KID: Not if I gotta be purple.

MICHELLE [*beside herself*]: God!! Are you stupid!! I mean I knew your IQ was lower than mine, Ben—but I had no idea!!

KID: What's stupid? Tell me.

MICHELLE: First of all, if you cut off your head you will die. Second—

KID: My answer to your first question is, "So what?"

MICHELLE: You want to die?

KID: Let me put it to you this way. I've been living now for five years and . . . it's not so hot. I'm embarrassed to go out and play. Mom's embarrassed—

MICHELLE: She is not.

KID: Sure she is.

MICHELLE: Well maybe Mom's embarrassed, but Dad isn't.

KID [*surprised*]: You spoke to Dad? . . . What does he look like?

MICHELLE: Very distinguished. Like George Washington—only with brown hair. He's not ashamed of you Ben. He told me he was proud of you, because . . . because you're nice and . . . you laugh at my jokes and . . . [*Suddenly very angry*] And I'll tell you something else, Mr. Stupid. Mr. Stupid Headless Benjamin Schwartz! No matter how dumb. No matter how purple and no matter how fat you may grow up to be. Somewhere, someday, some stupid girl is going to want to kiss you. And if you cut off your head . . . she's not going to know where to do it!!

SCHEHERAZADE
by Marisha Chamberlain

Scheherazade was commissioned by the Cricket Theater in Minneapolis, and developed in the Cricket Works-in-Progress. The play, which premiered at the Victory Gardens Theater in Chicago, won the Foundation for the Dramatists Guild/CBS Award. The KTCA television broadcast of *Scheherazade* received the Corporation for Public Broadcasting Award for Best Locally Produced Drama and a Commendation Award from American Women in Radio and Television, as well as being the British Film Institute Festival Selection for Best of American Public Television.

Scheherazade explores the aftermath of a rape, the inner consequences of a brutal act. Ann is a young woman attacked as she is turning the keys to her apartment; she is not only sexually abused, but when she unmasks her attacker, he threatens her at knifepoint. Through Ann's resourcefulness, the rapist is apprehended by the police. One of the arresting officers, Weldon, remains with Ann, and the drama continues. The attacked becomes the attacker as Ann, in her fury and confusion, mimics her assailant, threatening to kill Weldon. Weldon, in his struggle to help Ann begin the long process of dealing with her pain and anger, learns important insights into his own life and his relationship with women.

ANN: Do you have any daughters?

WELDON: No. I'm not even married . . . I have a girlfriend.

ANN: Where is she?

WELDON: At home.

ANN: Why isn't she with you?

WELDON: I'm at work.

ANN: What's she doing right now?

WELDON: I don't know. Sleeping.

ANN: Maybe somebody's got her.

WELDON: No. She's got security—locks and things.

ANN: So—he met her outside and made her open them. That's all.

WELDON: That's not likely.

ANN: I think she's dead.

WELDON: Nah.

ANN: What's her name?

WELDON: Alice.

ANN: Call her and check. [*She offers him the phone. He shows her the cut cord. She doesn't respond. He decides to play along. Dials.*]

WELDON: Hello, Alice? I'm sorry to wake you up, but this is very important. I want you to give me some advice. There's a girl here in the room with me—a good person—she's just been through a rape. [*Turns to her*] A nice person. A pretty girl with a lot of common sense . . . [*Ann gathers up her love letters, dumps them in the trash.*] Alice, I want you to marry me. I know I'm a cop. Marry me anyway. You aren't the only one to worry. I worry about you all the time—are you all right. I worry about you day and night . . .

ANN: I could feel it in my throat. The knife was here. Do you see a slice here? Did he cut me open?

WELDON: Oh, God—

ANN: No! Not "oh, God". You don't say that or you can't think. Just think, *think!* He cut me here. [*Unbuttons raincoat.*] Write this down. Draw this.

[*She looks at her chest, doesn't find the stab wounds she expects to see.*] No, don't be writing. Look at me! I don't see the stabs! Am I alive? Can you hear my voice?

WELDON: Oh, God. Yes! If someone did this to Alice, I swear to god I'd kill him with my own two hands.

ANN: But you didn't kill him. You just talked to him.

WELDON: I know that.

ANN: Because I'm not Alice.

WELDON: That's not what I'm saying to you.

ANN: Well, won't you kill him with your own two hands for me? Or do I have to do it myself?

WELDON: Look! Will you look at yourself for a minute? Look at you! You're looking at me. You're talking to me. You're breathing. You are alive.

ANN: I have to show you something. [*Goes to the terrarium, gets the tortoise, puts it down in front of him.*]

WELDON: Looks like a turtle.

ANN: It's a tortoise, actually.

WELDON: What the hell happened to him?

ANN: I killed him, actually. Yeah, I thought I was going to die, so . . .

WELDON: So you thought you'd take him with you.

ANN: You know, he didn't have to die . . . he could still be alive . . . What? No, it wasn't that. Are you kidding? What do you think I am, a moron? He couldn't have come with me. Not where I was going. No, it was just another thing to do. I was trying to keep busy. But you see that now. He didn't have to die. [*His radio squawks.*] I wish I was dead. I wish my turtle was alive. That would be better. That would be better.

WELDON: 332. We'll be down in a couple of minutes. [*Takes her by the arm*] We're going to go, now. C'mon, let's go. We'll get somebody else to help you. Someone who knows something.

ANN [*frees herself from his grip*]: You're giving me to someone else.

WELDON: No. You're right. Listen, I don't want to be familiar. Look, my name is Weldon. Why don't you call me Weldon.

ANN [*with quiet sincerity*]: Maybe my name could be Weldon. My name is Weldon, too. [*Defeated, he regards her. Nods in sympathy. Faint morning birdsong can be heard.*] You want to dance?

WELDON [*sits down on the couch, pats the cushion beside him*]: Come here . . .

ANN: It's not over just because I want it to be over. [*She goes to him, climbs into his lap. He's startled, resists her embrace, at first. Then, embraces her. The timer rings. She slips the knife from his jacket.*] See, I can be nice when I want.

WELDON: Sure, sure.

ANN: I'm in the wrong, aren't I? I hurt your feelings.

WELDON: Oh, no, it's okay—I'm fine—I'm supposed to be here.

ANN: There's no excuse for hurting your feelings. I'm very tired. Would you please get it over with? I'll be on the bottom, I don't mind. Could you please go slow, because I really hurt. He rammed me.

WELDON [*pulls away from her*]: Oh, no—no—no—that's not what I meant! [*She has the knife at his throat.*]

ANN: It's too late. You thought I was too slow to use this, too slow, too scared, too stupid—I'll show you. Sooner or later, I'm going to use it. Now, you just hold still. [*Tenses to cut.*]

WELDON: Okay, final report. Final report: An alleged rape, followed by the murder of a police officer. There is speculation that the rape was staged in order to ambush the officer, who died in the line of duty. Funeral rites will be held for Officer Weldon Hayes at St. Stanislas day after tomorrow. He is survived by his mother, Maureen.

ANN: And his girlfriend, Alice.

WELDON: They won't let me say that.

ANN: Oh, that's very sad.

WELDON: The alleged rapist and the girl who murdered the police officer—are both in custody and will be arraigned—

ANN: I'm just as bad as he is. I thought that might be.

WELDON: That's up to you. [*She gets up. He retrieves the knife.*] I'm fine. We're gonna be fine.

ANN: Thank you. You can go now. I can't believe I did that.

WELDON: You didn't. You almost did, but you didn't. There's a difference. That's the difference between you and him. You see that? I'm all right, Alice.

ANN: I'm not Alice. [ANN *leaves the apartment. We hear the next-to-last measures of the Rimsky-Korsakov "Scheherazade."* ANN *comes out on the street, sits down, heavily.* WELDON *picks up her keys, locks the apartment, comes out on the street. Very early morning, birds are singing more loudly.*]

WELDON: Did I say Alice? I'm sorry. Don't you want to lock up?

ANN [*ghostly*]: What's the point of a lock? [*Throws the keys into the street.*] Please give me a minute. Don't look at me. [*No longer aware of him, speaks to herself, in dialogue: a stern self to an agonized self.*] You should thank god. Oh, no. So what! Get up! I can't, I can't. Get up!

WELDON: We could call up one of your friends.

ANN: No. That's the lazy way. [*To herself*] Come on, get up. I can't. I just can't. [*He turns to her, steps toward her, checks himself, turns quickly away. She staggers to her feet, after a beat, crosses to him and grabs him from behind.*] Don't touch me! [*He tries to draw away.*] Don't let go! [*He relaxes, puts his arms on her arms, holding her to him.*]

WELDON: All right. You're home free.

ANN: Am I?

WELDON: I don't know.

ANN: Okay. Lock the door—don't let go. [*He turns around, clutching her to him, takes a step toward the keys.*] Don't let go.

WELDON: Ready?

ANN: Don't let go. [*He tries to walk, holding her to him.*]

WELDON: I'm going to carry you . . . [*He lifts her up above him a moment. She clings to him, wrapping her arms around his head, and they freeze there. She unscrews her face and opens her eyes.*]

ANN: Oh, my god—it's morning.

ROMANCE LANGUAGE
by Peter Parnell

Romance Language was originally commissioned by Playwrights Horizons in New York City and opened in their mainstage theater in a production directed by Sheldon Larry. Regional theaters, including the Mark Taper Theater in Los Angeles, have subsequently produced the play.

Set in 1876, *Romance Language* departs from historical fact to portray a world of imagination where people and ideas from America's literary and historical heritage collide on the great stretches of the Western frontier. Characters such as Emily Dickinson, Walt Whitman, Henry David Thoreau, Ralph Waldo Emerson, Huck Finn, and General George Armstrong Custer are thrown together in search for the American dream . . . and love. The many characters come together for Custer's defeat at Little Big Horn. The play revolves around the interlocking dreams of these characters—big dreams, idealistic dreams, obsessive dreams, American dreams—and, like the rout at Little Big Horn, the ultimate failure of these dreams.

True to the play, the following seduction scene between Louisa May Alcott and General Custer is not realistic, but high farce—high spirited and highly physical. In the scene, Louisa May Alcott—the prim writer of *Little Women* (who, like the real Alcott did, also writes racy potboilers under a pseudonym)—tries to seduce Custer, acting out her fantasy of being the exotic Moorish dancer, Minnie Montez, a character straight out of one of her potboilers.

Outside the saloon. Night. LOUISA MAY, *as* MINNIE *in gypsy attire, enters quickly.*

LOUISA MAY: I don't understand this. George Armstrong Custer raped me. I, Louisa May Alcott, the renowned author of *Little Women, Little Men,* and *Jo's Boys and How They Turned Out,* as well as half a dozen or more lurid thrillers written under a pseudonym, have finally acceded to my darkest nature, run off to the Rocky Mountains disguised as Minnie Montez, and experienced for the first time the sins and pleasures of the flesh as no woman from respectable Concord ever has before. [*Pause*] And it was better than even I'd imagined!

[CUSTER *enters. He grabs* LOUISA MAY *roughly, kisses her. She slaps him, turns away. He grabs her again more forcibly, pulls her to him, kisses her. She hits him harder, turns away. He grabs her, throws her to the ground, flings himself on top of her. They embrace, he passionately, she resisting. They roll around on the ground. She slaps him hard. He grabs her wrists, climbs on top*

[*of her. She knees him. Exhausted, she crawls off. Pause.*]

MINNIE: Does your wife go through this every night?

CUSTER: She don't resist so much. I wish she did. [*Pause.* CUSTER *looks at* MINNIE.] You're a very beautiful woman. MINNIE/LOUISA MAY *looks at him with a sultry expression. She speaks with a light gypsy accent.*]

MINNIE: Tell me more.

CUSTER: I noticed you the second you rode in here.

MINNIE: You had to. There's only one other woman in the camp.

CUSTER: You know what I mean.

MINNIE: What do you want from me?

CUSTER: You know that, too. [*Pause*]

MINNIE: So I am to be concubine to the great hero!

CUSTER: Others have done worse.

MINNIE: Others have not come so far.

CUSTER: *Where* have you come from? *Who* are you, really?

MINNIE: Those answers are for myself, and myself alone, to know!

CUSTER: And for that Negro scout who follows you around like a lost puppy?

MINNIE: He is not Negro! He is Tahitian! And he is just a boy!

CUSTER: Man enough to satisfy you, it seems. [MINNIE *goes to him as if to strike him.* CUSTER *grabs her.*] Strike me again, would you?!

MINNIE: Yes! As often as it would take to make you understand!

CUSTER: That you are strong?

MINNIE: Independent!

CUSTER: And incapable of love?

MINNIE: Not—incapable . . . [*She moves away, swiftly, clenching and unclenching her fists.*] Not incapable at all . . . [*Pause*]

CUSTER: Then there is someone else?

MINNIE: There is no one else! [*Pause. She looks at* CUSTER.] There was someone once, who . . . would not love me the way I loved him. *Could not* love me that way.

CUSTER: And so you left him?

MINNIE: Yes! I tore him from my heart and came out here to start a new life for myself! [*Pause*] But something about you . . . reminds me of him . . . something in your eyes. [CUSTER *goes to her; embraces her.*]

CUSTER: I could love you that way.

MINNIE: For how long?

CUSTER: Forever.

MINNIE: Until your hated Red Man is destroyed and you can march back to your wife?

CUSTER: I'll take you with me! [MINNIE *laughs.*] All the way to the White House! I am going to be President, Minnie Montez.

MINNIE: Yes. So I read in the papers.

CUSTER: We can say you're my long-lost gypsy sister. You can stay with us. We could see each other late at night. Ride through the streets of Washington and make love. [*Pause*]

MINNIE: I can see the future. You're going to have your hands full as President.

CUSTER: I *am* the Future.

MINNIE: Perhaps.

CUSTER: What else can you see?

MINNIE: I can't say.

CUSTER: You're lying! You can't see anything at all! [*Pause*] *I* am the one who sees! There's a reason for that! The same reason I became a general when I was only twenty-three! I risk, Minnie, and that's what this nation is founded on.

MINNIE: To risk, yes . . .

CUSTER: These hands are the strongest this side of the Mississippi! [CUSTER *goes to* MINNIE *and touches her face with his hands.*]

MINNIE: Maybe that's why they tempt me so . . . [CUSTER *kisses* MINNIE. *They embrace passionately. Pause. She turns away.*]

MINNIE: How old are you?

CUSTER: Thirty-six!

MINNIE: You *are* a boy!

CUSTER: No, I'm not!

MINNIE: I'm eight years older than you!

CUSTER: So what? This is primitive territory. [LOUISA MAY *points to her heart.*]

LOUISA MAY: So is this . . . [*Pause*] You must go . . .

CUSTER: I will find out who you really are, Minnie Montez. And I will make sure you never forget me . . . [CUSTER *leaves. Pause.*]

LOUISA MAY: Finally, a man of action! Oh, Henry David, it was never like this! [*She looks up at the sky.*] A dream. It is all like some sensational dream . . .

THE ART OF DINING
by Tina Howe

The Art of Dining, co-produced by the Kennedy Center in Washington, D.C., and the New York Shakespeare Festival, premiered at the New York Shakespeare Festival, in a production directed by A. J. Antoon. The play has become a popular regional theater piece.

Ellen and her husband, Cal, have converted the ground floor of a nineteenth-century townhouse on the New Jersey shore into a fabulously successful restaurant, The Golden Carrousel. Business has been *so* good that Ellen, as sole "chef extraordinaire," and Cal, handling just about everything else, are in way over their heads, as the following scene reveals.

(Note: As you might expect, the scene need not be done realistically to work. Simple props and a bit of miming can be as effective, if not more effective, than preparing an actual meal.)

ELLEN *is more frantic than ever. She has several bass out and is dressing them.*

CAL [*bursting in*]: One oxtail . . . one Billi, one bass, one duck, one Floating Island, and one pears!

ELLEN [*eyes closed, reciting*]: One oxtail, one Billi, one bass, one duck, one Floating Island, and one pears! . . .

CAL: One oxtail, one Billi, one bass, one duck, one Floating Island, and one pears! . . .

ELLEN: You do the shrimp and I'll do the eggs! [*She starts whipping egg whites with an automatic mixer as* CAL *removes the shrimp from the refrigerator and dumps them into the Cuisinart. He turns it on. They both make a fearful clatter.*]

ELLEN [over the din]: Heavy cream!

CAL: How much?

ELLEN: Half a cup.

CAL [*starts pouring it into the Cuisinart*]: Watch . . .

ELLEN: That's enough. [*They finish their chores simultaneously.*] You slice the mushrooms and I'll finish the mousse! [*She pours the mousse out of the Cuisinart and carefully folds in the egg whites she's just whipped as* CAL *slices the mushrooms with lightning speed and precision.*]

ELLEN: You cut the grapes and I'll do the soups. . . . [*She returns to her soups on the stove.*]

CAL: I'll cut the grapes. . . .

ELLEN: While I do the soups . . .

CAL: Where are the grapes?

ELLEN [*muttering as she works on the soup*]: One oxtail . . . one Billi, one bass, and one duck . . .

CAL: Where are the grapes?

ELLEN: Second shelf of the refrigerator.

CAL: Of course. [*Starts rooting around in the refrigerator.*]

ELLEN: One oxtail . . . one Billi, one bass, and one duck . . .

CAL: Second shelf.

ELLEN: That's right. . . . [*Tastes the soup.*]

CAL: It's not there.

ELLEN: Then look in the bin. . . .

CAL [*thumping around*]: Nope.

ELLEN: Try in the door.

CAL [*making more and more noise*]: Nothing.

ELLEN: Check the top shelf.

CAL: I already did.

ELLEN: They're not with the pears?

CAL: Not with the pears.

ELLEN: Not in the bin?

CAL: Not in the bin.

ELLEN: Start taking things out.

CAL [*does*]: I am!

ELLEN: They're not in the back?

CAL: Not . . . in . . . the back!

ELLEN: Under the bass?

CAL: Nowhere in sight!

ELLEN: Try by the cream.

CAL: I already have. [*He's now spread a great arc of food around the refrigerator.*]

ELLEN: They've got to be there.

CAL: Ellen, I'm looking!

ELLEN: Next to the stock.

CAL: Nowhere in sight!

ELLEN: Oh, honey, I need them!

CAL: Yes, I know. . . .

ELLEN: Should I come and help?

CAL: Son of a bitch!

ELLEN: I can't do the duck. . . . [*Reaches for the salt and notices the bowl of empty grape stems.*] OH, NO!

CAL [*picking over the mess strewn on the floor*]: They've got to be here!

ELLEN: *I don't believe this!* [*She lifts up the bowl to show* CAL.]

CAL [*his back to her*]: I remember seeing them. . . .

ELLEN: CAL, YOU ATE THEM!

CAL [*his back to her, finds something tempting, starts eating it*]: Mmmmmmmm . . .

ELLEN [*holding up an empty branch*]: There's nothing left but the stems!

CAL: What *is* this?

ELLEN: LOOK!

CAL [*facing her*]: What?

ELLEN: You ate all the grapes.

CAL: No, I didn't. I didn't eat those.

ELLEN [*waving the branch*]: CAL!

CAL: I didn't eat any grapes.

ELLEN: I saw you!

CAL: Why would I eat those grapes?

ELLEN: I don't know, but I saw you!

CAL: I don't even like grapes.

ELLEN: I asked you to stop, don't you remember?

CAL: I'd never eat grapes.

ELLEN: CAL, YOU ATE THOSE GRAPES, I SAW YOU!

CAL [*in a whisper*]: Not so loud, they'll hear you out front.

ELLEN [*whispering*]: How are we going to serve Duckling in Wine with Green Grapes?

CAL: I didn't do it.

ELLEN: You've ruined the dish.

CAL: You've made a mistake.

ELLEN: I can't go on like this. . . .

CAL: Serve it with something else.

ELLEN: What's scary is, you don't even know you're doing it.

CAL: Peaches or cherries.

ELLEN: It's like a disease. . . .

CAL: Roast duck with Bing Cherries is a classic!

ELLEN: YOU ATE THE BING CHERRIES THIS MORNING! [*She starts to cry.*]

CAL: Well, we have peaches, don't we? Substitute peaches!

ELLEN: Cal, I can cook. I can *really* cook!

CAL: It's even better with peaches!

ELLEN: I could win us three stars, maybe even four!

CAL [*starts opening cupboard doors*]: Now where are those peaches?

ELLEN: I've trained with the best . . .

CAL [*thumping in one of the cupboards*]: I know they're in here somewhere. . . .

ELLEN: . . . cooked with the best!

CAL [*finds a can of peaches*]: You see!

ELLEN: But I can't do this alone. I need you to help.

CAL [*starts opening the can*]: You golden babies . . .

ELLEN: You always had such good taste. . . . [*The lid off, he inhales the fragrance, then reaches down for one, lifts it up, and pops it in his mouth.*]

ELLEN: . . . a razor sharp instinct. I need it, Cal!

CAL: There's nothing wrong with canned peaches, they're just as good as fresh. [*He then takes a swig of the juice.*] I don't know when I've tasted such a delicious peach. . . .

ELLEN: Do you still have it? [*She rushes to a cupboard and sweeps down an armful of spice tins.*] SHOW ME IT'S THERE, SHOW ME YOUR TALENT! [*Concealing its identity, she pours out a heaping teaspoon of mustard and offers it to him.*] Taste this!

CAL [*offering her a large syrupy peach, still garbled*]: I really wish you'd try this, it's . . .

ELLEN [*fierce, forces the teaspoon of mustard into his mouth*]: *Taste!*

CAL [*spitting*]: What you are doing?

ELLEN [*shoveling in another batch*]: I SAID, TASTE IT!

CAL [*sputtering*]: Jesus, what is this?

ELLEN: You tell me. Cal!

CAL [*gagging*]: It's poison.

ELLEN: Try again! [CAL *is certainly strong enough to overpower her, but it is food and he can't resist anything that's put into his mouth. Coughs.*]

ELLEN: What is it?

CAL: How am I supposed to tell, my mouth is on fire?!

ELLEN: Well, you'd better be able to tell if you want to stay in business, my dear! [*Forces in another spoonful.*]

CAL [*weakly*]: It's . . . curry powder!

ELLEN: Wrong!

CAL: Paprika . . .

ELLEN: Wrong!

CAL: Clove . . .

ELLEN: Wrong!

CAL [*in pain*]: . . . Horseradish.

ELLEN: Think, Cal. Think!

CAL: Soy sauce?

ELLEN: Wrong!

CAL: Saffron?

ELLEN: Wrong!

CAL: Ginger?

ELLEN: Wrong!

CAL [*with a sob*]: I don't know!

ELLEN: IT'S MUSTARD, CAL. SIMPLE MUSTARD! [*She pours out another teaspoon of spice and puts it in his mouth.*] . . . And this?

CAL [*spits it out*]: Uuugh! You've gone crazy.

ELLEN: You don't know, do you!

CAL: Dill . . .

ELLEN: You're so glutted, you can't even tell! . . .

CAL: Cinnamon.

ELLEN: You can't even tell bitter from sweet.

CAL: Coffee?

ELLEN: It could be dirt for all you know! [*Shoves in another taste.*]

CAL: Nutmeg?

ELLEN: Unbelievable!

CAL: Anise? . . . Brown sugar? . . . Oregano? . . . Coriander? . . . Tarragon? . . .

ELLEN: It's salt, Cal. [*The doorbell rings.*]

CAL: No!

ELLEN: What are we going to do?

CAL: It didn't taste anything like . . .

ELLEN: *Salt!*

CAL [*pouring some in his hand*]: Salt . . .

ELLEN: You drank all the Floating Island. . . .

CAL: It didn't taste anything like salt!

ELLEN: You ate all the grapes. . . .

CAL [*tastes the bit in his palm*]: Son of a bitch . . .

ELLEN: And now, canned peaches . . . *canned*!

CAL: You know, that is amazing. I never would have guessed it was . . . salt. . . .

ELLEN: It makes no difference to you anymore. You'd eat *anything* and like it. [*The doorbell rings again. ELLEN goes back to stirring her oxtail soup, tastes it, pours the remaining beaten egg yolk into the Billi Bi, tastes that, adding spices. She starts to cry.*] There's someone at the door, you'd better get it. . . .

CAL: I'm sorry, El. . . . I'll watch it from now on. . . . I didn't realize. . . .

ELLEN [*crying softly as she stirs the soup*]: I can't do it all by myself, I just can't. . . . It's too hard . . . so much to do. . . . I get lost sometimes, afraid I've done something wrong. . . . I need you to help me. . . . Reassure

CAL [*wraps his arms around her, rocks her*]: Sssshhhh, come on El. . . . It will be all right. . . . We can still do it. . . . We'll work it out. . . . I'll watch the eating. . . . They love you out there. . . . They're breaking the doors down. . . . Listen me, Cal. . . . Tell me it's good. . . . Tell me it's fine. . . . Give me that strength. . . . Tell me it's fine. . . . to them . . . baby . . . baby . . . please . . .

[*The doorbell rings again and again . . .*]

2.

Scenes for Two Women

THIRD AND OAK:
THE LAUNDROMAT
by Marsha Norman

The Laundromat was first presented by the Actors Theater of Louisville as the first act of *Third and Oak*—two related short plays about the chance meetings of lonely people in a downtown laundromat and an adjacent pool hall. The play was subsequently produced by Ensemble Studio Theater in New York City and broadcast on National Public Radio's "Earplay." The cable television production of the play stars Carol Burnett and Amy Madigan.

At three in the morning, Alberta has come to an all-night laundromat to wash the shirts of her husband who died suddenly of a heart attack the winter before. The only other customer is Deedee, who lives across the street from the laundromat in an apartment above the Old Mexico Taco Tavern (because her husband "hates running out for beer late"). She has come to the laundromat with clothes that don't really need washing to get away from her apartment, to escape the realization that her husband of just over two years is fooling around with a woman who teaches at Weight Watchers, who is so thin "even her hair is thin." As they wash, dry, and fold their clothes, the two women gradually reveal their great loneliness, and they help each other to go on with—and possibly change—their lives.

ALBERTA: I didn't miss him till I put the cake in the oven. Guess I thought he was checking his seed beds in the garage. I yelled out, "Herb, do you want butter cream or chocolate?" And then I saw him. Lying in the alley, covered in my cabbage soup. It was his heart.

DEEDEE: Did you call the . . .

ALBERTA: I picked up his head in my hand and held it while I cleaned up as much of the stuff as I could. A tuna can, coffee grounds, egg shells . . .

DEEDEE: You knew he was dead, not just knocked out? [*Carefully*]

ALBERTA: He'd hit his head when he fell. He was bleeding in my hand. I knew I should get up, but the blood was still so warm.

DEEDEE: I'm so sorry.

ALBERTA: I don't want you to be alone, that's not what I meant before.

DEEDEE: Looks like I'm alone anyway.

ALBERTA: That's what I meant.

DEEDEE: Sometimes I bring in a little stand-up mirror to the coffee table while I'm watchin' TV. It's my face over there when I look, but it's a face just the same.

ALBERTA: Being alone isn't so awful. I mean, it's awful, but it's not that awful. There are harder things. [*The dryers stop.*]

DEEDEE [*watching Alberta take a load of clothes from the dryer, holding them up to smell them*]: I'd probably eat pork and beans for weeks.

ALBERTA [*her back to Deedee*]: I found our beachball when I cleaned out the basement. I can't let the air out of it. It's [*turning around*] his breath in there. [*Sees* DEEDEE *is upset.*] Get your clothes out. They'll wrinkle. That's amazing about the shoes.

DEEDEE: The shoes?

ALBERTA: Remember I was telling you what Herb had on? Gray suit . . .

DEEDEE: . . . white shirt, red tie with a silver stripe through it . . .

ALBERTA: I hang onto the shirt he died in, and I don't even know if he's got shoes on in his coffin.

DEEDEE: Well, if he's flyin' around Heaven, he probably don't need 'em. [*Pauses*] You bought him all black socks.

ALBERTA: It was his idea. He thought they'd be easier to match if they were all the same color.

DEEDEE: Is it?

ALBERTA: No. Now I have to match by length. They may be all black, but they don't all shrink the same. I guess I don't really have to match them now, though, do I? [*Continues to match them.*]

DEEDEE: I'd like to lose all Joe's white ones. [*Holding them up over the trash can, then thinking maybe it's not such a good idea.*]

ALBERTA [*going back for her last load of clothes*]: Deedee . . . your lights are on. [*Looking toward the window*] In your apartment. All the lights are on now.

DEEDEE: You sure?

ALBERTA: Come see. [DEEDEE *walks over to the window.*]

DEEDEE: You're right.

ALBERTA: Yes.

DEEDEE: So what do I do now?

ALBERTA: I don't know.

DEEDEE: Should I rush right home? Ask Joe did he have a good time bowling a few games after his double shift? Listen to him brag about his score? His score he didn't make in the games he didn't bowl after the double shift he didn't work? Well I don't feel like it. I'm going next door. Play some pool. Make him miss me.

ALBERTA: You should go home before you forget how mad you are. You don't have to put up with what he's doing. You can if you want to, if you think you can't make it without him, but you don't have to.

DEEDEE: But what should I say? Joe, if you don't stop going out on me, I'm not ever speaking to you again? That's exactly what he wants.

ALBERTA: What you say isn't that important. But there is something you have to remember while you say it.

DEEDEE: Which is?

ALBERTA: Your own face in the mirror is better company than a man who would eat a whole fried egg in one bite. [DEEDEE *laughs*.] But it won't be easy.

DEEDEE [*cautiously*]: Are you gonna wash that other shirt ever?

ALBERTA: The cabbage soup shirt? No, I don't think so.

DEEDEE: Yeah.

ALBERTA: Maybe, in a few months or next year sometime, I'll be able to give these away. They're nice things.

DEEDEE: People do need them. Hey! [*Leaving her laundry and going to the bulletin board.* ALBERTA *is loading up her basket.*] I told you there ain't a garden for miles around here. You better hang onto these hoes. It's gettin' about time to turn over the soil, isn't it?

ALBERTA: Another two weeks or so, yes it is. Well, [*taking the card*] that's everything. I'll just get my soap and . . .

DEEDEE [*hesitantly*]: Mrs. Johnson?

ALBERTA: Alberta.

DEEDEE: Alberta.

ALBERTA: Yes?

DEEDEE: I'm really lonely.

ALBERTA: I know.

DEEDEE: How can you stand it?

ALBERTA: I can't. [*Pause*] But I have to, just the same.

DEEDEE: How do I . . . how do you do that?

ALBERTA: I don't know. You call me if you think of something. [*Gives her a small kiss on the forehead.*]

DEEDEE [*asking for it*]: I don't have your number.

ALBERTA [*backing away toward the door*]: I really
    wanted to be alone tonight.

DEEDEE: I know.

ALBERTA: I'm glad you talked me out of it.

DEEDEE: Boy, you can count on me for that. Hey!
    Don't go yet. I owe you some money.

ALBERTA: No. [*Fondly*] Everybody deserves a free
    load now and then.

DEEDEE [*trying to reach across the space to her*]: Thank
    you.

ALBERTA: Now, I suggest you go wake up Sleepy back
    there and see if there's something he needs to talk
    about.

DEEDEE: Tell you the truth, I'm ready for a little peace
    and quiet.

ALBERTA: Good night. [*Leaves.*]

DEEDEE [*reaching for the Dr. Pepper she put on the
    washer early on*]: Yeah, peace and quiet. [*Pops
    the top on the Dr. Pepper.*] Too bad it don't come
    in cans. [*She stands there looking out the window.*]

CHOCOLATE CAKE
by Mary Gallagher

Originally produced at the Actors Theater of Louisville, where it received a Heidemann Award, *Chocolate Cake* was produced Off-Broadway at the Prov-
incetown Playhouse as part of *Win/Lose/Draw*, three
plays by Mary Gallagher and Ara Watson.

    Annmarie Fitzer and Delia Baron are attending a
conference of women's issues in a dying industrial city
in the dead of a New England winter. Both women are
intelligent, strong, funny, but neither woman has re-

ally been touched by the women's movement. Each in her own way is passive, submissive to her husband. Annmarie is shy, overweight, with a low self-concept; Delia is bright, neurotic, savvy . . . and bulimic. For these two women, food provides comfort, love, assurance; eating is a retreat, an escape from unhappy marriages. In Annmarie's motel room, they talk about their lives and their compulsive eating—the Oreos dipped in Cool Whip, the Frosted Flakes eaten right out of the box, even cutting a Sara Lee cheesecake with the car keys in midtown traffic and digging right in. And at night the loneliness and the attendant craving for *anything* chocolate.

DELIA [*rises; moving restlessly*]: What time is it?

ANNMARIE [*looks at clock*]: Twenty after seven.

DELIA: Oh God, and dinner's over! What are we going to do for the rest of the night? It's like an ice cave out there! Am I making this up, or is it always night in Massachusetts? . . . I'd kill for a chocolate bar. A giant Hershey's chocolate bar, with almonds!

ANNMARIE: The Sav-Mor's closed by now.

DELIA: I know it's closed! They shooed me out into the snow, and I heard them lock the door behind me. God, that depressed me, that sound! Why didn't I buy something while I was there? I knew I wanted chocolate! I walked up and down the aisles, picking up boxes and packages and feeling the weight in my hands. But I put them all back. And I told myself, "No. I won't do this tonight. There's someone who will talk to me. I'll go and stay with that girl until I'm tired enough to sleep." But now I've got that feeling . . . when you'd kill someone for something chocolate, rich and dark and sweet . . . God, I hate the night, don't you? [DELIA *is prowling, increasingly anxious and tense.*

ANNMARIE *watches her nervously, but with fellow feeling. She considers something, tests* DELIA.]

ANNMARIE: Delia . . . if you *had* bought something chocolate at the Sav-Mor, you know, and you had it here . . . you'd share it with me, wouldn't you?

DELIA [*misinterpreting this; wryly*]: You think I'm holding out on you, so you won't ask me for it? I wish to God I were! I'd do that, too. If I had ten pounds of chocolates and I gave a pound to you, it would just about kill me to do it. And I wouldn't rest until I got it back again. [*This convinces* ANNMARIE *to keep her mouth shut about the cake.*] Pretty, isn't it? Maybe you thought you'd get control of it as you got older. But it doesn't work like that. I have less and less control. I really scare myself. [*Slight pause.* ANNMARIE, *quite disillusioned now, looks wistfully at the telephone.* DELIA *sees this.*] Thinking of calling Spuds again?

ANNMARIE [*nodding*]: I really miss him, you know? This is the first night in five years that I've ever been away from him. We always sleep cuddled up together. I guess that seems strange, when we don't . . . make love . . . But that's the best part of the whole day, when he cuddles up and holds me . . . And I feel like, I don't know, I have to *try* . . . change *something* . . . so if I just call him and I say to him, "Robbie, can't we talk about—"

DELIA: Don't call him! Wait!

ANNMARIE: But—

DELIA: When I go away, I stay there, and I wait. And sooner or later, he calls me, and he asks me to come back.

ANNMARIE: He does?

DELIA: He always has before. The first time I left, he called four times before I even got there. Four messages were waiting for me. "Please come home. Love, Bill."

ANNMARIE: And now . . . ? [*Pause.* DELIA *doesn't an-*

swer. *Gently*] This conference only lasts a week.
Where will you go, if he doesn't . . . ?

DELIA [*at a loss; then, a desperate hope*]: Maybe I
could come to your house! Just for a couple days.

ANNMARIE: Gee . . . I don't know . . . we only have
one bedroom. . . .

DELIA: Oh, I could sleep on the couch. I hate going
into a bedroom and turning off the light. There's
something so final about that. I like to keep the
TV on and lie on the couch and watch it with my
clothes on, even my shoes, till I fall asleep. It's
like I don't really mean it, you know, I'm not
really alone in the dark. And back in New York,
in our building, there's a deli that's open all night.
So even if there's nothing rich and heavy in the
house, I can go to sleep, because I know that all I
have to do is go down to the lobby and open my
purse, and I can buy it all. The one thing that
sends me into a panic is knowing that I can't go
out and bring back what I need. Everything is
locked up tight! Everyone is gone! [*Clutching at*
ANNMARIE *pleading*] Please, I can't go back to my
room alone. I didn't think it would get this bad, I
thought I could control it, but . . . Can I sleep
here tonight? I won't talk or anything. I'll just sit
here quietly and you can read your book. I know
you're getting tired of this. It's depressing, listening to me . . . and you wanted help, and I didn't
help you . . .

ANNMARIE: No, it isn't that. But I don't think—

DELIA: I scare you a little, don't I? But that's why you
can understand. You'll let me sleep here, won't
you? Just once, just tonight.

ANNMARIE: No. I . . . I would . . . I really would . . .
but I might not stay. I'm going to call my husband. And then I might go home. [*Rejected*, DELIA
turns away, moves around the room in rising panic;
ANNMARIE *goes on*] Delia, why don't you go home,
too? You say your husband loves you—

DELIA [*not heeding this, obsessed*]: If I just had one small thing to get me through the night! Something sweet . . . so I know it's there, when I'm alone . . . [ANNMARIE *snatches the cake plate out of the suitcase, extends it toward* DELIA.]

ANNMARIE: Here! this is all I have. [*Delia turns, stares, lets out a cry, rushes at the piece of cake.* ANNMARIE *hastily sets the cake plate on the floor and backs away.*]

DELIA: Aaaaaaaaaaah!!! [*Pouncing on the cake plate, rises, clutching it to her; then*] Oh, my dear! You are a friend! [*Beat; then realizes that there must be more, a whole cake, somewhere in the room.*] But . . . are you sure you want me to take it all? Don't you want to keep half . . . in case . . .

ANNMARIE [*embarrassed, guilty*]: Oh, no no . . . I don't need it now.

DELIA [*knowing better*]: I see. Well, thank you. Thank you. [*Exuberant, gets coat and purse; then, as* ANNMARIE *opens the door, suddenly sets down the things.*] Listen. I want to give you something in return, because you've been so generous.

ANNMARIE: Oh, no—

DELIA: Yes! You asked me why I don't gain weight. But I didn't tell you my secret. I could tell you now.

ANNMARIE: What is it? [*Quickly closes the door.*]

DELIA: It's really all you need. If you know one little trick, you can eat everything, every night! And there won't be a sign of it on your body!

ANNMARIE: But that's like a miracle! You really mean it? I could just go crazy every night?

DELIA: Oh, ten times, twenty times a night! You can eat like a mad thing, twenty-three pancakes, gallons of ice cream, a whole chocolate cake . . . you can gorge till your heart's about to burst, till the sweat breaks out and you can hardly swallow! And when you can't eat anymore, and you're so exhausted, you know that you will sleep . . . you do your little trick, and . . . [*Shrugs; beat; then*] Of course it takes a little time. Longer and longer, *hours*, sometimes, for me. But then I'm older now . . . But when you're done, you're safe! No one will ever know. You can start all over if you want to.

ANNMARIE: Yeah . . . I might. If I was sure it wouldn't show, and nobody would know what I was doing to myself . . . there'd be nothing to stop me. [*This is rather frightening. She looks at* DELIA, *steadily.*] Delia . . . why didn't you buy lots of chocolate at the Sav-Mor, and stay up all night eating it, and then . . . do your trick, like you just said?

DELIA [*slight pause; then, simply*]: Because it makes me sad.

ANNMARIE: Then . . . why . . . ?

DELIA: It's my salvation, too. For people like us, it's the only state of grace. [*Holds the look between them; then, rising, briskly*] Shall I show you?

ANNMARIE [*hovers on the brink; then*] No. No, I don't want to know.

DELIA [*Beat; then, gracefully*]: All right, dear. [*Getting the cake plate and her coat and purse, goes on*] But if you change your mind, just come and knock. Even very late tonight. I'll know who it is. [*Goes to door, opens it.*] See you soon. [*Indicating cake on plate*] Enjoy. [*Goes out, closes door, goes up the stairs and exits; we hear the upstairs door open and close and the blast of the TV.* ANNMARIE *immediately rushes to the door and locks it. She takes a deep breath, lets it out. Then she goes to the oven, takes out the cake in its box, takes it to the wastebasket* DL *and dumps it in. She starts for the telephone,* DR, *does an about face and takes the cake out of the wastebasket. With rising conflict, she takes the cake out of the box, tries to throw part of it in wastebasket, can't make it leave her hand. She dumps the cake back in the box, drops the box in the wastebasket, removes a slipper and*

stomps on the cake three times, violently. Then she
stops, and lets out a cry of loss. But it's done now.
Slowly, nervously, she turns and looks at the phone,
knowing that the next thing she has to do is call her
husband . . . but not knowing whether she will do
it. She hesitates.]

INDULGENCES IN A
LOUISVILLE HAREM
by John Orlock

Indulgences in a Louisville Harem was co-winner of
the first Great American Play contest at the Actors
Theater of Louisville. Popular with regional and community theaters, the play has been produced in New
York at The Theater in a production directed by Susan Gregg.

Viola and Florence are sisters, two Victorian ladies
of early middle age, lonely, eccentric spinsters ram-
bling about their deceased father's graceful Louisville
house. The sisters' usual concerns are limited to the
church committee and whether or not Louisville is
within the breeding range of gladiolas. That is until
the mailman delivers "Mrs. Whiting's New Book of
Eligible Gentlemen," a catalogue of social introductions and promises of possible matrimony, and the
sisters' lives are changed forever with the arrival of
two strange but charming con men, Amos Robillet
and Winfield Davis.

VIOLA: Did you pay the butcher bill?

FLORENCE: Yes. Last week. I'm going to get the mail. [*Crosses to "door" area; finds the package.*] Viola?

VIOLA: Yes?

FLORENCE: Did you order anything?

VIOLA: No. Is that for us?

FLORENCE [*returning to table*]: It has our address: Four, Seven, Two Norwich Avenue . . .

VIOLA: Then it *is* for us.

FLORENCE: No. There's no name on this package. The writing begins with four, seven, two . . .

VIOLA: Let me see. Curious.

FLORENCE: It's probably a mistake.

VIOLA: It's probably for uncle.

FLORENCE: Oh. Probably. There's no name.

VIOLA: Perhaps, we should open it. [*Pause*] Let's open it. [*They carefully but enthusiastically open the package. Three books are revealed to be the contents.*]

VIOLA: Books.

FLORENCE [*reading the first title*]: Paris Poses.

VIOLA [*slowly paging through the first volume*]: This looks interesting.

FLORENCE: It looks like some sort of art book.

VIOLA: Turn the page.

FLORENCE [*taken aback by the "picture"*]: Oh! This isn't for us.

VIOLA: I just want to see something.

FLORENCE: Some things are private, and we can get along fine without them.

VIOLA: Maybe some of it's art.

FLORENCE [*taking the book from* VIOLA]: Perhaps. It's going into the furnace and that's that. And what's this?

VIOLA [*looking disappointedly through the next book*]: Gladiolas. "How to Raise and Breed Gladiolas."

FLORENCE: Now, that's nice.

VIOLA: Oh, Florence . . .

FLORENCE: Well, it is. Someone has gone through a lot

of trouble to put all of this information together . . . about gladiolas.

VIOLA: I suppose.

FLORENCE: This is research.

VIOLA: They can't grow in Louisville; we're beyond the range of gladiolas.

FLORENCE: We'll look it up. [VIOLA *gives her the book, and begins to look at the one remaining.*]

FLORENCE: Let's see . . . breeding range . . . pages 42–43 . . .

VIOLA [*absorbed in the new book*]: Sakes . . .

FLORENCE: Zone four: Indiana . . .

VIOLA: Curious.

FLORENCE: Missouri . . . Kentucky . . . There you are: *Kentucky.*

VIOLA: This is unbelievable . . .

FLORENCE: Viola, you're wrong. We're well within the breeding range.

VIOLA [*reading*]: "Mrs. Whiting's New Book of Eligible Gentlemen."

FLORENCE: What is?

VIOLA: This is.

FLORENCE: What is this?

VIOLA: Look. "Mrs. Whiting's New Book . . .

FLORENCE: These are pictures of men! Who are these men? What is this?

VIOLA: I think this is . . . Yes. These are men who are eligible.

FLORENCE: Nonsense.

VIOLA: Look! A doctor.

FLORENCE: I'm not sure that this . . .

VIOLA: I wonder how this works.

FLORENCE: Let me see.

VIOLA: There's a picture of Mrs. Whiting.

FLORENCE [*reading*]: Include letter of introduction, with names and numbers of selections . . .

VIOLA: Let's look.

FLORENCE: Viola.

VIOLA: We're only looking. Turn the page.

FLORENCE: This horrible book is a catalog of men.

VIOLA: Turn the page. They all look respectable. Here's a lawyer. Randolph Brooks, attorney at law, Belleville, Maryland. He looks like Fred Lacey.

FLORENCE [*grabbing book*]: Good-bye, Mr. Brooks. These are off to the furnace.

VIOLA: Wait a moment. It won't hurt us to look a bit further. Bankers. Carriage brokers. Oh, Florence, wouldn't it be wonderful to have a carriage broker!

FLORENCE: To *have* for *what*?

VIOLA: Why to have for . . . for . . . [*Perplexed pause.*]

FLORENCE: Exactly. This new book may be new in Belleville, Maryland, but here it is nonsense, it is social garbage, and it is probably immoral.

VIOLA: Excuse me, but they are all respectable *gentlemen.* It says so right here: Certified, acknowledged, and approved gentlemen. References available.

FLORENCE: References from who?

FLORENCE: And look at these faces. Honestly, Florence, I don't see the reason for all of your fussing. Testimonial letters! [*Reads*] Dear Mrs. Whiting: I have met a remarkable woman, a veritable paragon of my dreams, through your agencies, a person of most fine thoughts and even disposition. Our *nuptials* are to be celebrated before the end of the year, a fact warranting my heartfelt and constant gratitude to both you and your publication. I remain yours, both truly and sincerely, T. Charles Albany, Esq.

FLORENCE: How do we know that this T. Charles Albany really married this woman?

VIOLA: He'd have to be rather foolish not to marry the paragon of his dreams. Doctors, lawyers . . .

FLORENCE: Are there any Indian chiefs currently wooing through Mrs. Whiting?

VIOLA: Florence, be serious. This is a serious publication.

FLORENCE: This is a catalog of men.

VIOLA: And what's the matter with that? Aren't Sears and Roebuck respectable?

FLORENCE: Are they in there?

VIOLA: Let's try it out.

FLORENCE: We will do no such thing.

VIOLA: It says here that each prospective entry is personally interviewed by Mrs. Whiting, a woman long towering among the social structures of Dayton, Ohio. Sit down.

FLORENCE: You can't order men from a catalog.

VIOLA: This is the twentieth century. Now, tell me when you see someone interesting.

FLORENCE: This is . . .

VIOLA: *Tell* me. [*They begin to browse.*]

FLORENCE: Not so fast. Who was that?

VIOLA: That was . . . Sanders P. Krewsin, Professor of Literature.

FLORENCE: At where?

VIOLA: Brown University.

FLORENCE: That does sound respectable.

VIOLA: See. I told you so.

FLORENCE: Wait a minute: didn't Gussie Anderson's sister marry a professor of literature?

VIOLA: The one who drank whiskey and read Italian stories.

FLORENCE: The poor woman.

VIOLA: She wouldn't listen to anyone.

FLORENCE: Poor soul. [*After brief pause, they continue their browsing.*]

VIOLA: Wait. [*They look at picture.*] A purveyor of clocks? [*Brief thought, then dual rejection.*] No. [More page turning]

FLORENCE [*her eye catching an interesting face among the pictures*]: Who was he?

VIOLA [*reading*]: Amos N. Robbilet. Professor of Sciences. St. Louis, Missouri.

FLORENCE: That's a long way from here.

VIOLA: Any mention of Italian?

FLORENCE: Physics. Mathematics. No, just physics,

mathematics, and St. Louis. [*Pause*] Maybe he'
hiding something.

VIOLA: [*moving into action*]: He's been personally in
terviewed. Let's see . . . one application woul
cost us . . .

FLORENCE: You're not serious?

VIOLA: One dollar.

FLORENCE: We are *not* doing anything.

ISN'T IT ROMANTIC
by Wendy Wasserstein

Isn't It Romantic was commissioned in 1979 by The
Phoenix Theater in New York City. Playwrights Horizons presented a rewritten version of the play, which
moved to an extended run at the Off-Broadway Lucille Lortel theater.

The play traces the life decisions and romantic trials
of two New York friends. Janie Blumberg is a fledg-
ling writer, a bright, insecure Jewish girl who doesn't
know what she wants out of life . . . or love. Harriet
Cornwall, a cool, sleek WASP, a successful account
executive, knows exactly what she wants. She wants a
perfect life—marriage, career, outside interests, a life
right out of the magazines. Over lunch at the exclusive
Four Seasons restaurant, Harriet discusses her future
with her mother, Lillian, a powerful senior executive.
Many years before, Lillian chose a career over a husband, and she's relatively happy with her decision,
despite a certain loneliness, despite the nights spent
watching James Garner on "The Rockford Files."

Four Seasons Restaurant. HARRIET *and* LILLIAN *seated at a table. They have finished eating their entrees.* HARRIET *is distracted.*

LILLIAN: Everything all right with you?

HARRIET: Fine. I guess. I made a presentation to my boss a week ago. He told me my ideas were too theoretical. Then the next day, at a meeting, my friend Joe Stine said my boss presented my ideas as his own and he got them through.

LILLIAN: Good for you.

HARRIET: Mother I work very hard. I don't want that man stealing my ideas.

LILLIAN: You think it would be better to be married and have your husband steal your ideas?

HARRIET: What?

LILLIAN: I was just cheering you up with a depressing alternative. Look at Jean Harris. That guy would have manipulated her for the rest of her life. Do me a favor, baby. Go in tomorrow and tell your boss, whoever he is, Ron, Rick, Dick, I am sorry but you stole my idea and I hold you accountable. [*Pause.*] Do you want dessert? Have some chocolate velvet cake and I'll take a taste.

HARRIET: Mother, you haven't finished not eating your lunch. You haven't picked all the salad dressing off your salad or removed all the potatoes from your plate.

LILLIAN: Tom, we'll have the chocolate velvet cake.

HARRIET: I remember when you took me here as a little girl. I told everyone in my class we were going to the Four Seasons for lunch 'cause you told me it was very special. And I always loved coming here and I thought you were very beautiful in your subtle blue suits, calling all those grown men, Tom, Dave. I mean, they never really knew the other women in the room, but they knew my mommy. My mommy was important.

LILLIAN: She is. Harriet, you can't blame everything on me. I wasn't home enough for you to blame everything on me.

HARRIET: Clever.

LILLIAN: I thought so. [*Waves to someone.*] Hi, Bill.

HARRIET: Are you proud of me?

LILLIAN: Of course I'm proud of you. Are you proud of me?

HARRIET: Yes. Very.

LILLIAN: I didn't cheat you too much.

HARRIET: No.

LILLIAN: Have children, Harriet. It's one of the few things in life that's worthwhile. [*She waves at another man.*] Hi, Kip.

HARRIET: Mother, when do you stop hoping that there will be some enormous change, some dam breaking and then you'll start living your life? You know what I'm tired of? I'm tired of the whole idea that everything takes work. Relationships take work, personal growth takes work, spiritual development, child rearing, creativity. Well, I would like to do something simply splendidly that took absolutely no real effort at all.

LILLIAN: Harriet, your thinking is all over the place today. What is it? Are you having an affair or something?

HARRIET: My boss's boss. The one you said should be further along. But it's nothing.

LILLIAN: Forty percent of the people at McKinsey are having affairs.

HARRIET: I know that.

LILLIAN: See how nice it is to have a daughter in your own field. If you want me to, I'd like to meet this guy.

HARRIET: It's over. He once had an interview with you. He said you have balls.

LILLIAN: Don't be offended baby. Your father said the same thing. [*She waves again.*] Hi, Ken. Where's our cake? I have a meeting at two thirty.

HARRIET: Mother. . . ?

LILLIAN: What is this, "Youth wants to know"? Honey, I'm an old lady. I don't know all the answers to these things.

HARRIET: I have just one more question. Just one.

LILLIAN: To get to the other side.

HARRIET: What?

LILLIAN: I was giving you the answer.

HARRIET: That's not funny.

LILLIAN: I'm not a funny woman. Ask me, baby, I've got to go. Where is that man? I can't sit around here like this.

HARRIET: Calm down.

LILLIAN: What's your question? Harriet, I'm in a hurry.

HARRIET: Mother, do you think it's possible to be married or living with a man, have a good relationship and children that you share equal responsibility for, and a career, and still read novels, play the piano, have women friends and swim twice a week?

LILLIAN: You mean what the women's magazines call, "Having it all"? Harriet, that's just your generation's fantasy.

HARRIET: Mother, you're being too harsh. Listen to me, what I want to know is if you do have all those things, my generation's fantasy, then what do you want?

LILLIAN: Needlepoint. You desperately want to needlepoint. [*Pause*] Life is a negotiation, Harriet. You think the women who go back to work at thirty-six are going to have the same career as a woman who has been there since her twenties? You think someone who has a baby and leaves it after two weeks to go back to work is going to have the same relationship with that child as someone who has been there all along? It's impossible. And you show me the wonderful man with whom you're going to have it all. You tell me how he feels when you take as many business trips as he does. You tell me who has to leave the office when the kid bumps his head on the radiator or slips on a milk carton. No, I don't think what you asked me is possible.

HARRIET: All right. When you were twenty-nine, what was possible for you?

LILLIAN: When I was your age, I realized I had to make some choices. I had a promising career, a child, and a husband; and believe me, if you have all three, and you're very conscientious, you still have to choose your priorities. So I gave some serious thought to what was important to me. And what was important to me was a career I could be proud of and successfully bringing up a child. So the first thing that had to go was pleasing my husband 'cause he was a grown-up and could take care of himself. Yes, baby, everything did take work; but it was worthwhile. I never dreamed I'd be this successful. And I have a perfectly lovely daughter. Baby, I have a full, rich life.

HARRIET: Mommy, what full, rich life? You watch Rockford File reruns every night.

LILLIAN: If a man more appealing than James Garner comes into my life, I'll make room for him too. O.K., Baby?

HARRIET: Well, I've made up my mind. I'm going to try to do it. Have it all.

LILLIAN: Good for you. For your sake, I hope you can. [*Pause.*] What's the matter, Harriet? Did I disillusion you?

HARRIET: No, I'm afraid I'm just like you.

LILLIAN: Don't be afraid. You're younger.

HARRIET: Mother, you're trying my patience.

LILLIAN: You sound just like me, dear.

HARRIET: If you were younger, I'd say something nasty.

LILLIAN: Whisper it late at night. It will give you guilt and anxiety. Your sweet old mom who worked for years to support you.

HARRIET: Fuck off, mother.

LILLIAN: Don't tell that to your boss. Pay the bill, will you. Comb your hair, baby. I like it better off your face. Call me Sunday. Pretend it's Mother's Day. [*To waiter*] This young lady will take the check please. I love you, Harriet. [*Lillian kisses her on the cheek.*]

HARRIET: I love you, too.

LILLIAN: Sometimes.

HARRIET: Sometimes.

LILLIAN [*as she exits*]: Lovely lunch, Tom. Thank you. [*Harriet takes out her American Express Gold Card and lays it on the table.*]

SALLY AND MARSHA
by Sybille Pearson

Sally and Marsha was workshopped at the O'Neill Center's National Playwrights Conference and subsequently produced at the Yale Repertory Theater and SUNY/Purchase before opening at the Manhattan Theater Club in a production starring Bernadette Peters and Christine Baranski, directed by Lynne Meadow.

Sally and Marsha traces the growing friendship of two very dissimilar women who live across the hall from each other in a West Side apartment building in New York. Sally is a caring, warm South Dakota housewife, whose pregnancy we follow throughout the play. Marsha is a neurotic, overly ambitious, friendless New Yorker, deep into therapy. Down-to-earth Sally helps Marsha learn what years of analysis could not: to

be at ease with other people, to accept and return
affection, to comfort and be comforted.

---

*A tape cassette playing a hard rock instrumental and a
half gallon of Chablis are on the bookcase.* MARSHA
and SALLY *dance.* MARSHA *is a good, practiced dancer.*
SALLY, *whose pregnancy is now very evident, loves to
dance but hasn't much style.*

SALLY: [*dancing*]: You know how to do the squirm?

MARSHA: No.

SALLY: You got a treat coming to you. [*She demonstrates, pulling* MARSHA *in close to her.*] He pulls
you close and you look like you're squirming away,
but not really. Got to squirm with your hips.
[MARSHA, *uncomfortable, spins out.*]

MARSHA: Dumb. [*They dance alone.*]

SALLY: I'd like to be an ocean girl, a surfer girl . . .
This is hot music. Ted's going to get a Cousin
tonight. It's a sure shot!

MARSHA: Right on!

SALLY: We got to get rid of those men more often.
He's great in bed but he can't dance. [*She spins*
MARSHA.] Too much. Makes me feel like summer.
You taking me to the ocean this summer?

MARSHA: I want to like summer.

SALLY: That's my time!

MARSHA: I'd like it if I liked my legs.

SALLY: You got good legs.

MARSHA: From the knees down. My thighs look like
chenille bedspreads.

SALLY: Let's see. [MARSHA *stops dancing and turns
music off.*]

MARSHA: We're going to wake up your kids.

SALLY: What are you getting red for? [*She pulls her
own skirt up.*] I got knock knees.

MARSHA [*barely looking*]: Your thighs are firm.

SALLY: But they join my knees. [MARSHA *pours herself more wine.*]

MARSHA: I hate thighs. They're walking Rorschach tests. [SALLY *tickles* MARSHA *as she gets more wine.*]

SALLY: They should lock up Heintz and give me the key. [SALLY *sneaks behind* MARSHA *and* quickly lifts her skirt.] Peek-a-boo!

MARSHA: No. [MARSHA *takes umbrella off rocker and holds it in front of her as she sits.*]

SALLY: Honey, you got sexy legs. What you bring an umbrella for?

MARSHA: I never go out drinking without an umbrella. The act of remembering it keeps me in perfect control. [SALLY *laughs, takes glass of wine, and lies across couch.*]

SALLY: That's one for Dad. Imagine him carrying it into the saloon.

MARSHA: You know, one day, you're going to get in touch with your anger at that man and it's going to come pouring out.

SALLY [*laughing*]: At Dad?

MARSHA: Have you ever thought why you carry that piece of dress everywhere you go?

SALLY: It's a good dish cloth.

MARSHA: It's a constant reminder of the instability of your youth. That rag is a piece of repressed anger. The same as your not graduating high school was a defense mechanism against the repressed rage you felt to your father. [SALLY *is collapsed in laughter.*]

SALLY: GD!

MARSHA: God, are you in massive denial.

SALLY: Honey, not everyone's the same as your Mom and Dad.

MARSHA: But can you look at *your* mother? That woman must want to kill him.

SALLY: That's sure as H not Mom. She's got the trick. Knows how to keep herself alive.

MARSHA: How?

SALLY: She's got Dad. She keeps him alive. He couldn't
make a move without her.

MARSHA: Fat good that does her.

SALLY: She's got it! She's got the power you get from
keeping someone alive and the life you get inside
you when you love someone.

MARSHA: More babies?

SALLY [*shakes head, no*]: Deep inside you. [MARSHA
*turns the music on and dances aggressively alone.
It is Donna Summer's "Hot Stuff."*]

MARSHA [*while dancing*]: Why the fuck do I have to
be the one to keep my mother alive? [MARSHA
turns music up higher. After a beat, SALLY *turns
music off.*]

SALLY: Thanksgiving didn't work out for you, did it?

MARSHA: When was Thanksgiving?

SALLY: Your mom didn't like the food I made for you?

MARSHA: She had two Miltowns for dessert.

SALLY: Why?

MARSHA: Because I didn't love her enough to ask
HER for her stupid stuffing recipe.

SALLY: Come on. Teach me the New York Funk.

MARSHA: What the fuck did you shove in that turkey?

SALLY: Just celery, bread, giblets . . .

MARSHA: You two get together? That's what she said.

SALLY: What you think I put in?

MARSHA: I told her eggplant.

SALLY [*laughs*]: Eggplant! You don't put eggplant in a
turkey.

MARSHA [*upset*]: That's all I could think of. You should
have told me what was in it.

SALLY: So you said it was eggplant. Next time . . .

MARSHA: No next time. No next time. I'm never seeing
her again because I hate her and I don't like her and
I hate her and I don't like her and I . . . [SALLY
holds MARSHA.]

SALLY [*rocking*]: Come on. Come on.

MARSHA: Bitch.

SALLY: Ssssshhh.

MARSHA: I wanted it to be good.

SALLY [*rocking*]: I know.

MARSHA: Whatever I do, it's never enough.

SALLY: I see that. [SALLY *hums "Hot Stuff" and rocks. After a long beat, she speaks.*] Next time, you tell her it's cat shit. [*The two women laugh together.*]

MARSHA: I can feel the baby.

SALLY: Tell Marsha to shut up and go to sleep.

MARSHA: Marsha?

SALLY: Why not?

MARSHA [*touched by gesture*]: It's not a beautiful name.

SALLY [*sits on couch*]: She'll get by with it.

MARSHA: Are you joking?

SALLY: No.

MARSHA [*excited*]: I want to hear her. [MARSHA *runs to couch. She puts her ear to* SALLY's *stomach.*]

SALLY: She'll break your ear drums.

MARSHA [*closing one ear to hear better*]: Can you hear me? She said, "Yes!"

SALLY: She's going to talk as much as you do too.

MARSHA [*after a comfortable beat*]: Can you imagine. She doesn't have to keep anybody else alive now. [MARSHA *stays with her head on* SALLY's *stomach until stage directions say she rises.*]

SALLY [*resting head on back of couch*]: Maybe I was lucky being the oldest, being my own mother since I was three.

MARSHA: I'll never be a good mother.

SALLY: Heintz tell you that?

MARSHA: They never say never, but some things you have to accept.

SALLY: Everybody's got strange reasons to have kids.

MARSHA: You don't have strange reasons.

SALLY: Mmmhmm.

MARSHA: Tell me.

SALLY: I told Joni and she said I was dirty.

MARSHA: You can tell me.

SALLY: I love being touched by babies.

MARSHA: Sexually?

SALLY: Different, but it's sexy.

MARSHA: They turn you on? [*As* SALLY *speaks, she absently traces the actions on* MARSHA'S *face.*]

SALLY: Mmmmmhmmm. Their soft hair on the curve of my neck and their strong fingers pushing in and pulling out when they're at my breast, and then they put their fingers in your ears and run them over your face and they got a sweet smell. They make my body alive, gives me the chills. [MARSHA, *uncomfortable at being touched, rises abruptly and goes to tape cassette.*]

MARSHA: I've never felt that way. [*After a beat,* SALLY, *hurt, throws pillows off couch and makes up foldout bed.*]

SALLY: That's just me and babies. It's eleven o'clock.

MARSHA: No. Alive. I've never felt that way.

SALLY: You never felt that way with Martin?

MARSHA: I don't think I have.

SALLY: You don't think. You know.

MARSHA: Maybe if I knew what it felt like, then I'd know it happened to me.

SALLY: You'd know.

MARSHA: Everybody says that! Nobody tells you what they know.

SALLY: It can't be put into words.

MARSHA: Why not? Because it's another sorority secret?

SALLY: 'Cause it's different for everybody. My mother told me it was like lightning. If I'd taken her word, I'd never have tried it.

MARSHA: But she told you.

SALLY: There must be books. It's late. [SALLY *goes to closet to get bed pillows.*]

MARSHA: Of course, there are books. The last one said the glands of Bartholin become amazingly copious as sexual excitement increases. How the fuck does that help?

SALLY: You know you and Joni got more in common than you think. You both make me feel dirty.

MARSHA: I didn't mean to.

SALLY: OK.

MARSHA: No. I really didn't mean to.

SALLY [*smiles*]: OK. [*A silent beat of reconciliation.*]

MARSHA [*goes quickly to* SALLY]: So try for me.

SALLY [*after a beat she flops on bed*]: Floodwater. [*She laughs.*] See how dumb.

MARSHA: Go on.

SALLY [*doesn't lecture but enjoys herself as she thinks of how to say it and relives the feelings*]: Like you're a river and you've a fast current in you and you pick up power and keep picking up power till you come to the waterfall . . .

MARSHA: And you crash?

SALLY: You just hang there.

MARSHA: How long?

SALLY: You don't tell time. You just keep hanging!

MARSHA: That's it?

SALLY: Then all of you floats out. And then you float and stay floating . . .

MARSHA: Have you ever felt nauseous?

SALLY: Disgusted?

MARSHA: Like pain.

SALLY: If you don't become part of the water, you'd only feel the pressure. [*She demonstrates again.*] You got to move . . .

MARSHA: Forget the water! Is there pain?

SALLY: Yes. Part of it is like pain.

MARSHA: I always start like a river . . .

SALLY: OK.

MARSHA [*excited*]: Then I get to the pain part.

SALLY [*sharing excitement*]: OK.

MARSHA [*depressed*]: But then I get the feeling I'm going to throw up.

SALLY: That can be yours! I once thought I was going to pee all over him. You get so full, you think you're going to break, but you don't.

MARSHA: But I get so scared that I'm *really* going to throw up.

SALLY: OK. OK. That's when you tell Martin to stop.

Ask him to play a bit. Tell a joke. And don't worry if he gets soft. Take your time. You'll be feeling him hard again. And when you want him inside and you want to push through, just clear your head and let him put it in and take you there. [*She falls back dramatically on bed and looks up at* MARSHA, *who is shaking her head.*] Don't worry about him. He'll get it up for you again.

MARSHA: Who fucking worries about Martin? Someone told him at prep school what it was for and he does it. He needs nothing. He doesn't need a hot bath. He doesn't need a bottle of wine. I sometimes think he doesn't need me. It just goes up by itself. He's reading *The Wall Street Journal* and it's up. He eats his granola and it's up and if I'm there, it goes in and I feel nothing . . .

SALLY: He doesn't worry about you?

MARSHA: He doesn't know.

SALLY: You never told him.

MARSHA: I listen to the hottest rock and roll music in my head and it fakes him out every time.

SALLY: Why don't you tell him?

MARSHA: And have the only person who calls me a woman think I'm not!

SALLY: I wish I could take a broom and clean out your head and then show you, the life that's in you.

MARSHA: I don't want to talk about it anymore. [MARSHA *heads for refrigerator.*]

SALLY: I've faked.

MARSHA [*returns to Sally*]: You don't have to lie.

SALLY: I'm sure everybody has.

MARSHA: But it stopped for you.

SALLY: Only when it got so bad that it was all I was thinking about. It was either leave him or tell. And I told him it wasn't working and he told me he knew and that was the end of that.

MARSHA: Just telling him?

SALLY: Yes. And when it happens now, know what we

do? Play a couple of hands of Crazy Jacks and
then get back into bed.

MARSHA: You make it sound too easy.

SALLY: That's just our way. But I do think there's
something in laughing. [*She stretches out and leans
her head against* MARSHA.] I think even Burt Reyn-
olds got to get laughed into it sometimes. You
smell nice. What perfume is that?

MARSHA [*moving slightly*]: Miss Dior.

SALLY: Why do you always pull away from me except
when you're crying? [MARSHA *puts her head in
hands.*] Don't play baby.

MARSHA [*softly and not looking at her*]: Have you ever
fantasized about a woman?

SALLY: What they're like in bed?

MARSHA: In bed with you.

SALLY: More than like this?

MARSHA: Yes.

SALLY: You think I'm coming on to you?

MARSHA: No.

SALLY: Then why you pull away?

MARSHA: Do you think I'm a lesbian?

SALLY: Do you?

MARSHA: I'm not sure. I want to touch you.

SALLY [*easily*]: And to touch another woman is to be
a lesbian?

MARSHA: Yes.

SALLY: Heintz tell you that?

MARSHA: He never said I wasn't.

SALLY: He's full of bullshit. Come on. You hold me.

MARSHA: I don't know. [SALLY *pulls* MARSHA *to her
and places* MARSHA's *arms around her.*]

SALLY: One arm. Two arm. Legs on the bed . . .
That's nice.

MARSHA: I can't breathe.

SALLY: Sshh. Breathe with me. [*She shakes* MARSHA's
head.] Let your head loose.

MARSHA [*in hold*]: I've got the hiccups.

SALLY: Keep breathing.

MARSHA: I'll just go get some . . .

SALLY: No talking. Just breathe with me. [*The two women hold each other for a long quiet beat.* SALLY *does not release* MARSHA *until she can feel that* MARSHA's *body is calm. Gently releasing* MARSHA's *arms*] My sister and I slept in the same bed for ten years. [SALLY *moves* MARSHA *up to the pillows.* MARSHA *lies down.* SALLY *sits up with her arm around her. A comfortable silence.*]

MARSHA: I was in a pool once where the water was warm. It was an outdoor pool and it was winter, but inside me it was summer.

SALLY: Sounds nice.

MARSHA: She waited for Martin to put the turkey on the side so I could see her take the Miltowns.

SALLY: Ssshhhh.

MARSHA: She threatened to take an overdose once when I told her we were moving to . . .

SALLY: Come on. Come on. Put yourself back in your pool. [*The lights dim slowly on the two women.* MARSHA *falling asleep;* SALLY *awake. She rests her head on top of* MARSHA's *and smiles.*]

✗ INDEPENDENCE
by Lee Blessing

Developed in workshop at the Cricket Theater in Minneapolis and presented as a staged reading at the Eugene O'Neill Theater Center's National Playwrights Conference, *Independence* was given its professional premiere by the Actors Theater of Louisville during its Humana Festival of New American Plays.

Independence tells the story of the volatile relationship of Evelyn Briggs and her three daughters, Kess, Jo, and Sherry. Kess comes back to her family home in Independence, Iowa, after a four-year estrangement, called home by Jo, who claims that their mother, a former mental patient, tried to kill Jo when she found out Jo was pregnant. In the following scene, Kess confronts her mother about Jo's accusations.

EVELYN: Have a seat.

KESS: In a minute.

EVELYN [*sitting near Kess's bag*]: I will. I've been standing for hours. Out at the MHI. I work in the craft center, you know.

KESS: I heard.

EVELYN: I thought you'd be interested, since you were the one who brought me out there in the first place. Of course, now I'm helping other people, instead of being helped. They all like the projects I think up. Just simple things, really. Wood and yarn and paint and things. [EVELYN *opens* KESS's *bag and rummages inside.*] How long are you staying? Did you bring a lot with you?

KESS: What are you doing?

EVELYN: Looking at your things. [*Holding up a book*] What's this book? It's awfully thick.

KESS: It's a study of imagery in seventeenth-century Scottish border ballads.

EVELYN: What do you use it for? Do you read it?

KESS: I'm writing a book of my own.

EVELYN: Really? What's your book called?

KESS: "Imagery in Seventeenth-century Scottish Border Ballads."

EVELYN: Isn't that the same thing?

KESS: It's my view.

EVELYN [*laughs, continues rummaging*]: I'll never understand it.

KESS: Mom, why are you going through my things?

EVELYN: I haven't seen you. I'm trying to get an idea of who you are. How you've changed, I mean.

KESS [*retrieving her bag, moving it away from her*]: I haven't.

EVELYN: You came back. How long are you staying?

KESS: Jo and I are still talking that one over.

EVELYN: I hope you stay a long time. It's exciting to have all you girls together again. It's a rare treat.

KESS: Jo said you tried to kill her.

EVELYN: Why don't you sit down?

KESS: I'll sit down when I want to sit down.

EVELYN: Are you afraid to sit down? [*A beat.* KESS *sits in a chair.*] You always used to sit there. [KESS *immediately rises.*] It's so hard to know what to start talking about after four years, isn't it? Are you still a homosexual?

KESS [*a beat*]: Yes, Mother. I am still a homosexual.

EVELYN: I suppose that'll make it hard for you to give Jo much advice about this Don Orbeck fellow. She's awfully confused right now. She wanted to marry him, but I think I've pointed out the disadvantages of *that*.

KESS: What are they?

EVELYN: Oh—well, everyone counsels against getting married because of an inadvertent pregnancy. I mean, look at my own life. I married Henry Briggs just because we were expecting you, and that didn't work out so wonderfully, did it?

KESS: I guess not.

EVELYN: What is it about the women in this family? We get near a man, and the next thing we know we're pregnant. You're probably right to stay away from men.

KESS: Mom . . .

EVELYN: Are you sure you don't want to sit? I feel like I'm staring up at a big building.

KESS: I'll stand.

EVELYN: I hope you won't do any homosexual things while you're in town. I mean, it's your life, but . . .

KESS: [*moving toward the kitchen*]: I wonder if Jo needs help?

EVELYN: Oh, she's gone down to the bakery for some rolls.

KESS: She has?

EVELYN: She always does when she makes tea. It's one of our little sins.

KESS [*sighs, perches on the back of a chair*]: Oh.

EVELYN: It's been so long since we've talked. I admit, I wished you dead there for a couple of years, but I'm over that now.

KESS: Mom . . .

EVELYN: Jo's almost fully recovered, too. From her neck, I mean. So, I guess you'd say we're all doing very well at the . . .

KESS: Mom, can I say something?

EVELYN: Of course. We're having a talk.

KESS: As I was driving here, I was talking to myself—I was saying, "Mom's had four years. We both have. Four years of not seeing each other, not talking, not even writing. Maybe things are entirely different by now. Maybe we'll actually find that we've forgotten how we used to talk to each other. Maybe we'll invent a whole new way."

EVELYN: You talk to yourself in the car?

KESS: Why do we get into conversations like this?! Can't you just say, "Hello, Kess—it's nice to see you again"?

EVELYN: No.

KESS: Why not?

EVELYN: Because it isn't.

KESS [*a beat*]: Why not?

EVELYN: Isn't it obvious? You left this family long ago. You never visited, you never told us anything about your life . . .

KESS: I was trying to establish something for myself.

EVELYN: And then, four years ago, out of the blue, you came down here and decided I needed medical help.

KESS: You did.

EVELYN: In your opinion.

KESS: I found you sitting on the floor behind a chair, wrapped in a blanket.

EVELYN: And you gave me a hug. I remember; it was very sweet. Then you took me out to the MHI, and . . .

KESS: What did you want me to do? Take you up to Minneapolis with me? You wouldn't go. Quit my job? Move down here?

EVELYN: That could have been a start.

KESS: I'm a professional! I have a career. It takes all my time and energy—all my love to do it well. I'm not a hack teacher somewhere. I'm extremely good at what I do.

EVELYN: I know, dear. You're a specialist.

KESS: You were only in there three months.

EVELYN: How much love would you like, Kess?

KESS: What?

EVELYN: Isn't that what we're talking about? Really? You're not here for Jo. You're here for love. You want some of my love.

KESS: That would be nice.

EVELYN: Well, then, it occurs to me we may only be dickering about the amount. You're a specialist; maybe you don't need a lot of love from me. Maybe you only need a tiny bit. I think I could provide that.

KESS: Why did you try to kill Jo?

EVELYN: I didn't. I hit her.

KESS: She thinks you tried to . . .

EVELYN: You show me one mother who hasn't hit a child.

KESS [a beat.]: Well. I'm going to be here for a little while. I think Jo and Sherry could use whatever comfort and protection that would afford.

EVELYN: They do not need protection . . .

KESS: I think they do. I think they need that, and love.

EVELYN: You are just like Henry Briggs, you know

that? Only here when you want to create new tragedies.

KESS: Mom . . .

EVELYN: You have all his false appeal and his seeming logic. But just like Henry, you become part of this family only when it suits you, and—

KESS: Mother—

EVELYN: And one day you will leave for good. Won't you? Won't you?

KESS: Why did you hit Jo?

EVELYN: I never hit Jo! [*Rising*] I remember when a mother and daughter could converse like human beings about these things. You ask anybody in Independence about me. They'll say Evelyn Briggs is the sanest, most well-loved one among us. I am wonderful with those patients. I don't know what Jo may have told you, but it's . . .

KESS [*overlapping from "may,"*]: Jo has only been . . .

EVELYN: But it's not true! I am perfectly capable of functioning in a warm and loving universe. Which is what I try constantly to create! [*Pause. JO is heard in kitchen.*] I'd better go help Jo. Hope you like Constant Comment. [*She exits into the kitchen.* KESS *looks around the room, sighs and slumps on the arm of the couch.*]

FABLES FOR FRIENDS
by Mark O'Donnell

Fables for Friends opened at Playwrights Horizons in New York City.

    Fables for Friends is actually nine playlets, exploring young friendship, touching on those little epiphanies, turning points, changes, and rites of passage that are part of growing up. In the following piece, three high school girls, Libby, Liz, and Beth, have stopped at the local diner on the way home from school. As they wait for their food, they become increasingly uncomfortable over the fact that an older man is staring at them.

    (Note: The scene is for three actresses.)

Three P.M.: A diner. The three girls enter energetically.

LIZ: I could have died!

BETH: I could have died too!

LIBBY: I missed it.

BETH: Let's all order the same thing. Hi, Tony!

LIZ [*to the unseen Tony*]: We're fine.

BETH: I danced with Brian Culver on Sadie Hawkins night; he's a very sincere dancer.

LIBBY: He held the water fountain faucet for me once, after he'd had his drink.

BETH: Libby, you are too wonderful. [*Then, to* LIZ] But even if you are his confidante, big whoop! Who needs that?

LIZ: Things happen. I'm not gonna eat, are you?

BETH: Are you?

LIZ: If you are.

LIBBY: I can make something at home for free. I can use the blender or anything.

BETH: Libby, you are still too wonderful.

LIBBY: Beth, would you open your mouth on the very first kiss?

LIZ [*intruding*]: With a certain boy?

LIBBY: Yeah. Or in a certain life.

LIZ: Well, if he sincerely likes you—

LIBBY: What if he says he likes you, does that mean he does?

LIZ [*simultaneously with* BETH]: Yes.

BETH [*simultaneously with* LIZ]: No. [*Under such contradiction, they quickly reverse their stands and contradict each other simultaneously again.*]

LIZ: No.

BETH: Yes.

LIZ [*to settle it*]: Assume it's yes, you'll get more done.

BETH [*swiftly*]: Let's all order the same thing. That way they'll be no fighting once it comes. Yes? Three yeses? We'll all have the same thing like we were sisters eating at home.

LIZ: What if we all order the same thing and when it comes it's gross? I would die, that would be the end.

LIBBY: Yes, let's order different things. We can feed each other off our own plates.

LIZ: This is weird, there's a milk stain on the table from my ice water glass.

BETH: It's from the people before you. I'm going to have the burger plate. Maybe my zillionth one is free.

LIZ: The weirdest thing has been happening to me—

BETH: Like what, like that? Big whoop.

LIBBY: Are you all already to order?

LIZ: Yeah, I'll have the Brian Culver, no toast.

BETH: You wish. Oh, he's here. The burger plate. Amen.

LIZ: Yes, I'll have the—uh—slice of pizza plain—I forget, is that with cheese? And a *cola*. [*She laughs at the term.*]

BETH [*playing along*]: Oh, and a *cola* for me too.

LIBBY: Me too. Oh, is it my turn? And a donut.

BETH: No, make that your *diet cola*.

LIZ [*thrilled by the implicit mockery*]: For me too!

LIBBY: Me too! [*They watch the waiter go, and laugh simultaneously.*]

BETH: We're all having the same *beverage*!

LIZ [*imitating a nasal robot*] *Beverage! Beverage* with your *meal*! [Laughter]

LIBBY: We sure are having a good time, huh? [*This casts a pall on the proceedings. Then, to re-spark the conversation*] I love your new jacket, Liz. It's old, huh?

LIZ: Are you kidding? West Tech burned down ten years ago, I'd be going to a vacant lot!

BETH: What a goof! Liz the varsity quarterback.

LIZ: I found it in the Salvation Army.

BETH: It's so funny. I love the dumb colors, red and white.

LIZ: Look at this: "Skipper." If only they could have seen themselves back in those days.

LIBBY: Did they have anything green? I've decided I'm going to wear only green from now on so I can have an image.

LIZ: Wait'll you see, I bought somebody's old wedding picture, too. I'm going to hang it in my locker. My mother is so confused— She asked if I *knew* the people! Right, as if I were around in the nineteen thirties! [*Pause*] I'm gonna marry Tony and eat here for free.

LIBBY: We could eat here forever!

BETH: One thing I could not marry is that jukebox. It's slow, it is, it plays "I'll Never Tell You" slow somehow, and that song demands not a slow rhythm.

LIZ: Maybe the little men inside are tired of playing it for you.

LIBBY: Boy, it's a good thing we're nuts, huh! [*Another pall is cast.*] It helps to be nuts like us! [*Silence.* BETH *begins to hum "I'll Never Tell You." No recognizable tune emerges.*]

BETH [*joined by Libby*]: I'll never tell you, no, no, no, . . . See? It demands to be fast. [LIZ *has frozen, unnoticed by* BETH.] Remember that record album I played for you over the phone last week?

LIZ [*intensely*]: Sssh!

BETH: What?

LIZ: Shht! Everybody just act natural.

BETH: What's the matter?

LIZ: Nothing, everything is normal, don't turn your head.

LIBBY: If everything is normal, why do we have to act natural?

LIZ: Because that man over there is looking at us!

BETH: What!

LIZ: He's been staring at us!

LIBBY [*over-imagining the danger*]: Oh my God, and, please, angels—

LIZ [*sharply*]: Libby—

BETH: This is too weird. I'm sorry.

LIZ: He's looking. Don't look! [LIBBY *shuts her eyes.*] You can open your eyes, Libby, I mean don't look at *him*. Look how old he is! Don't look! At the counter.

LIBBY [*not looking*]: Oh my God!

BETH: Oh my water! [*Intentionally spills her ice water.*] Sorry, Libby, we better clean this up! [*She raises an unnatural fuss that allows her to steal looks at the counter.*] Napkins, napkins, here, let's shake off. Oopsy daisy!

LIBBY: It's fine, water doesn't stain.

BETH [*in a fake, loud voice*]: Thank goodness, huh! Thank goodness it doesn't stain! This is nice, did you get this at Peddler's Cove? I often go there! Sit. [*To* LIZ] I can't believe how old he is.

LIZ: I know, but he's not that old.

BETH: Some of his—I could see some gray hairs.

LIBBY: Is he kind of distinguished old, like he might have an important job?

LIZ: Come on, he's in Tony's.

LIBBY: Maybe he's from someplace foreign, where they look at each other.

LIZ: The stories you make up for people would make for a world of real dips.

BETH: He does look safe, though, not crazy.

LIZ: Are you trying to marry me to this guy?

BETH: He's staring at *you,* Liz.

LIBBY [*scared*]: Don't be scared, Liz!

LIZ: With my luck he's some gross uncle I was introduced to and forgot.

BETH: Have you ever had to handle a crush before?

LIZ [*She hasn't*]: Well of course. Of course I have. You're not around me every second. But this guy is so old. I can't tell him he'll find someone else.

LIBBY: Don't look back at him!

LIZ: I have to do something!

LIBBY [*"Think of your career"*]: You could be head of Debating Club next year!

LIZ: Let's not jump the gun here—

BETH: Don't do anything! What are you going to do?

LIZ: Okay. Tony has to bring the cokes. That'll be like something that happens.

LIBBY [*frightened*]: Then we tell Tony?

LIZ: I'll get up as if to stretch—and go find out what he wants.

LIBBY: Liz, don't talk to him!

BETH [*significantly: "D-Day"*]: Here are the cokes. [*They sit up painfully straight as the cokes are supposedly distributed. They watch* TONY *go.*]

LIBBY [*determined not to see him*]: Is he having coke?

LIZ [*peeking at the man*]: He's having coffee.

BETH [*factually*]: Gross.

LIZ: I'll ask to borrow the sugar.

LIBBY: Oh my God.

LIZ: Come on, it's four o'clock in the afternoon! [*They unwittingly exchange aviators' chocks-away glances. LIZ makes an unlikely stretch and goes.*] Geronimo!

BETH: Liz! [*To LIBBY, herself excited but trying to be calming*] Okay, okay now.

LIBBY: Okay, okay.

BETH: She's out of her mind!

LIBBY: Why are you grinning?

BETH: I can't help it. This isn't fun, I promise. Don't look! Is she talking to him?

LIBBY: No, he's talking to her, I can hear him. [*Both close their eyes and clasp hands, as if on a roller coaster.*]

BETH: Is that your heart or mine?

LIBBY: I don't know. [*Pause*] I wish I could save her.

BETH: Why did you ask before about if someone likes you? Does somebody *like* you?

LIBBY: No.

BETH: Who?

LIBBY: Terry Glauber. [*Pause. She lends an ear.*] Still talking.

BETH: He *should* like you, you're better than him.

LIBBY: He's supposed to stay in the hospital for another two months. Maybe then it would work out.

BETH: Oh, don't worry. I'm sure it'll be better than I think it'll be. [*Pause. Then, as an excuse to turn around.*] Tony! This isn't *diet* soda!

LIBBY: Don't turn around!

BETH: Are you trying to murder me by overweight? Ha-ha!

LIBBY: What are you doing?

BETH: The guy is writing something for her. His address!

LIBBY: Is she crazy? Does he know how old she isn't? I bet she told him she was her older sister. [*Pause. Sips her drink.*] This is *so* diet coke, it tastes like ashes.

BETH: I needed a reason to—shh, here she comes.

Come on, act like yourself. [*Silence.* LIZ *returns, sits, dazed. Silence.*]

LIBBY: Hi.

BETH: There's your coke.

LIBBY: Are you okay?

BETH: The guy's leaving. He's going. Liz—

LIBBY: [*absurdly, since* LIZ *is very still*]: Let her catch her breath.

LIZ [*finally*] The jacket belonged to his son.

BETH: Jacket? Your jacket? What about— Wasn't he watching you?

LIBBY: Are you all right?

LIZ: He saw the Skipper. This.

BETH: He thinks his son wants his letter jacket back? After ten years?

LIZ: No.

BETH: That's all he wanted, his son's jacket?

LIZ: His son was killed in a car crash. [*Awful silence, though not too long*]

LIBBY: Without the jacket?

BETH: Yes, without the jacket, sshh.

LIBBY: Oh, Liz.

LIZ: Some girl must have had it. He must've given it to some girl to wear who gave it to the Salvation Army eventually.

LIBBY: The dad didn't know who? [LIZ *shakes her head.*] Maybe she had to. Maybe she got married.

BETH: Are you giving it back?

LIZ [*nods*]: He was afraid I'd get cold. He said I should wear it home.

BETH: Oh. [*They all contemplate this opportunity briefly.*]

LIBBY: He did seem nice. [*Pause*] Though I never saw him. [*Pause*]

BETH: Oh, here's the food, uh, yes. [*Indicating* LIZ] That was her—I was the burger plate.

LIBBY: I was the donut.

LOOSE ENDS
by Michael Weller

Loose Ends was originally produced by the Arena Stage in Washington, D.C., in a production that subsequently moved to Circle in the Square on Broadway. The production starred Kevin Klein and Roxanne Hart and was directed by Alan Schneider.

Loose End chronicles the end of an era, the shift from the idealism and social awareness of the late sixties and early seventies to the careerism and cynical isolation of the "me generation" of the late seventies. The relationship of a young couple, Paul and Susan, spanning the years from 1970 to 1979, serves as the prism for the ideas of the play. When they first meet on a beach in Bali in 1970, Paul is a high-minded visionary just out of the Peace Corps and Susan is trying to find herself on a trip around the world. Although each can sense the other is very independent, the two end up living together in Boston. When Susan moves to New York to pursue her career as a still photographer, Paul joins her. But career pressures continue to chafe at the relationship. Paul becomes obsessed with the idea of having a child, but Susan believes that being a mother will undermine her career. When she finds out she is pregnant, she has an abortion to protect her lifestyle, but doesn't tell Paul, an action that helps bring about a permanent estrangement. In the following scene, set in Paul and Susan's New York apartment, Susan confides in Paul's associate Selina (who is also attracted to Paul) that she is pregnant.

SELINA: You feeling O.K.?

SUSAN: Huh? Oh, yeah, I'm fine. I guess I had too much wine or something. Maybe it's the monosodium.

SELINA: Maybe you ought to lie down.

SUSAN: No, I'm O.K. Lawrence'll be here in a minute. I'll be all right.

SELINA: You don't look all right.

SUSAN: Excuse me. [*Rises, starts out. Stops. Breathes deep. Returns. Sits.*] False alarm.

SELINA: Are you pregnant or something?

SUSAN: Yeah.

SELINA: Really?

SUSAN: Really.

SELINA: Paul didn't say anything.

SUSAN: I just found out, and don't say anything until I get a chance to tell him, O.K.?

SELINA: Man, I'd really like to be pregnant right now. I was thinking of just doing it, you know. Since it doesn't look like I'm having too much luck finding a guy I can put up with for more than a day or two. Just get someone to, you know, just contribute. Are you happy?

SUSAN: I had such an incredible feeling when I got the results of the test. Just . . . there you are, it finally happened. I was totally serene, just sort of floated home and I had this whole fantasy, you know, all those pregnant women you see walking around with that funny little smile on their face, the big secret . . .

SELINA: . . . and huge tits . . .

SUSAN: God, Paul would love that. Oh, and I got this idea for a series of self-portraits all through the pregnancy, the different stages. You could do it with a permanent camera in the bedroom so everything would be the same in the picture except I'd be getting bigger and bigger. But the thing is, when I started thinking about it I realized I was really into the idea of the photographs, but I wasn't really all that into the idea of being pregnant.

SELINA: You don't really want to tell him, do you?

SUSAN: Of course I want to tell him. I mean. O.K., I guess maybe I just want to get comfortable with the idea first so I know how I feel about it. We're the ones who have to do all the work, right?

SELINA: Yeah, I guess.

SUSAN: I don't know. It's just so nice the way things are now and the thing is he hasn't said anything about a baby for like . . . well, ever since his business started doing well. Not one word. So I guess it really was some kind of competitive thing. You know, I get pregnant so I can't work as much and that makes me less of a threat. The old story. Does that make sense?

SELINA: Oh, yeah. It makes sense. Sure.

SUSAN: So what do you think?

SELINA: About what?

SUSAN [*Pause*]: Why do you always take his side?

SELINA: Whose side?

SUSAN: Whenever I try to talk to you about something you always . . . like, I really thought you'd understand about this . . . sisterhood and all that. I mean I have a right to my own thoughts, don't I? It's not so terrible that I don't want to say anything to him until I know for sure how I feel about what my body is going to have to be doing for the next however many months and then when I know for sure I'll tell him about it and that way it won't get all messy with me getting my feelings all tangled up in the way he feels about it until we don't know who feels what about anything anymore, which is what always seems to happen with

us. But whenever I try to talk to you I feel like
you think I'm being . . . I don't know . . . like
you automatically think I'm doing the wrong thing.
Well?

SELINA: What are you asking me?

SUSAN: Yeah, you see? Like that kind of remark.
What's that supposed to mean? Oh, shit, Soolie,
listen to me. I sound like a witch. I'm sorry. I
really am sorry. I just, I don't know what to do
about this. [*Phone by* SUSAN *rings. She picks
up.*] Hello? Yeah, he can come up. [*Hangs up.*]
I'm thirty-three. If I don't have it now . . .
God, why is everything so fucking complicated?
They ought to have a course in making up your
mind. I'm sorry, but you see what I mean, don't
you?

SELINA: Oh. Sure. You have a problem, that's all. It's
O.K. You just have a problem.

SUSAN: I'm glad you think so.

SELINA: I don't really think anything, you know. All I
think is I'm always in the middle with you two.
Paul talks to me. You talk to me. Don't you ever
talk to each other? I don't know what you should
do. It's not my life. I mean I have enough of my
own stuff to figure out and I don't go around
asking people what I should do because they're
my problems and they're not very interesting unless you're me. In which case, they're mostly just
a pain in the ass. I'd like to move to New York,
for instance. I'd like to work for Paul. I think I'm
probably ready for it, although I think there must
be a lot of editors around as good as me and that
makes me wonder why you want me to move
here. Is it because I'm good at my job or because
you like me or because you and Paul don't know
how to deal with each other and you need me as a
middleman?

SUSAN: I didn't know you felt that way.

SELINA: You never asked. And I don't always feel that way either.

SUSAN: I think we better straighten this out.

SELINA: O.K.

LYDIE BREEZE
by John Guare

Lydie Breeze was first presented at the American Place Theater in New York City, in a production featuring Cynthia Nixon, Roberta Maxwell, Madeleine Potter, Josef Somer, Robert Joy, Ben Cross, and James Cahill, directed by Louis Malle.

Set in Nantucket in 1895, *Lydie Breeze* is a high Gothic tale of murder, guilt, and revenge, a fascinating blend of the humorous and the horrifying. Years earlier, Lydie Breeze's mother hung herself; Lydie has become a prisoner to everyone's memory of her mother. Over the course of the play, all of the players in the tragedy who are still living return to Nantucket, ready to act out the final curtain. One of the people who come back, Lydie's sister, Augusta (Gussie) Breeze, ran off to Washington, D.C., and became the "private secretary" to the powerful Senator Amos Mason. Now she has sailed back into town with Senator Mason on the fabled newspaperman William Randolph Hearst's yacht, "a yacht the size of the Oklahoma Territory." Like Mr. Hearst's yacht, everything about Gussie is very "American"—grand and slightly vulgar; and she fascinates the simple Lydie. In the following scene, Gussie, having just arrived at the Breeze house, tries to convince Lydie to run away from home, too, wooing her with promises of riches and great adventures in the world beyond Nantucket.

GUSSIE: Feel my dress. Can you feel the silk?

LYDIE: I never felt silk.

GUSSIE: Well, that's English silk, goddamit. And these are my beautiful English shoes. And these are beautiful English hairpins. I am doing so fine!

LYDIE: You went to England?

GUSSIE: Those English make me so mad. Can you imagine: We tell England to frig off in 1776. Not till 1894 does England finally decide to open an embassy in Washington. But Amos says I must forgive. So Amos and I had to return the honor and go over there.

LYDIE: Did you meet the queen? Is everything gold?

GUSSIE: I've been in Buckingham Palace. Saw Prince Edward. The Prince of Wales. He's Queen Victoria's son. The next king. We talked.

LYDIE: You talked to the next King of Wales?

GUSSIE: England! England! Are you an idiot? We were talking back and forth. If I ever get to England, I wouldn't mind looking him up. Buckingham Palace.

LYDIE: What did you talk about?

GUSSIE: Most of our chat revolved around the theater. When you meet people of that royal ilk, you have to have cultural things to talk about.

LYDIE: The theater?

GUSSIE: We saw *Frankenstein*. It was worth sailing an ocean for.

LYDIE: *Frankenstein?*

GUSSIE: Frankenstein is this wonderful scientist who cuts up old corpses . . .

LYDIE: Right on the stage?

GUSSIE: He makes this monster who's controlled by all the dreams of the parts he's made out of. Other people's dreams. Other people's nightmares. It scares the bejesus out of you. To hear all those tight-lipped English tiaras and white ties in the audience screaming like residents of Bedlam.

LYDIE: Is he hideous? Is he ghastly?

GUSSIE: No . . . Dr. Frankenstein must've got hold of the best-looking parts of all the corpses because the monster is . . . truly attractive. He pulls you toward him.

LYDIE: I don't want to go near him.

GUSSIE: In the last scene, the doctor goes up to the North Pole where he's chased the monster!

LYDIE: They have the North Pole right on stage!

GUSSIE: And they walk across the ice! And it's quiet . . . It's very still . . . [GUSSIE *spins* LYDIE *around.*] And you hear the wind swirling . . . And you know the monster is out there somewhere . . . Woooo . . . Woooo . . . ! [GUSSIE *hides.*]

LYDIE: Gussie? Gussie, don't scare me! [GUSSIE *sneaks up from behind* LYDIE.]

GUSSIE: And the monster leaps up . . . [GUSSIE *grabs* LYDIE. LYDIE *screams with pleasure.*] And he grabs Dr. Frankenstein and pulls him down, down under the ice. [LYDIE *and* GUSSIE *fall to the floor.*]

LYDIE: No!!

GUSSIE: And the monster looks out into the audience in the dark theater. "Come, my enemies, we have to wrestle for our lives. My reign is not yet over." Every evil ugly thing that ever happened woke up inside me. Ma killing herself. Pa going to prison. I got asthma worse than ever.

LYDIE [*hugging* GUSSIE]: I hate the evil ugly things inside of me.

GUSSIE: You're a goddamn little saint. You never did anything bad.

LYDIE: Ma killed herself. Maybe over something I did.

GUSSIE: You were just a baby. Ma killed herself because she was still in love with the other man.

LYDIE: Dan Grady. I know the name of Dan Grady.

GUSSIE: Pa killed Dan Grady and Pa went to prison. And then Pa came home and then Ma died. It was all for love. All for love.

LYDIE: Gussie, were you ever afraid of Pa?

GUSSIE: Yes, I was afraid of Pa. After he came home from jail, I could never sleep at night. If I was a bad girl, I was sure Pa would come in and kill me the same as he did to Dan Grady.

LYDIE: Is that why you left home?

GUSSIE [rises] I dream all the time I'm going to be killed. I'd rather be killed by a stranger than have Pa be the one.

LYDIE: Don't say that about Pa. [GUSSIE takes a comb from her purse and goes to the mirror to adjust her hairdo.]

GUSSIE: Sometimes I wish they left Pa in that Charlestown prison. What'd he ever do for any of us? Look at you. What's he doing for you? You can't read.

LYDIE: I can. A bit.

GUSSIE: You get decent grades in school?

LYDIE: I don't go to school.

GUSSIE: Do you know your ABCs?

LYDIE: Beaty teaches me.

GUSSIE: Those letters you write to me.

LYDIE: They're love letters.

GUSSIE: I can't read your letters. Zulus in darkest Africa send out better love letters.

LYDIE: It's very hot in here.

GUSSIE [taking LYDIE's arm]: How're you going to learn shorthand if you don't even have any long hand?

LYDIE [pulling away]: I don't want to learn shorthand.

GUSSIE: Don't you care about your life?

LYDIE: I care! I'm fine!

GUSSIE: Don't Pa care?

LYDIE: Pa cares.

GUSSIE: Some people even say Pa is not your real father. Amos Mason says Dan Grady is your father. If he is, I envy you.

LYDIE: You never come home. You never answer my letters.

GUSSIE: Baby, maybe I have kind of ignored the family the past few years. But I come back—see this—I think Ma'd like you travelling with me.

LYDIE: But Ma is here. I hear Ma's voice everyday.

GUSSIE: I only hear my own voice. And my own voice is saying that I want you to learn shorthand so bad. That's the ticket. When I went down to Washington, I just showed up at the Capitol building. Amos could've thrown me out with a gold piece. But he didn't. He took me in and he's taught me to read and recognize the good things. [*She strokes* LYDIE's *face.*]

LYDIE: Your hand feels so nice.

GUSSIE: Oh, baby, I'd love you to meet Amos. You'd score a bull's-eye, Lydie. A pretty young girl in Washington. And you could keep me company.

LYDIE: But I have to stay here with Pa . . .

GUSSIE: Pa!? Pa lost Ma. Pa lost me. Pa lost Amos as a friend. Pa won't even notice you're gone. Baby, electricity's been invented. I'm introducing you to power. You got a bag? I'm packing you up and taking you away.

LYDIE: I don't want to be like you. I don't want to go into bed with everybody.

GUSSIE: What do you know about going to bed?

LYDIE: Beaty tells me about going into bed.

GUSSIE: Beaty don't know nothing! Hills of beans have flags in them announcing what Beaty knows!

HOOTERS
by Ted Tally

Hooters was first performed at Playwrights Horizons in New York City.

Cheryl has dragged her friend Ronda to Cape Cod for the weekend for a little sun, for a little breather from Cheryl's overbearing boyfriend, and, perhaps, for a little "recreation." Unpacking the car, Cheryl has attracted the attentions of a college-age Casanova, Ricky. A few fancy maneuvers on the beach *et voilà*: Cheryl and a very reluctant Ronda are going out for dinner with Ricky and his friend, Clint.

Saturday Evening. The women's room. They are almost finished dressing to go out. They wear pretty summer dresses, high heels, jewelry, etc. CHERYL *smokes, puts on makeup.*

RONDA: Where's my bracelet?

CHERYL: I haven't seen it.

RONDA: I let you wear it yesterday. You were the last to see it.

CHERYL: I gave it back.

RONDA: You did not.

CHERYL: Yes I did.

RONDA: When?

CHERYL: Last night, when we were unpacking.

RONDA: You better not have lost that bracelet.

CHERYL: Ronnie.

142

RONDA: If you have I'll murder you. Jerry Potts gave me that bracelet. It's very special.

CHERYL: It must be around here somewhere.

RONDA: I've looked everywhere. It's gone.

CHERYL: Well, you must've put it in with your makeup and your other jewelry. Did you look in here?

RONDA: Of course I looked in there! I'm really not a total moron, thanks a lot.

CHERYL [*looking in makeup bag*]: Ronnie, why are you being so hostile?

RONDA: I'm not being hostile. I just want that bracelet you stole.

CHERYL: If you didn't want to go out tonight you could've just said something.

RONDA: Oh sure. I could've said excuse me, but I really think both you guys are total creeps. They wouldn't have even heard me—you were *panting* too loud for normal conversation.

CHERYL: I see. We should've stayed in our room tonight and watched the light bulb burn out.

RONDA: How in the world you could just stand there and pretend you *believed* that crap about the movies—it was enough to turn my stomach!

CHERYL: Ronnie, it was fun! Didn't you think it was fun to let those two kids think they could impress us into going out to dinner?

RONDA: But we *are* going out to dinner!

CHERYL: So?

RONDA: So who's so smart?

CHERYL: When he started talking about Paul Newman it was all I could do to keep a straight face. And when he did that scream—? [*Imitates* RICKY'*s expression and arm-flapping.*] Could you just *die*? [*She laughs.*]

RONDA: Great logic. He can throw a spastic fit on a public beach, so he must be a good date. What does he have to do to be the father of your children—dribble down the side of his chin?

CHERYL: I think you're getting a little carried away here. It's just a dinner date.

RONDA: Terrific. And who do I get, the bodyguard?

CHERYL: I think he's cute too.

RONDA: Great. Remind me to go down on him under the table.

CHERYL: I don't know how you can be so cynical. Don't you ever just want to have a good time?

RONDA: A quickie on Cape Cod with a couple of jerky strangers is not my idea of a good time.

CHERYL: Who said anything about a quickie?

RONDA: Oh don't tell me the thought hadn't occurred to you.

CHERYL: Ron, they're *kids*!

RONDA: Don't tell me it hasn't occurred to them.

CHERYL: Of course it has. It's the only thought their little heads are capable of holding at one time. That's the fun part.

RONDA: *Fun* part?

CHERYL: Leading them by the nose.

RONDA: Or whatever else is straight and sticks out.

CHERYL: Sure!

RONDA: You're not back in junior high, even if you act like it.

CHERYL: And you're not the principal, even though you talk like him.

RONDA: You make me sound like some kind of prude.

CHERYL: You are.

RONDA: I've slept with men!

CHERYL: Two.

RONDA: Three!

CHERYL: Well. Two and a half.

RONDA [*angrily*]: You leave Jerry Potts out of this! He's suffered enough.

CHERYL: I didn't say anything.

RONDA: Anyway it doesn't matter who I've slept with. It's not something you keep a scorecard in!

CHERYL: Of course not.

RONDA: Even though you think it is.

CHERYL: I do not!

RONDA: I don't know how you could do this to David. You're practically *engaged* to him.

CHERYL: Oh-ho! Now it's David.

RONDA: I think this is just a crude attempt to score points on him in some kind of dumb game you've made up. I'd ask myself what I was after if I was you.

CHERYL: *David* wants me to feel middle-aged. David wants me to be the mother of three in a ranch wagon on my way to the PTA! Well forget that.

RONDA: Try your real age.

CHERYL: Oh, okay, what's that? How are you supposed to act when you're twenty-five? You tell me, you're the expert—does it mean you're still allowed to have fun, but not quite as much? Or you can *have* it, but you can't let it show?

RONDA: Being a kid and acting immature are not the same thing.

CHERYL [*Pause*]: You know what you are, Ron? You're a conscientious objector. When the trumpets sounded for the sexual revolution, I think you just charged in the opposite direction.

RONDA: Maybe I just refused to be drafted!

CHERYL: Well you can relax now, the revolution's over. This is just a mopping-up operation.

RONDA [*very upset*]: I hate it! I hate being so *free* that I'm *compelled* to do something I never asked for the freedom to do in the first place! I never *asked* for it, so thanks a lot! And something that somebody as pretty as you could've always done anyway. Well where does that leave me if I don't want to? Where does that leave *me*?

CHERYL [*Pause*]: You really are getting very worked up over a crummy little seafood dinner. A couple of shrimp and a lousy clam roll? [*She laughs.*]

RONDA: Where's my bracelet?

CHERYL: Ron, talk to me.

RONDA: If I'm going to have zits all over my face from

seafood, I can at least wear something shiny. Maybe it'll distract them.

CHERYL: You're really mad at me, aren't you?

RONDA: [*Pause*]: I thought I came to the beach to be with you. I thought you wanted to get *away* from guys for one weekend, and we'd talk. Maybe get some sun, and talk things out. [*Pause*] This isn't fair, Cheryl.

CHERYL: I'm sorry, Ron. [*Pause*] I guess I got a little carried away here. [*Pause*] Listen. We'll have a couple drinks, we'll eat, we'll say goodnight and come home together. Alone. Okay?

RONDA: Do you mean it?

CHERYL: Yes.

RONDA: But do you really mean it?

CHERYL: I promise.

RONDA [*Pause*]: Okay.

CHERYL: Okay. [RONDA *runs to* CHERYL, *hugs her impulsively. The doorbell rings.*]

RONDA: Oh God it's them. The epileptic and his bodyguard. Cher, what am I going to do?

CHERYL: Get the door.

RONDA: Right. [RONDA *goes off to answer the door.* CHERYL *smoothes her clothes.*]

A LIE OF THE MIND
by Sam Shepard

A Lie of the Mind was first performed at the Promenade Theater in New York City. The production, directed by Sam Shepherd, included Harvey Keitel, Aidan Quinn, Amanda Plummer, Will Patton, Geraldine Page, Karen Young, James Gannon, and Ann Wedgeworth.

A brooding, epic play, *A Lie in the Mind* smashes domestic tragedy against bitter comedy to expose the myth of the American family. Jake, an angry, restless man, has badly beaten his wife, Beth. He thinks he has killed her, but she has survived, and her family has taken her back to her native Montana. Jake's family, meanwhile, has provided the tormented man with a haven, too. In his boyhood bedroom, complete with a single bed that's too small for him and dusty model airplanes hanging from the ceiling, his mother Lorraine, vainly tries to comfort him with childhood games and cream of broccoli soup. But when Jake realizes Beth may still be alive, he heads off to Montana, leaving a disconsolate Lorraine and his sister, Sally, to argue over Jake and another family renegade: Jake and Sally's father, who left his wife and children years before and whose death on a highway has remained a mystery, a miasma of guilt and denial for the family.

SALLY: Didn't you ever wonder about him? About what became of him?

LORRAINE: Who?

SALLY: Dad.

LORRAINE [*sitting up*]: Wonder? Did I ever wonder? You know a man your whole life. You grow up with him. You're almost raised together. You go to school on the same bus together. You go through tornandoes together in the same basement. You go through a world war together. You have babies together. And then one day he just up and disappears into thin air. Did I ever wonder? Yeah. You bet your sweet life I wondered. But you know where all that wondering got me? Nowhere. Absolutely nowhere. Because here I am. Here I am. Alone. Just the same as though he'd never even existed.

SALLY: I thought you said he was still in you.

LORRAINE: Not him. Some disease he left behind.

SALLY: But there must've been a time when you loved him. Before.

LORRAINE: Love. Whata crock a' shit. Love! There's another disease. Only difference is it's a disease that makes ya feel good. While it lasts. Then, when it's gone, yer worse off than before you caught it.

SALLY: Well, I don't think there's a whole lot we can do about it, is there?

LORRAINE: Yes there is. Oh, yes there is. You can resist. You can look it right square in the kisser and resist. [LORRAINE *lies back down. Pause.*]

SALLY: Maybe. Maybe, *you* can. That's what Jake tried to do. He's a lot like you I guess. He started squirming in that trailer. Making up reasons why we had to get outa here. Get back across the border before it got dark. Dad kept wanting us to stay but he didn't have anything to offer us. And that's when Jake made a desperate move. He didn't even know he was doing it. He was so desperate to get out of that situation, that he stands up and he offers to take Dad and me out to a bar. For a drink! I couldn't believe it. Dad's whole face lit up. I've never seen his face like that. He smiled like a little kid and grabbed his hat.

LORRAINE: You can't stop a drinkin' man from drinkin'. All he needs is an idea and he's gone. Just the idea of straddling a bar stool in some honky-tonk somewhere in his mind. He's gone. [LORRAINE *slowly pulls herself up to a sitting position and listens more intently to* SALLY.]

SALLY: They started right off with double shots of tequila and lime. At first it was like this brotherhood they'd just remembered. But then it started to shift. After about the fourth double shot it started to go in a whole different direction.

LORRAINE: That figures.

SALLY: There was a meanness that started to come outa both of them like these hidden snakes. A terrible meanness that was like—murder almost. It *was* murder.

LORRAINE: Whadya mean, murder?

SALLY: Their eyes changed. Something in their eyes. Like animals. Like the way an animal looks for the weakness in another animal. They started poking at each other's weakness. Stabbing. Just a little bit at a time. Like the way that rooster used to do. That rooster we had that went around looking for the tiniest speck of blood on a hen or a chick and then he'd start pecking away at it. And the more he pecked at it the more excited he got until finally he just killed it.

LORRAINE: Yeah, we had to boil that one. Tough son of a gun.

SALLY: They looked into each other like there was nobody else in the bar. At first it was all about sports. About which one of them could throw a hardball faster. Which one could take the toughest hit in football. Which one could run the fastest and the longest. That was the one they decided would be the big test. They decided to prove it to each other once and for all. So they downed a couple more tequilas and crashed out through the doors of the place into the street.

LORRAINE: I thought you said he could barely stand up.

SALLY: Who?

LORRAINE: Your father.

SALLY: That was before. Before he'd had a drink. Now it was like he'd had a transfusion or somethin.' That tequila went right into his blood and lit him on fire. He crouched down in a racing position right beside Jake. And they were both deadly serious. And then they took off. Dad took about four strides and fell flat on his face in the street but Jake never stopped. He ran like a wild colt and never once looked back. Straight into the next bar up the block. I went over and tried to help Dad up but he turned on me and snarled. Just like a dog. Just like a crazy dog. I saw it in his eyes. This deep, deep hate that came from somewhere far away. It was pure, black hate with no purpose.

LORRAINE: That was him all right.

SALLY: He wouldn't let me help him. He just crawled up the street toward the bar that Jake went into. And there I was following along behind. I felt so stupid. He kept turning and snarling at me to keep back. But I didn't wanna fall too far back 'cause I was afraid somethin'—[*she starts to break down but stops herself.*]

LORRAINE: What?

SALLY [*trying to control it*]: I was afraid somethin' bad might happen to him and—it happened anyway.

LORRAINE: What happened?

SALLY: Jake came up with a brilliant idea. He said, since we were only about a mile from the American border we should hit every bar and continue the race until we got to the other side. First one to the other side, won. First one to America! But we couldn't miss a bar. Right then I knew what Jake had in mind.

LORRAINE: What?

SALLY: Jake had decided to kill him.

[*Pause*]

LORRAINE [*throws the blankets off and struggles to sit up*]: What in the world are you talkin' about!

SALLY: It was just the same—it was just the same as if he'd had a gun. He knew what was gonna happen. Dad couldn't even walk anymore. He couldn't stand. His knees were all bloody. Jake knew that all he had to do was push him over the edge. Just a few more drinks and he'd be gone.

LORRAINE [*struggling to stand by bed, supporting herself*]: That is the most lame-brained, idiotic piece of claptrap I ever heard in my life! Jake might be a lot a' things. He might be crazy. He might be wound a little loose in some areas but he would never, ever, in this world, try to kill his own father! How can you say somethin' like that?

SALLY: I was there! I was right there and I saw every inch of it. I saw him killed! I saw it happen. I saw him splattered all over the road like some lost piece of livestock. He was trying to run down the middle of a highway. He was trying to beat his own son to the border. He didn't even know what country he was in anymore! Jake murdered him! And he never even looked back. He was already sitting in some bar down the road ordering the next round of drinks. He never even got up when he heard the sirens.

LORRAINE: It was an accident! That's all. Just an ordinary accident. Couldn't be helped.

SALLY: No, Mom. It was no accident.

LORRAINE: He didn't know what he was doin', any more than his father did!

SALLY: He knew. He still knows. He made me promise. That's how come he didn't tell you face to face. That's why the cop came to your door.

LORRAINE: He is not a murderer! My son is not a murderer! Why is everyone trying to make him into this criminal. First, that woman of his. He never shoulda got tied up with that woman in the first place. She's the cause of all this. And now you've turned against him.

SALLY: I'm just tellin' you what I saw with my own eyes.

LORRAINE: What you saw? What you saw! You stood there and watched your own father get run over by a truck in the middle of a Mexican highway and you're tryin' to tell me that Jake murdered him?

SALLY: That's the way it happened.

LORRAINE: What about you! Jake was nowhere near

him you said. What were you doin'? Standin'
there helpless? You were the only one sober and
there was nothin' you could do? Is that the story?

SALLY: Dad wouldn't let me near him. I couldn't get
near him.

LORRAINE: You couldn't have gone for help? Were
your legs broke or somethin'?

SALLY: There was nowhere to go! Jake had the keys.

LORRAINE: Jake! Jake! Jake! *You're* the one who killed
him, not Jake!! You're the one. If he was that
drunk, you could've taken care of him. You coulda
got him off the road. You coulda dragged him.
You coulda done somethin' other than just stand
there and watch. It was you. Wasn't it? It was you
that wanted him dead. It's you that wants Jake
dead too!

SALLY: No!

LORRAINE: It's you that wants to undermine this entire
family! Drag us down one by one until there's no
one left but you.

SALLY: I'm just sick of coverin' up for him. I'm sick to
death of covering everything up. I'm sick of being
locked up in this room. In our own house. Look
at this room. What're we doin' in here? This was
Jake's room when he was a kid. What're we doin'
in this room now? What're we supposed to be
hiding from?

[*Long pause.* LORRAINE *stands there staring at* SALLY,
*then slowly turns her head up and stares at the
model planes.*]

LORRAINE [*staring at planes*]: I know one thing for
sure. All these airplanes have gotta go. All these
airplanes are comin' down. Every last one of 'em.
All the junk in this house that they left behind for
me to save. It's all goin'. We'll make us a big
bonfire. They never wanted it anyway. They had
no intention of ever comin' back here to pick it
up. That was just a dream of theirs. It never
meant a thing to them. They dreamed it up just to

keep me on the hook. Can't believe I fell for it all those years.

SALLY: I didn't want him to die, Mom.

LORRAINE: Doesn't matter now. He was one a' them hopeless men. Nothin' you can do about the hopeless. [*Pause*] You know what I miss more than anything now?

SALLY: What?

LORRAINE: The wind. One a' them fierce, hot, dry winds that come from deep out in the desert and rip the trees apart. You know, those winds that wipe everything clean and leave the sky without a cloud. Pure blue. Pure, pure blue. Wouldn't that be nice?

3.

Scenes for Two Men

MINNESOTA MOON
by John Olive

Among its many productions, *Minnesota Moon* has been performed by the Circle Repertory Company in New York City, as well as in Scotland's Edinburgh Festival.

The play takes place in Maple Lake, a small town in southern Minnesota, in the early 1970s. Two friends, Alan and Larry, are saying good-bye—Alan is heading off to school in Minneapolis; Larry is deciding whether to continue his job at a gas station in Maple Lake or enlist. They spend their last night together drinking beer in the moonlit yard of a deserted farmhouse. During the course of the night, they work their way to confronting something they have never been able to talk about: the recent death of their friend, Terry.

LARRY: Remember the dances, Al?

ALAN [*laughs.*]: You 'n me, Terry, Winkie, Jim. What a bunch of rowdies. The time Terry decided he was gonna dance with every girl in the place. Where was that?

ALAN [*still laughing*]: I can't remember. Somewhere by Lake Crystal.

LARRY: Five minutes and two fights.

ALAN: You looked real sexy with your fat lip.

LARRY: What a crazy fucker Terry was.

ALAN: Really.

LARRY: With his practical jokes, his runnin'. He had
   . . . he had . . .

ALAN: Creativity.

LARRY: He had a lotta that, yeah.

ALAN: The most creative person I ever knew. Everything he did he did his way, his style.

LARRY [*counting on his fingers*]: May, June, July—

ALAN: Four and a half months.

LARRY: Huh?

ALAN: It's been four and a half months.

LARRY: Since Terry. . . . [*Still counting*] Yeah, right.
   Four and a half. . . . [*After a pause*] Alan?

ALAN: Yes, Lawrence?

LARRY: Hey, fuck you.

ALAN: What.

LARRY: I sorta wouldn't mind talkin' 'bout Terry.
   [*Pause.* ALAN *gets up and opens a beer.*] Because I
   think about him all the time and maybe one a the
   reasons I don't know what the fuck I'm doing is
   because I can't get Terry off my mind.

ALAN: Yeah, yeah, yeah.

LARRY: I mean, it shouldn't take four and a half months
   to—

ALAN: You want one?

LARRY: Huh? No, I got half a one here. You miss him
   as much as I do? Al?

ALAN: Whaddaya think?

LARRY: You pissed?

ALAN: No.

LARRY: Seen his ma lately?

ALAN: Yeah, today. Went over to say good-bye.

LARRY: Yeah? How is she? How's the place look?

ALAN: She's fine, place looks like shit.

LARRY: No one around to—

ALAN: She's gonna sell it and move up with her
   daughter.

LARRY: In California?

ALAN: No, the one in Duluth.

LARRY: Oh, yeah. So . . . You said good-bye.

ALAN: Yep.

LARRY: She cry, or anything?

ALAN: Hey—

LARRY: What?

ALAN: You think life's a movie?

LARRY: I dunno what life is.

ALAN: Just somethin' for you to—

LARRY: All I asked—

ALAN: It was a private . . .

LARRY [*overlapping*]: Did she . . . ?

ALAN: . . . conversation! Jesus.

LARRY: Okay, you don't have to tell me. I ain't your friend, I wasn't Terry's friend, I'm just a nosy sonofabitch who can't keep his mouth shut.

ALAN [*after a pause*]: We talked about Minneapolis, about how hard I would have to study and would I have enough money.

LARRY: You talk about Terry?

ALAN: Yes, we talked about Terry.

LARRY: And?

ALAN: She's against motorcycles and how there should be a law, like in Florida, that cyclists always have to wear helmets.

LARRY: She say that?

ALAN: Yes.

LARRY: Helmet wouldn't a helped Terry. That truck squashed him flat.

ALAN: Well, maybe she didn't know that.

LARRY: Why? Didn't she . . . ?

ALAN: They didn't give her the gruesome details or maybe she didn't ask.

LARRY: But didn't she read the . . . ?

ALAN: Larry.

LARRY: "You dumb shit."

ALAN: Yeah.

LARRY: Anything else?

ALAN: None of his scholarships came through.

LARRY: What!? Shit! He was good, man. The hurdles, the dashes, every time he ran the 880 he cleaned up.

ALAN: He got beat.

LARRY: Well, there was just that nigger-guy from Rochester.

ALAN: Maybe the "nigger-guy" got the scholarships.

LARRY: He was good!

ALAN: Guess he'll just hafta work his way through college.

LARRY: Pisses me off.

ALAN: The dinky schools we usually ran against didn't—

LARRY: But he was—

ALAN: Good, yeah. He really was. He was a runnin' fool.

LARRY: Shit, you too. Both of you crazy fuckers were always—

ALAN: Impromptu footraces.

LARRY: Slam on the brakes, out the door and, bam, you were off.

ALAN: Middle a winter.

LARRY: You guys really scared the shit outa Winkie that one time.

ALAN: Terry lived for that. Running and laughing and yelling and running. He'd let me get ahead then I'd hear this "Whoo! Whoo! Whoo!" behind me and he'd be shootin' past, yellin' with every stride. Collapse into a snowbank, laughing, barking huge clouds of white breath up at the cold moon, the air like fire in our lungs.

LARRY: Yeah. Hey, how fast he do the hundred?

ALAN: Hm? Oh, I dunno. Ten somethin'.

LARRY: I could never break twelve.

ALAN: I never tried.

LARRY: Fucker could run.

ALAN: Fucker could run.

LARRY: What's it feel like to be dead? What're you lookin' at me like that for?

ALAN: I'm not—

LARRY: One chuckle and I'll stomp yer ass.

ALAN: Hey.

LARRY: Okay, okay.

ALAN: When you're dead you don't feel. Question is: what's it feel like to die?

LARRY: I guess that's what I meant.

ALAN: Maybe you don't feel anything. Maybe your body sees it comin' and just . . . shuts down. You're fallin' and fallin' and your body sees the ground rushin' up and it transmits a message to every cell: "This is it, guys." Bam, you're dead. Dead before you even hit the ground.

LARRY: Yeah?

ALAN: Yep. Your body'd never let you suffer alla that pain. It'd kill itself for you, put you outa your misery.

LARRY: You think that's what happened to Terry? Died even before the truck hit him?

ALAN: Sure.

LARRY [*after a pause*]: Musta hurt like a bastard.

ALAN: Yeah.

LARRY: Shit.

ALAN: Drink your beer. Notice how quiet it is? That's because all the bugs 'n birds're depressed. Let's change the subject.

EXECUTION OF JUSTICE
by Emily Mann

Execution of Justice was originally commissioned by the Eureka Theater in San Francisco. The play had its first professional engagement at the Actors Theater of Louisville. Before its broadway premiere in 1986, the play was trimmed and honed at Baltimore Center Stage, the Berkley Repertory Theater, and the Guthrie Theater.

Execution of Justice dramatizes the murder trial of Dan White, the former San Francisco supervisor and ex-cop, who in 1978 assassinated the mayor, George Moscone, and fellow supervisor, Harvey Milk, the nation's first openly gay elected politician. The events of the play are authentic, culled not only from transcripts of the trial, but from taped interviews with various citizens of San Francisco. In the following scene, Inspector Frank Falzon asks Dan White to recount the events that led up to the shooting of the mayor and Harvey Milk.

FALZON: Dan, can you tell Inspector Erdelatz and myself, what was your plan this morning? What did you have in mind?

WHITE: I didn't have any devised plan or anything, it's, I was leaving the house to talk, to see the mayor and I went downstairs, to, to make a phone call and I had my gun down there.

FALZON: Is this your police service revolver, Dan?

WHITE: This is the gun I had when I was a policeman. It's in my room an ah . . . I don't know, I just put it on. I don't know why I put it on, it's just . . .

FALZON: You went directly from your residence to the mayor's office this morning?

WHITE: Yes, my, my aide picked me up but she didn't have any idea ah . . . you know that I had a gun on me or, you know, and I went in to see him an, an he told me he wasn't going to, intending to tell me about it. Then ah . . . I got kind of fuzzy and then just my head didn't feel right and, I, then he said: "Let's go into the, the back room and, and have a drink and talk about it."

FALZON: Was this before any threats on your part, Dan?

WHITE: I, I never made any threats.

FALZON: There were no threats at all?

WHITE: I, I . . . oh no.

FALZON: When were you, how, what was the conversation, can you explain to Inspector Erdelatz and myself the conversation that existed between the two of you at this time?

WHITE: It was pretty much just, you know, I asked, was I going to be reappointed. He said, no I am not, no you're not. And I said, why, and he told me, it's a political decision and that's the end of it, and that's it.

FALZON: Is this when you were having a drink in the back room?

WHITE: No, no, it's before I went into the back room and then he could obviously see, see I was obviously distraught an then he said, let's have a drink an I, I'm not even a drinker, you know I don't, once in a while, but I'm not even a drinker. But I just kinda stumbled in the back and he was all, he was talking an nothing was getting through to me. It was just like a roaring in my ears an, an then em . . . it just came to me, you know, he . . .

FALZON: You couldn't hear what he was saying Dan?

WHITE: Just small talk that, you know, it just wasn't registering. What I was going to do now, you know, and how this would affect my family, you know, an, an just, just all the time knowing he's going to go out an, an lie to the press an, an tell 'em, you know, that I, I wasn't a good supervisor and that people didn't want me an then that was it. Then I, I just shot him, that was it, it was over.

FALZON: What happened after you left there, Dan?

WHITE: Well, I, I left his office by one of the back doors, I was going down the stairs and then I saw Harvey Milk's aide an then it struck me about what Harvey had tried to do an I said, well I'll go talk to him. He didn't know I had, I had heard his conversation and he was all smiles and stuff and I went in and, you know. I, I didn't agree with him on a lot of things, but I was always honest, you know, and here they were devious. I started to say you know how hard I worked for it and what it meant to me and my family an then my reputation as, as a hard worker, good honest person and he just kind of smirked at me as if to say, too bad an then, an then, I just got all flushed, an, an hot, and I shot him.

FALZON: This occurred inside your room, Dan?

WHITE: Yeah, in my office, yeah.

FALZON: And when you left there did you go back home?

WHITE: No, no, no I drove to the, the Doggie Diner on, on Van Ness and I called my wife and she, she didn't know, she . . .

FALZON: Did you tell her Dan?

WHITE [*sobbing*]: I called up, I didn't tell her on the phone. I just said she was work . . . see, she was working, son's at a babysitter, shit. I just told her to meet me at the cathedral.

FALZON: St. Mary's?

WHITE [*sobbing*]: She took a cab, yeah. She didn't know. She had knew I'd been upset and I wasn't even talking to her at home because I just couldn't explain how I felt and she had no, nothing to blame about it, she was, she always has been great to me but it was, just the pressure hitting me an just my head's all flushed and expected that my skull's going to crack. Then when she came to the church, I, I told her and she kind of slumped and she, she couldn't say anything.

FALZON: How is she now do you, do you know is she, do you know where she is?

WHITE: I don't know now. She, she came to Northern Station with me. She asked me not to do anything about myself, you know that she, she loved me an she'd stick by me and not to hurt myself.

FALZON: Is there anything else you'd like to add at this time?

WHITE: Just that I've been honest and worked hard, never cheated anybody or, you know, I'm not a

crook or anything an I wanted to do a good job,
I'm trying to do a good job an I saw this city as
it's going, kind of downhill an I was always just a
lonely vote on the board and try to be honest an,
an I just couldn't take it anymore an that's it.

GLENGARRY GLEN ROSS
by David Mamet

The Pulitzer Prize-winning *Glengarry Glen Ross* premiered at the Cottesloe Theater, part of the National
Theatre complex in London, where it was distinguished
as the Best Play of the season. A production of the
play opened on Broadway, with a pre-Broadway run
at the Goodman Studio Theater in Chicago.

In *Glengarry Glen Ross* a group of driven, hard-
driving Chicago salesmen make their living selling ques-
tionable Southern real estate to gullible Northerners.
Survival of the fittest is the law; the salesmen are
jackals who will do anything they can to close a deal—
lie, cheat, even steal. The best salesmen get the premium leads, the worst salesmen get the leavings.
Levene, an aging salesman down on his luck, becomes
involved in a scheme to burglarize the real estate
office he works for and sell the premium leads to a
rival agency. The morning after the robbery, Levene,
full of bravado because he thinks he just closed a
major deal, comes down hard on the office manager,
Williamson, about Williamson's ruining a deal for another salesman. In the process of bawling out Williamson, he unwittingly reveals his complicity in the robbery.

LEVENE: You *are* a shithead, Williamson . . . [*Pause*]

WILLIAMSON: Mmm.

LEVENE: You can't think on your feet you should keep your mouth closed. [*Pause*] You hear me? I'm *talking* to you. Do you hear me . . . ?

WILLIAMSON: Yes. [*Pause*] I hear you.

LEVENE: You can't learn that in an office. Eh? He's right. You have to learn it on the streets. You can't *buy* that. You have to *live* it.

WILLIAMSON: Mmm.

LEVENE: *Yes.* Mmm. *Yes. Precisely. Precisely.* 'Cause your partner *depends* on it. [*Pause*] I'm *talking* to you, I'm trying to tell you something.

WILLIAMSON: You are?

LEVENE: Yes, I am.

WILLIAMSON: What are you trying to tell me?

LEVENE: What Roma's trying to tell you. What I told you yesterday. Why you don't belong in this business.

WILLIAMSON: Why I don't . . .

LEVENE: You listen to me, someday you might say, "Hey . . ." No, fuck that, you just listen what I'm going to say: your partner *depends* on you. Your partner . . . a man who's your "partner" *depends* on you . . . you have to go *with* him and *for* him . . . or you're shit, you're *shit*, you can't exist alone . . .

WILLIAMSON [*brushing past him*]: Excuse me . . .

LEVENE: . . . excuse you, *nothing*, you be as cold as you want, but you just fucked a good man out of six thousand dollars and his goddamn bonus 'cause you didn't know the *shot*, if you can do that and you aren't man enough that it gets you, then I don't know what, if you can't take *some thing* from that . . . [*blocking his way*] you're *scum*, you're fucking white-bread. You be as cold as you want. A *child* would know it, he's right. [*Pause*] You're going to make something up, be sure it will *help* or keep your mouth closed. [*Pause*]

WILLIAMSON: Mmm. [LEVENE *lifts up his arm.*]

LEVENE: Now I'm done with you. [*Pause*]

WILLIAMSON: How do you know I made it up?

LEVENE [*Pause*]: What?

WILLIAMSON: How do you know I made it up?

LEVENE: What are you talking about?

WILLIAMSON: You said, "You don't make something up unless it's sure to help." [*Pause*] How did you know that I made it up?

LEVENE: What are you talking about?

WILLIAMSON: I told the customer that his contracts had gone to the bank.

LEVENE: Well, hadn't it?

WILLIAMSON: No. [*Pause*] It hadn't.

LEVENE: Don't *fuck* with me, John, don't *fuck* with me . . . what are you saying?

WILLIAMSON: Well, I'm saying this, Shel: usually I take the contracts to the bank. Last night I didn't. How did you know that? One night in a year I left a contract on my desk. Nobody knew that but *you*. Now how did you know that? [*Pause*] You want to talk to me, you want to talk to someone *else* . . . because this is *my* job. This is my job on the line, and you are going to *talk* to me. Now how did you know that contract was on my desk?

LEVENE: You're so full of shit.

WILLIAMSON: You robbed the office.

LEVENE [*laughs*]: Sure! I robbed the office. Sure.

WILLIAMSON: What'd you do with the leads? [*Pause. Points to the* DETECTIVE'*s room*] You want to go in there? I tell him what I know, he's going to dig up *something*. . . . You got an alibi last night? You better have one. What did you do with the leads? If you tell me what you did with the leads, we can talk.

LEVENE: I don't know what you are saying.

WILLIAMSON: If you tell me where the leads are, I won't turn you in. If you *don't*, I am going to tell the cop you stole them, Mitch and Murray will see that you go to jail. Believe me they will. Now, what did you do with the leads? I'm walking in that door—you have five seconds to tell me: or you are going to jail.

LEVENE: I . . .

WILLIAMSON: I don't care. You understand? *Where are the leads?* [*Pause*] Alright. [WILLIAMSON *goes to open the office door.*]

LEVENE: I sold them to Jerry Graff.

WILLIAMSON: How much did you get for them? [*Pause*] How much did you get for them?

LEVENE: Five thousand. I kept half.

WILLIAMSON: Who kept the other half? [*Pause*]

LEVENE: Do I have to tell you? [*Pause.* WILLIAMSON *starts to open the door.*] Moss.

WILLIAMSON: *That* was easy, *wasn't* it? [*Pause*]

LEVENE: It was his idea.

WILLIAMSON: *Was* it?

LEVENE: I . . . I'm sure he got more than the five, actually.

WILLIAMSON: Uh-huh?

LEVENE: He told me my share was twenty-five.

WILLIAMSON: Mmm.

LEVENE: Okay: I . . . look: I'm going to make it worth your while. I am. I turned this thing around. I closed the *old* stuff, I can do it again. *I'm* the one's going to close 'em. *I* am! *I* am! 'Cause I turned this thing a . . . I can do *that*, I can do *anyth* . . . last night. I'm going to tell you, I was ready to Do the Dutch. Moss gets me, "Do this, we'll get well. . . ." Why not. Big fuckin' deal. I'm halfway hoping to get caught. To put me out of my . . . [*Pause*] But it *taught* me something. What it taught me, that you've got to get *out* there. Big deal. So I wasn't cut out to be a thief. I was cut out to be a salesman. And now I'm back, and I got my *balls* back . . . and, you know, John, you have the *advantage* on me now. Whatever it takes to make it right, we'll make it right. We're going to make it right.

WILLIAMSON: I want to tell you something, Shelly. You have a big mouth. [*Pause*]

LEVENE: What?

WILLIAMSON: You've got a big mouth, and now I'm going to show you an even bigger one. [*Starts toward the* DETECTIVE's *door.*]

LEVENE: Where are you going John? . . . you can't do that, you don't want to do that . . . hold, hold on . . . hold on . . . wait . . . wait . . . wait . . [*Pulls money out of his pockets*] Wait . . . uh, look . . . [*Starts splitting money*] Look, twelve, twenty, two, twen . . . twenty-five hundred, it's . . . take it. [*Pause*] Take it all. . . . [*Pause*] Take it!

WILLIAMSON: No, I don't think so, Shel.

LEVENE: I . . .

WILLIAMSON: No, I think I don't want your money. I think you fucked up my office. And I think you're going away.

LEVENE: I . . . what? Are you, are you, that's why . . . ? Are you nuts? I'm . . . I'm going to *close* for you, I'm going to . . . [*Thrusting money at him*] Here, here, I'm going to *make* this office . . . I'm going to be back there Number One. . . . Hey, hey, hey! This is only the beginning . . . . List . . . list . . . listen. Listen. Just one moment. List . . . here's what . . . here's what we're going to do. Twenty percent. I'm going to give you twenty percent of my sales. . . . [*Pause*] Twenty percent. [*Pause*] For as long as I am with the firm. [*Pause*] Fifty percent. [Pause] You're going to be my partner. [*Pause*] Fifty percent. Of all my sales.

WILLIAMSON: What sales?

LEVENE: What sales . . . ? I just *closed* eighty-two grand. . . . Are you fuckin' . . . I'm *back* . . . I'm *back*, this is only the beginning.

WILLIAMSON: Only the beginning . . .

LEVENE: Abso . . .

WILLIAMSON: Where have you been, Shelly? Bruce and Harriet Nyborg. Do you want to see the *memos* . . . ? They're nuts . . . they used to call in every week. When I was with Webb. And we were selling Arizona . . . they're nuts . . . did you see how they were *living*? How can you delude yours . . .

LEVENE: I've got the check . . .

WILLIAMSON: Forget it. Frame it. It's worthless. [*Pause*]

LEVENE: The check's no good?

WILLIAMSON: You stick around I'll pull the memo for you. [*Starts for the door*] I'm busy now . . .

LEVENE: Their check's no good? They're nuts . . . ?

WILLIAMSON: Call up the bank. *I* called them.

LEVENE: You did?

WILLIAMSON: I called them when we had the lead . . . four months ago. [*Pause*] The people are insane. They just like talking to salesmen. [WILLIAMSON *starts for door.*]

LEVENE: Don't.

WILLIAMSON: I'm sorry.

LEVENE: *Why?*

WILLIAMSON: Because I don't like you.

LEVENE: John: John: . . . my *daughter* . . .

WILLIAMSON: Fuck you.

IN PURSUIT OF THE SONG OF HYDROGEN
by Thomas G. Dunn

In Pursuit of the Song of Hydrogen was workshopped at the Playwrights' Center in Minneapolis, the Midwest Playwrights' Program in Madison, Wisconsin, the No Smoking Playhouse and New Dramatists in New York City, and George Mason University in Virginia. Since its premiere at Humboldt State University in Arcata, California, the play has been popular in college and semi-professional theaters across the country.

In Pursuit of the Song of Hydrogen traces the death of a young scientist, William, who has evolved a black hole theory of existence, a revolutionary theory that becomes the basis of a religious cult after the scientist's death. In the following scene William has spent the night in his laboratory, pondering the secrets of the universe through his telescope. It's morning, and William meets his brother Jack in Jack's driveway. A man obsessed with the infinite and the unknown, William has little interest in such smaller, earthbound concerns as family. This indifference becomes the center of the two brothers' conflict.

JACK: Billy . . . [*Backs off a bit.*] William, what in God's name are you doing standing out here in my driveway at this time of the morning?
WILLIAM: Waiting to talk to you.

JACK: Ah, I see. [*Slight pause. He lights a cigarette.*] Well?

WILLIAM: You're off to work early today?

JACK: I try to get in before ten on days that I golf after lunch.

WILLIAM: Ahh. Of course.

JACK: Not wanting to seem rude, but is there some reason why you're standing in my driveway this morning.

WILLIAM: Yes . . . you called. They took a message for me at the—

JACK: That was two weeks ago!

WILLIAM: Right . . .

JACK: And I called three times in two days. You never answered any of my calls.

WILLIAM: Mars seemed to be slowing up. It's the time of year when Venus and Mars should be lined up perfectly, and instead, for just a few days it looked to us as if—[*stops himself.*] You'll have to excuse me. I've been working all night, and I just came back from the most fantastic interview.

JACK: You just came back from a fantastic interview? At this time of the morning?

WILLIAM: What did you call about, Jack?

JACK: Why, Mum, of course. She hadn't heard from you in three months, and I promised her I would check in with you to make sure you were still of this earth.

WILLIAM: Barely, just barely.

JACK: Any chance of you getting home for the holidays? That's what she wants to know.

WILLIAM: I can't leave now. . . . Too much to wrap up.

JACK: Right. Well, should I tell her or will you?

WILLIAM: I think Margaret is calling her—we were thinking of sending the boys over there. Do you think Mum would like that?

JACK: She'd love it. Damn bastard . . . can't go yourself, so you send the two little cuddlies. William, someday this will all catch up with you.

WILLIAM [*innocent*]: What will?

JACK: This disregard for people. This sense that you're something special while the rest of us are not.

WILLIAM: Do you mean it?

JACK: Yes, I do mean it, dammit. [*Looks at* WILLIAM] I do mean it.

WILLIAM: You're not joking, are you?

JACK: Oh, you're impossible. So, how is Margaret doing? Last time I talked with her she was up to her neck in your work. Poor girl out of the hospital for less than a week and there she was hard at it.

WILLIAM: That poor girl understands more about my work than I do.

JACK: William, really.

WILLIAM: It's true. . . . Since I've been doing these guest lectures, I've been letting her literally write my speeches. She's fantastic. It's as if I'm way off somewheres with my thoughts, and she's walking along right behind me organizing them and making sense . . . of them.

JACK: In the clouds . . .

WILLIAM: What was that?

JACK: Nothing. I'm so glad to hear she's such a help. . . . if I was you I'd be a bit more careful of her.

WILLIAM: Careful of her?

JACK: Of her and the boys. You're lucky, William, damn lucky . . . and, as usual, you don't seem to have any conception of just how lucky you are. [*He gets out a cigarette and starts to light it.*]

WILLIAM: Are you going to have a cigarette?

JACK: Too early for a drink.

WILLIAM: I thought you were on your way to work.

JACK [*lights the cigarette*]: Well, yes, but you stopped me and started this chat.

WILLIAM: But I'm ready to go.

JACK: Well . . . [*Starts to take out cigarette and then*

puts it back in.] Fine . . . I'll smoke in the car. [*Starts to circle away.*]

WILLIAM: Jack?

JACK [*His patience is tried*]: Yes, William? [*Pause; no answer.*] Yes, William?

WILLIAM: If something were to ever happen to me . . .

JACK: Yes?

WILLIAM: A car accident or a divorce or something—would you promise me that you'd watch out for Margaret and the boys?

JACK: Sure. I'm their godfather.

WILLIAM: No . . . more than that. More than just watch out for them. Would you become me?

JACK: Billy! Would I become you? What kind of thing is that to say? I mean, that's just the way your ego works—always has. You don't give a damn about other people—you don't think two twits about them—you just expect that they'll move right along doing what you'd expect. [*Puts out cigarette.*] For Christ sake, of course I'll take care of Margaret and the boys. I'm embarrassed that you should even have to ask. But become you? Hah! Over my dead body on that one.

WILLIAM [*Pause. He shrugs.*]: Just thought I'd ask.

JACK: Anything else? I really have to get to work. I've got a tummy tuck consultation first thing this morning that just can't wait.

WILLIAM: A tummy tuck?

JACK: Some other time. Over a cool drink at the club . . . or over a nice Sunday dinner at your place.

WILLIAM: Jack? [*Slight pause.*]

JACK: Yes, William?

WILLIAM: I haven't been much of a brother for you . . . have I?

JACK: You've been different . . . maybe preoccupied is a better word. Yes, that's it . . . you've been a preoccupied brother.

WILLIAM: You've been perfect.

JACK: Huh?

WILLIAM: Whenever I hear the word "brother" . . . or whenever I stop to think about the concept of brother . . . I always think of you. You are, in my mind, the perfect brother. Older, wiser . . . doing things before me . . . great clothes. That's you, my brother.

JACK: William, for god's sake . . . we're in my driveway. It's 9:45 in the morning. What is going on?

WILLIAM [*looks for a moment as if he is going to hug* JACK.] Just wanted to return your call.

JACK: Well, thank you for that. [*Takes out a cigarette and circles around* WILLIAM—*as if he's getting ready to enter a car.*] Good seeing you.

WILLIAM: Do you know Jane Fonda?

JACK: I know who she is.

WILLIAM: I think she's fantastic. Everything that is America right now is Jane Fonda.

JACK: Well, I don't know about that, but she is—

WILLIAM [*pats his arm and exits quickly*]: Good talking to you, Jack, old brother. Good talking to you.

JACK: The same, I'm sure.

SPLIT SECOND
by Dennis McIntyre

Split Second was first produced by The Amistad World Theater in cooperation with John McDonald and Gus Fleming. The play subsequently was produced at Theater Four in New York City.

Val Johnson, a black New York City cop, arrests a white car thief. Val handcuffs his prisoner and radios in for assistance. As they wait, the car thief tries to cajole Val into letting him go free; when Val won't, the car thief lets loose a stream of racial slurs. Val shoots him dead, then makes it seem as if the car thief had tried to pull a knife on him. Val spends the next two days torn between confessing and covering up what actually happened. His father, a former cop, argues for strictly abiding by the law; his wife argues for his freedom, saying that the white world will never understand a black cop's motives for killing the car thief. Val becomes more and more confused as to what is "right." The following confrontation between Val and Williams, the bigoted white car thief, is raw, brutal, shattering; its impact resonates throughout the rest of the play.

A New York City side street, 28th and Eleventh Avenue. VAL JOHNSON, *a black New York City cop, street clothes, and* WILLIAM H. WILLIS, *white, street clothes.*

VAL: Freeze, motherfucker! Freeze it! [VAL *stands upstage, breathing hard, his service revolver drawn, holding it with both hands, pointing at* WILLIS. WILLIS *stands farther DS, panting, gasping for breath, slowly raising his hands.*] You move, you even sweat, and you're wasted pal! You want two more seconds of light, start staring at the green Caddie! Don't take your mind off it! Start thinking about the fucking ride, shithead! Just pretend I'm not here! Man, you should have been more picky. Going to jail for an Oldsmobile, now that's dumb, real stupid. You didn't even have to grow up to do that, did you?

WILLIS [*starts to turn around*]: Look—

VAL: I said freeze, fucker, you ever want to blink again! You'd better keep your eyes on that green Caddie! I'd do that, if I were you, I really would! I'd start thinking about horsepower! I'd start think-

ing about chrome! That's what I'd do! I wouldn't
want to make two mistakes in one night! No, I
wouldn't want to do that, not with me behind
you! [VAL *moves DS to* WILLIS.]

WILLIS: I mean, is this really necessary?

VAL [*moving closer to* WILLIS]: Uh, huh.

WILLIS: Can't we, like, talk it over?

VAL [*closer to* WILLIS]: Nope.

WILLIS: Have a heart, would you? It's the Fourth of
July, for Christ's sake!

VAL [*right behind* WILLIS]: Just another night to me,
fucker. [VAL *pushes* WILLIS *forward and kicks his
legs apart.*]

WILLIS: You don't got to do that, do you?

VAL [*pushes* WILLIS *against fence*]: You want to bet?

WILLIS: Just where the hell am I going to go? Tell me
that.

VAL [*holsters his revolver*]: That's the point, asshole.
[VAL *begins to frisk* WILLIS.]

WILLIS: I'm clean. Really. Hey, be a little more careful, would you? I'm a citizen.

VAL [*takes a large pocketknife out of* WILLIS' *right pants
pocket*]: I'll keep that in mind.

WILLIS: You'd better keep that in mind, man. [VAL
*puts the knife in a jacket pocket. He takes a wallet
out of* WILLIS' *left back pocket, throws it SL on
floor.*] I got an explanation. I do. I can explain.
You got it all wrong. I wasn't messing with the
Olds. I got an explanation. Really.

VAL: Left hand! [*Removes handcuffs from his belt and
snaps them on* WILLIS, *one at a time.*]

WILLIS [*as his left hand is cuffed*]: You don't need
cuffs. I'm stranded, man. This is Eleventh Avenue. I'm not going anyplace.

VAL: Right hand!

WILLIS [*as his right hand is cuffed*]: The last cab I saw,
it was two days ago. You got to go to Eighth, you
want a subway. I couldn't make it to Eighth, not

with you chasing me. I'm out of shape. You know that.

VAL [*backs away from* WILLIS, *removes a Miranda card from his pocket, reads from the card*]: You have the right to remain silent. You are not required to say anything to us at any time or to answer any questions. Anything you say can be used against you in court.

WILLIS: What do you think? I don't go to the movies? This is fucking out of sight, man! You know that? It was my cousin's car. Really.

VAL [*replaces the card in his pocket, squats, picks up wallet and puts it in right jacket pocket*]: We'll talk about it. As soon as we call your cousin.

WILLIS: He gave me the keys. He got a ride out to the Shore.

VAL: It must be nice, the Shore. I mean, if you live around here.

WILLIS: Look, he didn't need his car. I had his keys. Honest.

VAL [*takes knife, opens it*]: What'd you do? Drop them?

WILLIS: Yeah, that's right. They must have fell out of my hand.

VAL: I'm real sorry about that.

WILLIS: I had them. I did. I didn't know who the fuck you were. You scared the shit out of me.

VAL [*closes knife, puts it in his left jacket pocket*]: You didn't even see me.

WILLIS: Right. I'll admit that. You guys are fast. Real fast. I know that. But I heard you. That was enough. This is a shit neighborhood. I mean, I told my cousin to get a garage. I told him I'd split it with him. I use his car a lot.

VAL: Real generous, your cousin.

WILLIS: He is. He's terrific. You should meet him.

VAL [*takes out his two-way radio and crosses to* WILLIS, *pulling him off fence. As he does so*]: I won't be here. You know, when he gets back from the

Shore. [*transmitting*] Officer Johnson. Holding one. Request transportation. West 28th Street, off Eleventh. 500 block [VAL *crosses USL.*]

WILLIS [*crosses SR to C*]: A fucking Oldsmobile?! Jesus Christ, man! We could have talked things out! We still can— You? One of you guys?! Shit, no wonder I didn't see you!

VAL: Surprise.

WILLIS: Look, now we can talk. What do you say? We can make a deal. Fuckin' a, all this time, I thought you were white. You got a white voice, you know that?

VAL: No deal.

WILLIS: And you're not that dark either. Really. The right light, sunset, real early in the morning, you put a hat on your head, shit, man, no kidding, you could have come over on the fucking *Mayflower.*

VAL: You want to shove it back up your ass?

WILLIS: I was trying to compliment you, that's all I was trying to do. Ever since I was a kid, I've tried to concentrate on the positive aspects of life. You know what I mean?

VAL: [*crosses US to arch*]: You're not going anywhere. Concentrate on that.

WILLIS [*crosses to* VAL]: All the crime in this fucking city, and we're talking about a fucked-up car. I'll bet there's three throats being slit, just while we're standing here. That's the kind of action you should be jumping on. A lot of people, they'd be real grateful not having their throats slit. Look, man, be realistic. What'd I do? I mean, really, brother? It was a '77 Oldsmobile. Nobody misses a fucking Oldsmobile, not in this neighborhood. They left it there to lose it. It would have been doing the city a favor. You know how much it costs to tow away a piece of fucking junk like that? Of course you do. You do it. Or your pals do. Shit, the muffler was hanging out all over the street. Spark city, brother, that's all it was. What if the guy'd tried to pass one of those propane trucks? We'd be missing twenty blocks. There would have been fingers and toes in Connecticut. And there was a puddle of oil, maybe ten feet. I'm lucky I didn't kill myself.

VAL: You are.

WILLIS: I mean, talking about an abortion. Two of the tires were skinny, and the other two needed air. One of them had seven patches on it. I've never seen seven patches on a tire. That's why I counted them. The doors were open, brother, all four of them. I don't mean unlocked. I mean OPEN. The guy was just begging me to cart it away. If he knew who I was, he probably would have sent me the registration.

VAL: We'll check it out. See what he feels about it. How's that sound?

WILLIS: Check it out? You got to speak Spanish, you want to check it out. That was a spic buggy if I ever saw one. It has Jesus doing pushups on the rear-view mirror. It had fifty-two Virgin Marys all over the dashboard, for Christ's sake! If he'd had room, it would have had a palm tree! You don't want to take me in over a spic buggy. Not you. I mean, do you? Really?

VAL: No law against decorating your dashboard.

WILLIS: You couldn't see to drive it. There's got to be a fucking law.

VAL: It was parked. Remember?

WILLIS [*crosses DSR*]: I don't understand it. I really don't understand it. You know what?

VAL [*crosses DSL*]: What's that?

WILLIS: You got no sense of fair play. That's one thing you don't have, brother. [*Gestures*] Now, if I'd been fiddling around with the Caddie over there, you might have had ample cause. It's an '81. It's got respect written all over it. [*Spells it*] R-e-s-p-e-c-t! But an Olds, a '77 goddamn Olds—that's a

one-night stand, brother. You get up the next
morning, you wouldn't even wipe your ass with it.

VAL: You're a real pisser, aren't you?

WILLIS [*crosses US to C*]: No, see, it's like this, I'm the
black sheep in the family. No offense there, *bro,*
but I've been in trouble before. You're going to
find out. You've got computers. I know that. But
it's all been small stuff. Nothing big. Like the
Olds. That's my style. I don't beat up grandmoth-
ers, man. I don't rip off purses. I don't even own
a gold chain. I never took heroin in my life. I
don't even know what the shit looks like. Somebody offers me coke, I turn it down. That knife,
it's for my protection. It's a tough city. You can
understand that. You carry a gun, don't you? Look
at my fucking wardrobe. People don't dress like
this, not when they're in the money. I mean, do I
look like I'm part of the cash flow? Do I look like
crime pays? [*His suit*] This is one step above May's.
The spics are breathing down my neck. They're
starting to dress better than me. That car, that
heap, that was to buy a new suit. So I could go to
court. So I could look decent. So I could make a
favorable impression. My ex, she's breaking my
balls. Alimony. Child support. You might appreciate that. I've been around black chicks. Mar-
lene, my ex, she's just like a lot of black chicks.
Gorgeous in bed, real nifty, you know what I
mean, right? But one step away from the sheets,
all of a sudden, she's putting a bat between your
legs, just for fucking practice.

VAL [*low*]: You're not helping your case.

WILLIS [*crosses DSC*]: Look, brother—

VAL [*low—dangerous*]: Don't call me fucking brother.

WILLIS: What else am I supposed to call you? You and
me, we're in the same category.

VAL: The fuck we are!

WILLIS: No, listen, we're deprived, that's all I'm saying.
Economically deprived. We always have been—

always will be. My father was a prick. Yours just happened to be colored, right? Look, you get me to a phone booth. One block over. It's not busted. 29th. Back on Tenth. I'll give you a number. You dial it, there's a thousand bucks waiting. All you've got to do is dial 348-5745—no—it's 398-5745. My brother's place. He's got a large insomniac problem. He's always up late. He owns two dry cleaners. He keeps a lot of cash in his house. He doesn't trust the night deposit. A thousand bucks, brother! It's cheaper than bail. That's why he'll pay it. It's happened before. He always pays my bail, my brother— And then he screams at me. What do you say? Hell, it the Fourth of July, man! Have a heart. I got kids. Two girls. Six and ten. Real cute—[VAL *stares at* WILLIS.] All right, then lets talk about your twelve fucking kids, nigger! How's that?!

VAL [*crosses USC. Dangerous*]: I'd be real quiet, if I were you. Real quiet. [*Crosses DSL*]

WILLIS [*crosses US to* VAL]: Got you there, didn't I? Finally touched a nerve, right. I was beginning to think you didn't have no emotion, *bro*. Now, your kiddies, I'll bet they could use a couple thousand real fresh bucks, couldn't they? I mean, you could probably spring at least six of them. You know, fix it up with the prosecutor, as long as he's got big lips and frizzy hair, right? You got a wife on the side, brother? A couple thousand bucks, you and the little lady, you could get [*intentional dialect; crosses DSC*] "yourselves" a lifetime supply of penicillin, couldn't you? Why don't you give your foxy bitch a call? See what she thinks about it. You don't want to do that? No, I wouldn't want to do that either. Not this late. I wouldn't want to disturb her, not when her mouth's full. Or how about a two-thousand-buck transistor radio? I'll bet you've already got a hard-on just thinking about it. Five hundred fucking stations,

man! Wouldn't be nobody but nobody riding the
subways no more, would they? And I'll even throw
in a pair of earphones. Free. No extra charge.
Just call it a jigaboo bonus. How's that grab you?
Wait a minute. One more thing. A real package
deal. Six-foot shoes. Gold and orange. No, excuse
me. Make those roller skates. Purple and green.
Concentrate, brother! Get a fix on it! A 125th
Street, Saturday night, and you'd be the heaviest
fucking dude stomping the pavement!

AL: You keep talking, asshole, and you won't even
be able to fucking limp!

VILLIS: Is that a fucking fact?!

AL: That's a fucking fact!

VILLIS: What's wrong, *bro*? You don't want to talk to
a white man? You don't want to negotiate? William H. Willis, he's not good enough for you? No
dope, no deal? No pussy, no action? Fucking nigger cops! How'd you get the job, anyway? Suck
off another fucking spearchucker cop?! That's what
they call progress, don't they? They ought to take
all you nigger cops and ship you back to Africa.
That's what they ought to do. Let you be jungle
cops. Give you some beads and a spear. Let you
direct traffic in the jungle. Because that's where
you belong, nigger! Didn't you know that?! I mean,
like don't you miss the smell of elephant shit?!
[VAL *draws his service revolver.*] Just try it! Go
on! See where it fucking gets you! [VAL *slowly
holsters revolver.*] You don't got the balls, do
you? Well, I can understand that. Really. Most
niggers, they only come with one ball, that's what
I hear. Hey, I got a joke for you. You want to
hear a joke? What's the difference between a
nigger cop and a pile of shit. No difference, man!
Get it?! [VAL *draws his service revolver, points it
at* WILLIS, *and pulls the trigger. An explosion from
the revolver.* WILLIS *sags to the ground, jerks, and
then lies still.* VAL *replaces his revolver in holster,*

> turns away from WILLIS, takes several steps, and
> then stops. He turns back, stumbles to WILLIS
> searches in his own pockets for the handcuff key
> finds it, unlocks the handcuffs, locks them again
> replaces them on his belt, takes out WILLIS' knife
> opens it, wipes it with his jacket, puts the knife in
> WILLIS' right hand, and then begins to back away
> He remembers the wallet. He takes it out, wipes it
> on his jacket, moves back to WILLIS, and puts it in
> WILLIS' back pocket. He backs away again, pant
> ing, taking deep breaths. He draws his service re
> volver and begins moving upstage. Blackout.]

HOW I GOT THAT STORY
by Amlin Gray

How I Got That Story, a shattering comic strip of a
play, was performed for limited run at Second Stage in
New York City, directed by Carole Rothman, with
Bob Gunton and Daniel Stern. The play had an extended run at the Westside Arts Theater with Don
Scardino replacing Daniel Stern. The play received its
first production at the Court Street Theater, a workshop unit of the Milwaukee Repertory Theater.

A naive reporter from East Dubuque comes to
Am-bo Land (a.k.a. Vietnam) to cover the war. He
confronts a parade of people, some native, some
American—the twenty-odd characters the reporter
meets are all played by one actor. The reporter comes
in full of idealism, wanting to "understand" the
effect of the war on this third world nation. He ends
up drawn into the vortex of an overwhelming civil war
and begins a long slide, ending up in the gutters of

Saigon, a plundered soul who can neither go back home nor live in a country he can never "understand." In the following scene, the reporter has been captured and held for ransom by a guerrilla who has nothing but disgust for the reporter's cavalier attitude toward his war.

A small, bare hut. The REPORTER *is sleeping on the floor. His head is covered by a black hood and his hands are tied behind his back. A* GUERRILLA IN-FORMATION OFFICER *comes in carrying a bowl of rice.*

GUERRILLA: Stand up, please.

REPORTER [*coming awake*]: What?

GUERRILLA: Please stand up.

REPORTER: It's hard with hands behind the back.

GUERRILLA: I will untie them.

REPORTER: That's all right. I'll make it. [*With some clumsiness, he gets to his feet.*] There I am.

GUERRILLA: I offered to untie your hands.

REPORTER: I'd just as soon you didn't. When you know that you can trust me, then untie my hands. I'd let you take the hood off.

GUERRILLA [*takes the hood off*]: Tell me why you think that we should trust you.

REPORTER: I'm no threat to you. I've never done you any harm.

GUERRILLA: No harm?

REPORTER: I guess I've wasted your munitions. Part of one of your grenades wound up imbedded in my *derriere*—my backside.

GUERRILLA: I speak French as well as English. You forget—the French were here before you.

REPORTER: Yes.

GUERRILLA: You told us that you came here as a newsman.

REPORTER: Right.

GUERRILLA: You worked within the system of our enemies and subject to their interests.

REPORTER: Partly subject.

GUERRILLA: Yet you say that you have never done us any harm.

REPORTER: All I found out as a reporter was I'd never find out anything.

GUERRILLA: Do we pardon an enemy sniper if his marksmanship is poor?

REPORTER: Yes, if he's quit the army.

GUERRILLA: Ah, yes. You are not a newsman now.

REPORTER: That's right.

GUERRILLA: What are you?

REPORTER: What am I? [*The* GUERRILLA *is silent.*] I'm what you see.

GUERRILLA: What do you do?

REPORTER: I live.

GUERRILLA: You live?

REPORTER: That's all.

GUERRILLA: You live in Am-bo Land.

REPORTER: I'm here right now.

GUERRILLA: Why?

REPORTER: Why? You've got me prisoner.

GUERRILLA: If you were not a prisoner, you would not be here?

REPORTER: No.

GUERRILLA: Where would you be?

REPORTER: By this time, I'd be back in East Dubuque.

GUERRILLA: You were not leaving when we captured you.

REPORTER: I was, though. I was leaving soon.

GUERRILLA: Soon?

REPORTER: Yes.

GUERRILLA: When?

REPORTER: I don't know exactly. Sometime.

GUERRILLA: Sometime.

REPORTER: Yes.

GUERRILLA: You have no right to be here even for a minute. Not to draw one breath.

REPORTER: You have no right to tell me that. I'm here. It's where I am.

GUERRILLA: We are a spectacle to you. A land in turmoil.

REPORTER: I don't have to lie to you. Yes, that attracts me.

GUERRILLA: Yes. You love to see us kill each other.

REPORTER: No. I don't.

GUERRILLA: You said you didn't have to lie.

REPORTER: I'm not. It does . . . excite me that the stakes are life and death here. It makes everything . . . intense.

GUERRILLA: The stakes cannot be life and death unless some people die.

REPORTER: That's true. But I don't make them die. They're dying anyway.

GUERRILLA: You just watch.

REPORTER: That's right.

GUERRILLA: Your standpoint is aesthetic.

REPORTER: Yes, all right, yes.

GUERRILLA: You enjoy our situation here.

REPORTER: I'm filled with pain by things I see.

GUERRILLA: And yet you stay.

REPORTER: I'm here.

GUERRILLA: You are addicted.

REPORTER: Say I am, then! I'm addicted! Yes! I've said it! I'm addicted!

GUERRILLA: Your position in my country is morbid and decadent. It is corrupt, reactionary, and bourgeois. You have no right to live here.

REPORTER: This is where I live. You can't pass judgment.

GUERRILLA: I have not passed judgment. You are useless here. A man must give something in return for the food he eats and the living space he occupies. This is not a moral obligation but a practical necessity in a society where no one is to be exploited.

REPORTER: Am-bo Land isn't such a society, is it?

GUERRILLA: Not yet.

REPORTER: Well, I'm here right now. If you don't like that then I guess you'll have to kill me.

GUERRILLA: We would kill you as we pick the insects from the skin of a valuable animal.

REPORTER: Go ahead, then. If you're going to kill me, kill me.

GUERRILLA: We are not going to kill you.

REPORTER: Why not?

GUERRILLA: For a reason.

REPORTER: What's the reason?

GUERRILLA: We have told the leadership of TransPan-Global Wire Service when and where to leave one hundred thousand dollars for your ransom.

REPORTER: Ransom? TransPanGlobal?

GUERRILLA: Yes.

REPORTER: But that's no good. I told you, I don't work there anymore.

GUERRILLA: Your former employers have not made the separation public. We have made our offer public. You will not be abandoned in the public view. It would not be good business.

REPORTER [*truly frightened for the first time in the scene*]: Wait. You have to think this out. A hundred thousand dollars is too much. It's too much. You might get ten.

GUERRILLA: We have demanded one hundred.

REPORTER: They won't pay that. Take ten thousand. That's a lot to you.

GUERRILLA: It is. But we have made our offer.

REPORTER: Change it. You're just throwing away money. Tell them ten. They'll never pay a hundred thousand.

GUERRILLA: We never change a bargaining position we have once set down. This is worth much more than ten thousand dollars or a hundred thousand dollars.

REPORTER: Please—

GUERRILLA: Sit down.

REPORTER [*obeys; then, quietly*]: Please don't kill me.

GUERRILLA: Do not beg your life from me. The circumstances grant your life. Your employers will pay. You will live.

REPORTER: You sound so sure.

GUERRILLA: If we were not sure we would not waste this food on you. [*He pushes the bowl of rice towards the* REPORTER.]

REPORTER: How soon will I know?

GUERRILLA: Soon. Ten days.

REPORTER: That's not soon.

GUERRILLA: This war has lasted all my life. Ten days is soon. [*Untying the* REPORTER's *hands*] You will be fed on what our soldiers eat. You will think that we are starving you, but these are the rations on which we march toward our inevitable victory. Eat your rice. In three minutes I will tie you again. [*He goes out. The* REPORTER *eats as best he can.*]

OLDTIMERS GAME
by Lee Blessing

Workshopped at MidWest Playlabs, *Oldtimers Game* was first presented as part of the Actors Theater of Louisville Humana Festival of New Plays.

Oldtimers Game takes place in the locker room of the Northshore Otters, a minor-league baseball team.

The occasion, an oldtimers game, has brought together retired players, a current star from the major leagues, the new owner of the major league franchise and, of course, the present-day Otters. The retired players find themselves faced once again with the harshly competitive world of the minor leagues. Their nostalgia (both for Northshore and the game itself) is severely tested. In the following scene, Crab confronts John about his unwillingness to play in the oldtimers game.

JOHN *rises, holds his back and grimaces. He starts unbuttoning his uniform. After a moment we hear* CRAB *from the tunnel.*

CRAB [*off*]: Old John? Old John? Better get up here. [*Reenters*] Hey, Old John, where are you? They're going to start the introductions—what are you doing?

JOHN: Hm? I'll be right out.

CRAB: You're changing your clothes. What are you . . . Are you hurt?

JOHN: Hurt? No, I just . . . thought I might watch from the stands.

CRAB: What are you talking about? You're playing today.

JOHN: Nobody wants to see a forty-mile-an-hour fastball. I threw a little behind the house yesterday. Could've timed me with an hourglass.

CRAB: What's the matter?

JOHN: Well, it doesn't, I guess—you just scuttle back out there and tell them I'm sick or something.

CRAB: They just want to see you. It's like when the president used to throw out the first ball. No one cared what it looked like, it was who was throwing it.

JOHN: No one wants to see us dressed up in clown suits, rolling the ball to one another.

CRAB: I do! So do the fans. You're not even going to
stand out there, doff your cap?

JOHN: No.

CRAB: Just because you're afraid? [JOHN *stares at him.*]
People up there are ready to applaud you!

JOHN: I've made up my mind. Leave me alone.

CRAB: Sure. It's your mind—what's left of it. [*Pause*]
You know I once saw Ty Cobb at an oldtimers
game. In Detroit. He looked like he was about a
million years old. Could hardly hold his bat up.
Somebody had to run for him. God, it was pitiful.
It was the only time I ever saw him play, though. I
will never forget it.

JOHN: What are you talking about?

CRAB: Nothing, I just—

JOHN: Is that supposed to get me back out there? A
stupid story about Ty Cobb?

CRAB: No, it's just—

JOHN: Telling me about Ty Cobb will not get me to go
out there and pitch like that, and . . . end up
catching line drives with my face.

CRAB: Line drives? Is that what you're worried about?
Hell, they won't hit anything up the middle on
you—you're too damn slow! They're going to pull
their line drives right at third base, right at me.
I'll probably get killed. And even if I don't, I'm
still going to look like a pile. I know that. But I'll
tell you something. The fans know us better than
we do. And they invited Crab Detlefsen here. I
don't know why, but damn it, it's Crab Detlefsen
they're going to get—errors and all.

JOHN: You know, I still don't remember you.

CRAB [*suddenly tucking* JOHN's *uniform shirt back in,
buttoning it*]: Well, you don't have to.

JOHN: What are you doing?

CRAB: Getting you ready to meet your public.

JOHN: Wait a minute . . . Now, I said *no*—

CRAB: Why? Just 'cause you're afraid?

JOHN: *I am not afraid!*

CRAB: Then why?! Why'd you come today, if you weren't going to play?

JOHN: Because I . . . love baseball. It's the people I don't like. [*Embarrassed*] I don't like people. Why do you think I run a resort in northern Wisconsin? For the crowds?

CRAB: You don't like people?

JOHN: Well, it's not so strange. Some people don't like fish.

CRAB: But how do you . . . How do you live, if you . . . ?

JOHN: I just keep away from situations. That's all. Today I got tempted. Baseball always tempts me. It was a mistake to come.

CRAB: Why do you hate *people*?

JOHN: I don't hate 'em, I just don't like 'em. They don't know the first thing about baseball. They don't know why they're playing it. They don't know what it's for.

CRAB: I know what it's for.

JOHN: Ignore the beauty of an entire world, just to eke out another buck, or beat out somebody else, or . . . use somebody up.

CRAB: It's always been that way.

JOHN: I always hated it.

CRAB: Well . . . what the hell. It's not the people you're here for. Is it? It's the game. The game of baseball. [*Quietly resumes buttoning* JOHN's *shirt.*] That's all we're worried about today. Look. It's just a couple hours. We'll go out there and doff our caps, and do everything we used to do, only clumsier—and if people want to bother us and talk to us, well, we'll just let 'em, and we won't hear a word they say. 'Cause we came to play baseball. [*Finishing up*] OK? I'll stick close to you.

JOHN: What makes you think I like *you*?

CRAB [*points at* JOHN's *uniform*]: You look good in that. Come on, Old John. Just three innings, but it'll feel like a lifetime. [CRAB *and* JOHN *disappear up the tunnel.*]

THE SHAWL
by David Mamet

The Shawl premiered with another short play, *The Spanish Prisoner,* at the New Theater Company in Chicago. On a double bill with *Prairie du Chien, The Shawl* inaugurated the reopening of the Vivian Beaumont Theater at Lincoln Center in New York City.

The Shawl is a ghost story; in fact, David Mamet calls the play his "Twilight Zone" episode. John is a psychic, a flim-flam artist who in order to keep the affections of his male lover, Charles, tries to cheat a grieving woman out of her inheritance. Over the course of the play, he reveals the tricks of his trade to Charles—explaining the buzz words he uses, the library research he does, the playing off his client's vulnerable points, the use of logic, of intuition. Just when his lover, the woman he is trying to bilk, and the audience are sure he is a fraud, John does another act of mystification and we are left to wonder if he really does possess a certain telepathic power after all. In the following scene, John explains his "psychic powers" to Charles.

CHARLES: There'll be money when?

JOHN: Soon.

CHARLES: And how will we "get" this money. [*Pause*] How will this money *come* to us?

JOHN [*pause*]: It will come to us. At the *end.* When she *asks,* "How can I pay you?" We say, "Leave something. To help us with our work. Leave what you will . . ." They will ask and they will reward you. I told her to bring a photograph. Anything . . . Eh? This creates the habit. To bring something, to "bring" things to you . . . their thoughts . . . "money" . . . and when you don't *misuse* it, it creates confidence in them. And *when* we've helped her . . .

CHARLES: *When* we've *helped* her . . .

JOHN: Yes. These things take time.

CHARLES [*simultaneously with "time"*]: When we've helped her to *what*?

JOHN: I've told you. To . . . to do whatever that is she wants to do. To . . . *face* herself . . . as we *will* help her . . . and she *will* reward us. And we're *making* progress. As you saw.

CHARLES: I saw.

JOHN: Well, yes. You . . . you . . . she was won over. Didn't you see that?

CHARLES [*simultaneously with "see that"*]: Perhaps.

JOHN: Oh, no. SHE WAS WON OVER. She gave me the bill. She's going to bring the picture . . . slowly . . . slowly . . . you can't force the . . . coming to the Truth . . . [*Pause*] Don't you see that?

CHARLES [*simultaneously with "that"*]: You said she dreamed this meeting.

JOHN: . . . Ah. Did she foresee the meeting? We all dream of a wise man, one day . . . who will . . . I paint a picture. Looks like magic. You see her economic class . . . by the way: look at the shoes, anyone could buy a pricey dress . . . and we so we see an income of a certain magnitude. Suggests a summer house. Where? By the water is the obvious bet. And we suggest the mother nearby, you see? As the mother is the thing that draws her here. She's on her mind . . . and her mind . . . *freed* by "magic" . . .

CHARLES: . . . her mind freed by magic . . .

JOHN: Yes. By my "clairvoyance." Yes. Yes. Yes. You must give them a *mechanism*. To allow them to *trust* you. She wouldn't trust just "anyone." She comes in: "Show me you have psychic powers." Alright. "Read my mind. Tell me my complaint." Alright. I will. A troubled woman. Comes in. With a problem? What is it? It's *money*—illness— *love* . . . That's all it ever is. Money, illness or love. A deeply repressed woman. In her thirties. Unmarried . . . as you say . . . Matter of the Heart? No. *Illness*. Perhaps. Woman of an anxious nature, that is a good bet. But no. I say "the fear of death." Three times. And no reaction. In her eyes. And so. Health. No. Love. No. And that leaves "money."

CHARLES: And you said "the Law."

JOHN: I said a legal problem. How's this money come to her, a wealthy woman, but there's *contracts* . . . some legal . . .

CHARLES: You said "her mother's will."

JOHN: Yes. I did.

CHARLES: How did you know that?

JOHN: It was a guess. And an educated guess. Technique takes you so far, and then once in a while . . .

CHARLES: And that's all there . . . that's all there is. [*Pause*]

JOHN: What?

CHARLES: That's all there is to what you do.

JOHN: Well, I suppose we all want "magic," but our job, our *real* job . . . One moment. I'm sorry . . . [*Pause*] I'm sorry. You were speaking of money. I . . . I . . . what am I seeing . . . something came into my . . . evening . . . evening . . . eveningwear? A [*pause*] I see, what are they? Some stone? . . . Sapphire?

CHARLES: What is this?

JOHN: Someone . . . a gift . . . they were *yours* . . . a set of sapphire studs. They . . . parted from them . . . ? You . . . no . . . yes. Valuable set of studs. A . . . a . . . and your concern with money and . . . you pawned a set of Sapphire Studs. [*Pause*]

CHALRES: How do you know that?

JOHN: Two weeks ago . . . before we met. Did . . . did you do that?

CHARLES: You . . . how could you know that?

JOHN: I saw the pawn ticket. In your wallet. You see? Very simple, really. [*Pause*] If one is allowed to believe . . . Our job is not to guess, but to *aid* . . . to . . . to create an atmosphere . . . As I just did with *you* . . . to enable . . .

CHARLES: What were you doing in my wallet?

JOHN: Well. The man came with the *food,* I had to *tip* him . . . you were in the *shower,* I'm *sorry.* I did . . . I *certainly*

CHARLES: You should not have looked in my wallet.

JOHN: No, you're absolutely right. I should . . . I should not. I'm sorry. I'm *very* sorry. Charles. I'm *very* sorry. I took a *dollar*, the ticket fell . . . you're absolutely right. And I apologize. [*Pause*] I apologize. Will you forgive me? [*Pause*] Will you please forgive me? [*Pause*]

CHARLES: You're very nosy.

JOHN: Yes, I. And I suppose that it's a professional . . . you're *right*. And I apologize. And I'm sorry as it's obvious that it's a touchy . . .

CHARLES: I should *say* that it's a "touchy." *Yes*. It. Well, I would say that it . . .

JOHN: We are going to have money. I *promise* you. When she comes to *us* asks *us*: "How can I repay you?" We say, "Leave what you will. To aid us in our work . . . Some would leave fifty, some would leave a thousand." . . . We are going to . . .

CHARLES: When?

JOHN: Soon.

A SOLDIER'S PLAY
by Charles Fuller

A Soldier's Play was first presented by the Negro Ensemble Company in New York City. The play, later the Academy Award-nominated film *A Soldier's Story,* won the Pulitzer Prize.

Part murder mystery, part meditation on racial prejudice, *A Soldier's Play* revolves around Company B, 221st Chemical Smoke Generating Company, an all-black company stationed at Fort Neal, Louisiana, during World War II. The company leader, Sergeant Vernon C. Waters, a black man with an obsessive need to be accepted into the white world, has been found murdered. During the investigation a string of suspects, some white, some black, are interrogated; a galaxy of possible motives are uncovered. In the following flashback, Waters' prejudice against his own race is revealed as he talks to one of his men, Private James Wilkie.

(Note: By leaving out Wilkie's lines, this scene may be used as a monologue.)

WATERS: Wilkie? [WILKIE *rises, focuses front, listening to* WATERS.] You know what I'ma get that boy of mine for his birthday? One of them Schwinn bikes. He'll be twelve—time flies don't it? Let me show you something?

WILKIE [*to* DAVENPORT]: He was always pullin' out snapshots, sir. [WATERS *hands* WILKIE *a snapshot.*]

WATERS: My wife let a neighbor take this a couple of weeks ago—ain't he growin' fast?

WILKIE: He's over your wife's shoulder! [*Hands it back,* WATERS *looks at the photo.*]

WATERS: I hope this kid never has to be a soldier.

WILKIE: It was good enough for you.

WATERS: I couldn't do any better—and this army was the closest I figured the white man would let me get to any kind of authority. No, the army ain't for this boy. When this war's over, things are going to change, Wilkie—and I want him to be ready for it—my daughter too! I'm sendin' both of 'em to some big white college. [*Puts photo in wallet and replaces it in his pocket.*] Let 'em rub elbows with the whites, learn the white man's language—how he does things. Otherwise we'll be left behind—you can see it in the army. White man runnin' rings around us.

WILKIE [*sitting on the bunk*]: A lot of us didn't get the chance or the schoolin' the white folks got.

WATERS: That ain't no excuse, Wilkie. Most niggahs just don't care—tomorrow don't mean nothin' to 'em. My Daddy shoveled coal from the back of a wagon all his life. He couldn't read or write, but he saw to it we did! Not havin' ain't no excuse for not gettin'.

WILKIE: Can't get pee from a rock, Sarge.

WATERS [*crosses*]: You just like the rest of 'em, Wilkie—I thought bustin' you would teach you something—we got to challenge this man in his arena—use his weapons, don't you know that? We need lawyers, doctors—generals—senators! Stop thinkin' like a niggah!

WILKIE: All I said—

WATERS: Is the equipment ready for tomorrow's game?

WILKIE: Yeah.

WATERS: Good. You can go now, Wilkie. [WILKIE *is stunned.*]

WATERS: That's an order!

VIKINGS
by Steven Metcalfe

A popular play in regional and community theaters, *Vikings* received its world premiere at the Manhattan Theater Club, in a production directed by Lynne Meadow.

Three generations of Larsen men live under one roof: Yens, Yens' son Peter, and Peter's son, Gunnar. The arrival of the ailing Yens' nurse, Betsy, affects the uneasy truce the three men have made. Central to the conflict in *Vikings* is Peter's great anger: anger over his wife dying, compounded by Peter wanting only to be a carpenter like himself, not something "better." Peter's anger is manifested in his heavy drinking. In the following scene, Gunnar is alone in the kitchen after a birthday celebration with his grandfather when Peter comes home drunk, not having had the courage to keep his date with Betsy.

There is silence as PETER *drains the last of a can of beer and then inserts the can back into the plastic rings with the other empty cans. He looks out, not seeing the audience, lost in thought.* GUNNAR *has watched this. He addresses the audience.*

GUNNAR: He comes to a quiet place. A hill. A high elevation. A view. At night the lights of the town are spread out below like a bright carpet. Once upon a time, when my mom and dad were young and had just started going out, this was the place where the high school kids would come to park. This was their lovers lane. Back when. Police patrol it on a regular basis these days. High school kids were coming up here to smoke pot. Parked cars are asked to move on. [PETER *takes out some breath mints and pops one in his mouth.*]

PETER: Larsen, Larsen, he's our man . . . [*He looks at his watch.*] Jesus, what have I done . . . [PETER *exits.* GUNNAR *moves to the table. Light change.*]

GUNNAR: Dad? Is that you?

PETER [*entering, he is drunk*]: What are you doing up?

GUNNAR: Beating the house at solitaire. By cheating. How'd it go?

PETER: You should be in bed.

GUNNAR: I'm getting ready to call it a night. You have a good time?

PETER: I'm going to bed. G'night. [*He stumbles.*] What are you lookin at? Gunnar, you oughta be in bed. All right. I had a little too much to drink.

GUNNAR: I'll make you some coffee.

PETER: I don't want any coffee. Can't drink it without sugar. Goddam sugar. It's no damn good for you.

GUNNAR: Booze is?

PETER: Oh, shit, here it comes. Fingers to hammers and hands to skilsaws. Christ all mighty, leave me alone.

GUNNAR: What's her ceiling need, huh? Boards? Caulking? I'll help.

PETER: I don't want help.

GUNNAR: Dinner O.K.? You hungry? You want a sandwich?

PETER: No, I don't want a goddam—will you go to bed? [*Pause*] What kind of sandwich?

GUNNAR: How about P.B. and J.?

PETER: Peanut butter. My life's half over and I'm eating peanut butter. Just go to bed, Gunnar. Get out a here!

GUNNAR: You're gonna wake Yens up.

PETER: Wake him up? He's probably eavesdropping already and if he isn't, it's time for him to drag his ass to the toilet. Hey, Dad, you want a little prune juice?! [*Pause*] I wanted it to go well, Guns. She had on this nice pair a slacks and her hair . . . she looked terrific. I didn't go in. I couldn't get any further than the kitchen door. Your old man chickened out, Guns. He chickened out. What's this?

GUNNAR: Birthday cake. We were pretending.

PETER: Lotta good that does.

GUNNAR: You should have gone in.

PETER: I know. I got there and all I could do was watch through the window like some kind of peeping tom. I'd bought some beer and I stopped along the way to drink it . . . I was half in the bag. She would have taken one look at me and slammed the door in my face.

GUNNAR: No, she wouldn't have.

PETER: Gunnar, she was . . . she was wearing a silk blouse for chrissake.

GUNNAR: Call her.

PETER: Come off it. It must be two in the morning.

GUNNAR: Make an excuse. Make a joke. You gotta do something!!

PETER: Let's just drop it.

GUNNAR: You could tell her that—

PETER: Goddammit, drop it. Don't give me advice, don't lecture me. I don't find it appropriate. I'm the father here. I tried. I couldn't do it. I should a known. I'm going to bed.

GUNNAR: Why? So you can have more bad dreams? So you can yell in your sleep and wake us all up? I hear Yens creeping around here, half the time he's not going to the bathroom, he's trying to negotiate the stairs so he can get to you. Man, the old lady'd die all over again if she could see how her death has fucked you up. [PETER *strikes* GUNNAR. *A moment and then* GUNNAR *strikes him*

back, hard, across the mouth and sends him sprawl-
ing. A moment as they glare at one another.]

PETER: I want you out of the house by the middle of
next month. And you're off the job as of right
now. You're fired.

GUNNAR: Why?

PETER: Because you're my son and I don't want to see
you carrying tar paper and shingles up ladders. I
don't want to see you washing shit and grime
from your hands at the end of each day. You're
better than that.

GUNNAR: Why are you throwing me out of the house?

PETER: Because I don't want to see you playing nurse-
maid to a sick old man. I don't want you playing
babysitter to a middle-aged one. You need some
money, you let me know.

GUNNAR: Money. No, I don't need any money. [GUNNAR
exits.]

RICH RELATIONS
by David Hwang

Rich Relations premiered at the Second Stage theater
in New York City.

Hinson, a man in his early fifties, is visited by his
son, Keith, late twenties, who teaches debate in an
exclusive Connecticut prep school, in this scene from
Rich Relations.

HINSON: You know, your Uncle Fred—he may be a
small thinker, but he really likes you.

KEITH: Think so?

HINSON: He wants you to marry Marilyn.

KEITH: What?

HINSON: No—I'm serious—I'm telling you!

KEITH: Dad, that's ridiculous!

HINSON: It is one of the few times he has thought big!

KEITH: Dad—

HINSON: He's crazy. I know.

KEITH: Marilyn is my cousin!

HINSON: I know. I told you, he's crazy.

KEITH: Why would he . . . ?

HINSON: Oh—you don't know. After the kind of guys that she goes out with.

KEITH: What do you mean?

HINSON: You would be like manna from heaven.

KEITH: What kind of guys . . . ?

HINSON: And, then, you know, he—Fred—he thinks about being related to me, too.

KEITH: What?

HINSON: That would be a big thing for him.

KEITH: He's already related to you!

HINSON: Huh?

KEITH: He's already your brother-in-law!

HINSON: You see? Why do you think he married Barbara?

KEITH: Wait.

HINSON: You think for her looks? Of course not! Pleasant personality? Ha!

KEITH: Dad, just hold on, OK?

HINSON: He saw—there was an opportunity to get hooked up with some real money—

KEITH: Dad, quiet! [*Pause*] He's related to you now. Why would he want me to marry Marilyn?

HINSON: Double relations!

KEITH: That's the stupidest—

HINSON: No. Listen. Right now, he's only got my sister. OK, if they need money—sometimes, I say yes, sometimes I say, let them work it out themselves. Sometimes, I say, "Barbara, I know you're my sister, but shut up and go home." I say that. But with you—he knows I'll have to give you money if you ask.

KEITH: I never ask!

HINSON: If you married Marilyn, then you'd ask!

KEITH: I can't believe this.

HINSON: Stupid girl, Marilyn—anyway.

KEITH: You think everyone wants to marry me.

HINSON: They do.

KEITH: So they can be related to you.

HINSON: Not just that.

KEITH: Mostly, right?

HINSON: Don't sell yourself short. You're a good catch. Most men today—bums, derelicts, two steps above the gutter. No, really. I walk out there. Downtown. I go to lunch, I see them. They don't have good jobs, insurance, pensions—nothing. And even if they do, they don't have the good heart like you. They run around, sleep with everybody—fool around—bad upbringing. Not like you. It's not their fault. They didn't have your social privileges. You have manners, dating is no big deal, you don't have funny thoughts about other men. That's rare today. You're a real catch, son.

[Pause]

KEITH: Well, I think I'd better unpack.

HINSON: Of course, they want to be related to me, too.

KEITH: Dad, we'll discuss this some other time.

HINSON: I mean, being related to a real estate baron.

KEITH: You're not a baron!

HINSON: Yes, I am. You know, son—I have to tell you this—

KEITH: Dad, I want to unpack.

HINSON: Just wait. Wait a second, OK? Last week, this client—I'm supposed to meet her. She's the daughter of a big oil guy. This guy is worth—I don't know—thirty, forty million. I'm supposed to meet his daughter for lunch. She drives up—this big limousine—black—haaa—the biggest I've seen—

one of those big antennas on back. She steps
out—oh!—it's this young, pretty girl. Everyone in
my office looks at her. I get into the limousine
with her—into the back seat—she's just so beautiful—it makes my heart just go—top speed. The
car is driving—seventy, eighty down the freeway.
And I feel my heart—shaking—top speed. When
it's all over, she looks at me and says, "Hinson,
you're a baron."

KEITH: That's good. It's good that you're seeing women.

HINSON: You know what I said to her?

KEITH: Dad, I really—

HINSON: You know? I said, just like this—I said, "What's
a baron?"

KEITH: You don't know?

HINSON: I know. She told me. She said, "A baron is
like a king."

KEITH: Well, not exactly.

HINSON: So I'm a real estate baron.

KEITH: It's lower than a king.

HINSON: So what?

KEITH: It just is. I was just explaining—

HINSON: It's close enough. Once you get up there, who
cares how close it is? King, baron—it's all good.

KEITH: That's true.

HINSON: So, I'm having a sign made up for my office—
"Hinson Orr, baron."

KEITH: What?

HINSON: You like that? I'm going to hang it over the
light sculpture.

KEITH: Dad, see—baron, it has bad connotations.

HINSON: King? King has bad connotations?

KEITH: A baron's not a king!

HINSON: Why do you keep bringing that up?

KEITH: Baron implies you're shady.

HINSON: Shady? She called me shady?

KEITH: Not exactly.

HINSON: After what I did for her? In the back seat of
her car? She calls me shady?

KEITH: It's not bad to be shady in business.

HINSON: No, you're right. It's not. Sometimes, you got to bend the rules a little. Not like in your world.

KEITH: Anyway, I wouldn't put it on my wall. You don't want to tip off your clients, do you?

HINSON: Why not? I want them to know I'm honest. If I'm shady, I tell them—right away. People—they respect you for that.

[*Pause*]

KEITH: Look, I gotta unpack, OK? Just forget it.

HINSON: That's good. That you unpack. First thing. Shows you're organized.

KEITH: I guess.

HINSON: Not like me. I never know what to pack. I leave the clothes in my suitcase. They get wrinkled, smelly.

KEITH: Why don't you just take them out?

HINSON: I just can't. I had a bad upbringing.

KEITH: What does that have to do with it?

HINSON: Lots. We were brought up—like peons. Look at Barbara. You think that's a girl with social grace, class? Ha! She's lucky to get any husband at all, even an auto mechanic like Fred.

KEITH: OK, Dad.

HINSON: She's funny up here, Barbara.

KEITH: I'm going in now.

HINSON: Yeah. Me, too. It's late. For me. That's nine o'clock. Not like you, huh?

KEITH: Good night.

HINSON: Swinger.

KEITH: Dad!

HINSON: Look, come into my bedroom, and we can chit-chat.

KEITH: We just did.

HINSON: More! You just got here!

KEITH: Dad, you just fall asleep if I talk to you in bed.

HINSON: So? That's conversation. For your father—you should be happy to put me to sleep.

KEITH: Maybe tomorrow, Dad.

HINSON: OK. Well, good night.
KEITH: 'Night.
HINSON: Good to have my son home.
KEITH: Yeah. Nice to be here. [HINSON *exits.*]

WORMWOOD
by Amlin Gray

Wormwood is one of two short plays loosely based on the life and writings of Strindberg, produced under the title *Zones of the Spirit*. Theater for the New City presented the New York premiere of the play, in a production directed by Sharon Ott. It had previously been produced at the Milwaukee Repertory Theater.

The time is the 1890s; the place is the dusty back room of the Snout, a disreputable tavern in Stockholm. In this room Ossian Borg wrote his notorious memoir novels, writing only at night, wringing the anguish of his most intimate thoughts. To bring himself to a creative state, he would sip absinthe, which contains wormwood, a poison that causes fever, myopia, and persecution mania. Now he is married to a former artist, and has become a petit bourgeois who earns his living translating business letters. Lured back to the Snout, Borg realizes that he wants only to return to his writing, to be an artist again, with all its inherent dangers and dark exhilaration. The following scene reveals the artist at work, transforming reality to fit his vision. Johan Ekdahl, a waiter at the Snout, knew Borg's wife in art school; Borg, fueled by his jealousy, turns what was most probably an acquaintance into a great affair, creating a work of fiction, a fable penned in hell.

JOHAN: Mr. Borg, I met your wife by accident this afternoon. A former fellow-student had a show—we'd been all three at the institute together. When I told your wife I worked here, she asked if I could show her the back room, which she was curious to see—because of you, of course—well, why else? She was curious to see it—Mr. Borg.

OSSIAN: You knew my wife before I met her.

JOHAN: At the institute, that's right, sir. We were classmates.

OSSIAN: Back before I'd ever seen her, and before she'd ever seen me.

JOHAN: I think she'd graduated, sir, before she'd met you. I believe that's right.

OSSIAN: Are you a sapper and a miner, Johan?

JOHAN: Sir?

OSSIAN: Do you dig holes and plant explosives?

JOHAN: No.

OSSIAN: You've run a tunnel underneath my marriage, though, isn't that so?

JOHAN: No, sir, that isn't so. I haven't.

OSSIAN: You knew my wife before I knew her. Nobody should have known my wife before I did. Nobody should have known me before she did. Don't you think that's the best basis for a marriage?

JOHAN: Ideally I guess it is. But it hardly ever happens, does it? It *couldn't* happen. There's the parents, in the first place.

OSSIAN: Yes, her father. He's got the jump on me, and don't you think he doesn't know it.

JOHAN: I didn't really know your wife that well.

OSSIAN: You knew her. More importantly, she knew you.

JOHAN: She never really paid me any mind, to speak of.

OSSIAN: You say so, but you could be lying, couldn't you? Or you could be mistaken. It's a subject for conjecture. Happily, I don't conjecture anymore. I translate business letters—Swedish into French and German, French and German into Swedish. I improve on the originals in both directions. That's all the writing I do now.

JOHAN: There's nothing to conjecture about Mrs. Borg and me.

OSSIAN: There's always something to conjecture. You're a painter. Is there ever not something to look at?

JOHAN: No, but looking's not conjecturing.

OSSIAN: Painting is.

JOHAN: No, Mr. Borg. You just paint what you see.

OSSIAN: You look past what you see to what you know to be behind it and you paint that. Else why paint at all?

JOHAN: Your wife's stopped painting.

OSSIAN: That's right. In the name of simple decency.

JOHAN: I paint. Is that indecent of me?

OSSIAN: Not if you're completely without talent, as I'd guess you are.

JOHAN: What's talent got to do with it?

OSSIAN: A painter, or a writer, uses the people around him. The more talented he is, the more cruelly he exposes them. He strips the skin off his nearest and dearest, then offers the skin up for sale. He vivisects people like rabbits. He cuts the tail off his dog, eats the flesh, and gives the dog the bone to chew. What could be more loathsome?

JOHAN: He exposes himself too, doesn't he?

OSSIAN: He exposes himself most shamefully of all. That's hardly compensation to the people he humiliates. I wrote two novels in this room.

JOHAN: I know.

OSSIAN: Of course you know. Everybody knows, to my disgrace. The first one showed a father and his son—his wife's son—in a wretched symbiosis. It revealed the old man's martyrdom as the cramped manipulations of a crippled weasel. At the same time, it revealed the child's ingratitude as no less vicious. No quarter. No prisoners. Art in full deadly career, scything all before it into severed limbs and torsos.

JOHAN: I'm happy I'm not talented, if that's what happens.

OSSIAN: So you should be.

JOHAN: Your wife is very talented.

OSSIAN: Of course she is. If she'd been a dabbler like you, she could have gone on painting till the earth ran out of pigment.

JOHAN: You stopped her, though.

OSSIAN: She stopped herself. Her motives were the same as mine had been. Of course, there'd been some damage done already. My books were in print and some people had ogled her self-portraits.

JOHAN: They were staggering.

OSSIAN: No one but I should have seen them, and not even I. Not even Marika herself should have seen them. You surely shouldn't have. Better I should find you back here drinking with her.

JOHAN: Your wife and I drank absinthe in your honor.

OSSIAN: Absinthe?

JOHAN: Anisette. Real absinthe has been outlawed.

OSSIAN: Yes, I know. Quite rightly, too. Did you sit in my place, or was this glass Marika's?

JOHAN: That glass was hers.

OSSIAN: She hardly touched it.

JOHAN: She took a taste.

OSSIAN: It looks as thin as water. Absinthe used to swell with winding layers of greenish oil ready to suck at your tongue like a harlot.

JOHAN: There's some absinthe in that crate.

OSSIAN: Not real absinthe?

JOHAN: Yes.

OSSIAN: With wormwood?

JOHAN: Yes, sir. Malachi's illegal stock.

OSSIAN: I should have known he'd keep some back. One of the notes he sent me hinted that he had. It had been a grace to think there wasn't any wormwood left in Sweden—like dreaming that this room had caught on fire and burned to cinders. Do you have the key?

JOHAN: No. Malachi.

OSSIAN: The provider. If I drank a glass of wormwood, I might find out how you met my wife.

JOHAN: I've told you.

OSSIAN: You've told me too much and nothing at all.

JOHAN: I've told you all there is to tell.

OSSIAN: You've said you met at school, without my introducing you.

JOHAN: We met before you knew each other!

OSSIAN: Don't you see that only makes it worse? You were able to impress yourself on Marika before I'd even come into the picture. One person's consciousness has only so much space for unalloyed impressions. That space is filled early in life, before the gestures of the face have carved their creases. My image in Marika's mind lies over images of people she knew earlier. A former image might one day bleed through, and where will I be then?

JOHAN: I've told you Marika paid no attention to me.

OSSIAN: No attention to you?

JOHAN: None.

OSSIAN: What teachers did you both hate?

JOHAN [*automatically*]: Mr. Elstad— How did you know? Does she still talk about him?

OSSIAN: There always is one teacher all the students hate. He's usually the best.

JOHAN: Mr. Elstad was a rotten teacher. He taught history of art. When he explained a painting, I could hardly see the colors on the canvas for Elstad's description of them.

OSSIAN: Did you and Marika make fun of Mr. Elstad?

JOHAN: He had a stupid mustache. It stuck straight out sideways like the bristles on a pig. Marika said it would have made a fine pair of brushes.

OSSIAN: Did she?

JOHAN: Oh, she hated Mr. Elstad.

OSSIAN: Where were you when she joked about his mustache?

JOHAN: Where? I don't remember that.

OSSIAN: Of course you do. Think back. Were you at school?

JOHAN: Well, most likely we probably were.

OSSIAN: Only probably? Then you might have both been someplace else.

JOHAN: We might have.

OSSIAN: Where?

JOHAN: I don't know. What does it matter?

OSSIAN: It's grist for the mill.

JOHAN: What grist for what mill?

OSSIAN: You're hiding something, Johan.

JOHAN: No I'm not. I don't have anything to hide.

OSSIAN: Then tell me. Where did Marika make this mustache joke to you about poor Mr. Elstad?

JOHAN [*concentrates a moment*]: I don't think she made it just to me. I think she might have made it to a group of us.

OSSIAN: A group of students?

JOHAN [*"Yes"*]: All of us clustered around her when she talked down the teachers. She'd get really very nasty.

OSSIAN: Where did all you students cluster, if not at the institute?

JOHAN: Well, sometimes we'd go visit the museums together. Sometimes we'd go to the shore.

OSSIAN: The shore?

JOHAN: The beach, yes. During lunch, or in the evening.

OSSIAN: In the evening?

JOHAN: When the sun stayed out, in summer.

OSSIAN: On Midsummer Evening?

JOHAN: Maybe so. I don't remember.

OSSIAN: That's when the sun stays out the longest.

JOHAN: Yes, I think we all went to the shore together one year on Midsummer Evening. When our last class was dismissed we all trooped over.

OSSIAN: Did you stay all night?

JOHAN: I stayed all night. There were bonfires and dancing on the sand.

OSSIAN: Some of the others stayed all night too?

JOHAN: I think most of them.

OSSIAN: Did Marika stay?

JOHAN: I don't remember if she stayed till morning. She stayed pretty late. [*Explanatorily*] Midsummer Evening.

OSSIAN: It won't offend you if I drink from my wife's glass?

JOHAN: Of course not.

OSSIAN: If you drank from it, that would offend me very deeply. [*He sniffs the glass of anisette.*] Your pseudo-absinthe smells invisible, just as it looks. [*He drinks. Disapprovingly*] It tastes like licorice.

JOHAN: I like having the taste come from something that's clear. It's almost magical.

OSSIAN: If I think the wormwood into it—the taste like blackened sulfur from a burnt match—maybe we can manage our Midsummer Night. Now—we have a group of students, all clustered around Marika.

JOHAN: That wasn't on Midsummer Night, though. At least, I don't remember that it was.

OSSIAN [*Ignoring Johan's cavil, sips his drink, as he will continue to do at intervals*]: Gradually the group got smaller, didn't it? The students fell away in couples. There were Marika and you, and there were others, fewer and fewer as time went by. They fell away in couples.

JOHAN [*assents, as he comes under the influence of the picture Ossian is developing*]: It was Midsummer Night.

OSSIAN: You didn't fall away, though, did you?

JOHAN: I fell away.

OSSIAN: You fell away with Marika—and left the last few stragglers standing, young men and women making an odd number, a sad little number.

JOHAN: I didn't leave with Marika. I left alone, to walk along the water.

OSSIAN: And left Marika alone.

JOHAN: She was alone quite often. Yes, I think I see her standing up the bank a little way, alone.

OSSIAN: You'd been alone together, then, before you left.

JOHAN: She was comfortable with me. I wasn't jealous of her talent like the others.

OSSIAN: She stayed alone while you went down to walk along the shore.

JOHAN: She liked to stand among the trees. She did a painting of them once—several paintings.

OSSIAN: She liked it there among the shadows.

JOHAN: Yes.

OSSIAN: What else?

JOHAN: What else?

OSSIAN: There's more.

JOHAN: There's more what?

OSSIAN: There's more to the picture.

JOHAN: That's all I can remember. It's *more* than I remember.

OSSIAN [*begins filling the vacuum*]: There's the midsummer sun. You must remember that. The sun rode sideways until, right around eleven, it eased into the ocean at an angle almost flat with the horizon. The radiance it left beyond bled softly through the sky above the skerries and across the beach and up the wooded incline where she stood. She was alone. And then he came back.

JOHAN: Who came back?

OSSIAN: The young man.

JOHAN: Wait a minute. What young man?

OSSIAN: The painter. She was standing on the hillside by the shore and he came back.

JOHAN: Who was this painter? Was he me?

OSSIAN: Her fellow student.

JOHAN: And her fellow student's name was what?

OSSIAN: His name was Johan.

JOHAN: Mr. Borg, this story isn't true. You know that, don't you?

OSSIAN: What?

JOHAN: This story isn't true.

OSSIAN: Why not?

JOHAN: Why not? It isn't, that's all. It just isn't.

OSSIAN: Because it didn't happen?

JOHAN: Right, because it didn't happen.

OSSIAN: Aristotle knew two thousand years ago that history is inferior to poetry. History, he said, is just what happened. Poetry is what happens.

JOHAN: I didn't go to Marika on any hillside by the water.

OSSIAN: Why didn't you?

JOHAN: I *didn't*.

OSSIAN: But you might have.

JOHAN: No!

OSSIAN: Why mightn't you?

JOHAN: No reason, but—

OSSIAN: Why mightn't you have been a man of talent, even genius, a man whose will was just as strong as Marika's? You weren't, but that was purely accidental, just a random fact. It says nothing about anything. It doesn't help us fathom what the world is like.

JOHAN: I'm not a man of genius and I never was.

OSSIAN: You're like a cork that slips down in the bottle when I try to pop it out. Go get Malachi.

JOHAN: All right, I will, but—

OSSIAN: I don't want to hear you anymore. You've given me all that I needed.

JOHAN: Mr. Borg, I'm not the Johan in this fantasy.

OSSIAN: You're not, no. You're not worthy of yourself. You lack your own dimensions. I can't correct that with you standing here in front of me. Fetch Malachi and don't come back.

JOHAN [*starting out*]: I'll go. Just so you know—

OSSIAN: I won't know what I don't *believe*. Don't bother me with facts. They lie like algae on a lake. I want the close green depths to swim in—or to drown in, as the case may be. Vanish. Send in Malachi.

JOHAN [*at the door*]: I'm gone, but—

OSSIAN: You *are* gone. You're not there. Don't say another word. You're on the shore. Midsummer Evening. [*He empties his glass at a gulp and pays no further attention to the literal* JOHAN.] You're walking up the hillside from the beach with slow firm steps. You come to Marika, whose face, though it's addressed to you, seems not to see you. It's as if she heard you with her eyes. The color of her eyes has darkened, getting deeper in their fear of getting deeper which then makes them deeper still and still more fearful, then still deeper. . . . [JOHAN *makes to speak.*] You won't make another sound. You'll disappear and send in Malachi. [JOHAN *has only the strength of will to hesitate before silently obeying. He goes out and softly shuts the door behind him.*]

OHIO TIP-OFF
by James Yoshimura

Ohio Tip-Off was workshopped at New Dramatists and produced at Center Stage in Baltimore.

Every player on the Ohio Mixers, a Continental Basketball team, dreams of getting a "ticket to heaven," an invitation to play basketball for the majors. At an end-of-the-season game in Lima, Ohio, a scout for the Atlanta Hawks is there to watch. Dwight Anderson, a black who plays guard, is particularly anxious. Once a hot prospect, Dwight has had "bad luck" —accidents and setbacks—and at twenty-seven is passing his prime. That night on the court, Dwight's teammate and friend, twenty-four-year-old Gerald Sims, plays brilliant basketball and blows Dwight off the court. Gerald will be offered a "ticket to heaven." Dwight, bitter, taunts Gerald, telling him he'll be lucky to spend ten days in "heaven," warming the end of the bench. They fight. In the following scene, the two friends are reconciled.

DWIGHT: Do good, Gerald. A lot of pressure up there, but you'll handle it.

GERALD: I can't fuck up.

DWIGHT: You won't.

GERALD: I know you'll be coming after somebody's job next season.

DWIGHT: We'll see, huh?

GERALD: You're the best I've ever seen, Dwight.

DWIGHT: I was good once. [*Beat*] I went up against Magic Johnson one time. In L.A., third quarter. I was getting my minutes. I was greased. I had a good sweat. There I am, on a breakaway, and I'm running against someone.

GERALD: Johnson?

DWIGHT: I didn't know it was Magic just yet. I just felt someone leaning on me. I take off for the bucket, trying to shake free of whoever it is leaning on me. I get to the top of the key, and I take off. I'm flying.

GERALD: You got free of Johnson.

DWIGHT: Don't I wish. I take off, and this someone behind me, he takes off with me. I hear him. I hear his breathing. He's right on my neck. 20,000

people in the stands, screaming blood, and now I
can't hear them. Just Magic. Breathing.

GERALD: 20,000 and you hear his breathing, yeah.

DWIGHT [*smiles*]: I hear the fear in him.

GERALD: He's flying with you. He's up in the air.

DWIGHT: He's going to stuff the ball back in my face.

GERALD: From behind. He is.

DWIGHT: I wouldn't be his first victim, huh? [*Beat*] I
show him the ball in my left hand. I put the ball
out there to tease him.

GERALD: He goes for it.

DWIGHT: He's too smart for that. He's no slouch.
'Can't fake him.

GERALD: He's a mother of a player.

DWIGHT: He's a trademark. The best of the best.

GERALD: But you're taking it to him.

DWIGHT: He's breathing fear. [*Beat*] I turn the ball
over to my right hand. I do the switch on him, but
now I've got a problem. I'm flying in the air, and
I'm running out of room to fly. The basket is
coming right at my eyes.

GERALD: You got a problem.

DWIGHT: A shitload. I'm running out of room, I've got
Magic right on my ass, and he's reaching for the
ball. [*Beat*] We're in a rhythm now, and I gotta
break it. I'm waiting for him to take another
breath. Take that second breath, and you start to
come down. You gotta.

GERALD: You can't fly on that second breath.

DWIGHT: We're flying and flying, and I'm waiting, and
just when I feel I can't hold my time anymore, I
hear him take that second breath. And goddam! I
feel him moving away from me.

GERALD: He's coming down, you're still up?

DWIGHT: I am. [*Pause*] And then I don't know what,
why it happened, but I miss the shot. I beat Magic
Johnson, but I blow the shot. [*Pause*] I would
have made it. I would have stuck. It was enough
of one play, one moment. To make it for me. I

can still see the ball bouncing away from the rim.
Goddam.

GERALD: Goddam.

DWIGHT: All for missing that shot. [*Pause*] When you
get to Atlanta, inside a locker, I think it's the one
way in the corner, there'll be a mark inside the
door. I scratched a D on it. When you get there
maybe you'd look for it.

GERALD: I'll do that.

DWIGHT: They've probably painted over it.

GERALD: I'll look for it anyway.

DWIGHT: I scratched it in good. It's the corner locker.
It's quiet there. You can think and see everyone
else. If they have painted over it, you'll still be
able to make it out. I think. Open the locker up
halfway. The lights from overhead, they shine on
it at a certain angle, and that'll be me. That's my
D scratched there.

GERALD: For Dwight.

DWIGHT: None other. [DWIGHT *picks up his gear, and
begins to exit.*] You got lucky, Gerald.

GERALD: Everyone knows that. [DWIGHT *laughs, exits.*
GERALD *packs up his gear.*]

4.

Monologues
for Women

THE WAKE OF JAMEY FOSTER
by Beth Henley

A dark comedy of Southern manners, *The Wake of Jamey Foster* was presented on Broadway in a production directed by Ulu Grosbard.

The oddest gathering of family and friends have descended on Marshael Foster's house in Canton, Mississippi, for the funeral of Marshael's husband, Jamey, who died in the arms of Esmerelda Rowland, the woman he had moved in with. The young widow teeters on a fine, taut line between grief and hysteria. Totally losing it at one point, she confronts Jamey's corpse, and ends up holding on desperately to the memory of the first time he said he loved her because they were lying under the purple trees.

She is talking to herself and putting JAMEY's *clothes in a sack.*

MARSHAEL: All these ties. You never wore even half of 'em. Wasted ties. God, loose change. Always pockets full of loose change. And your Spearmint chewing gum sticks. Damn, and look—your lost car keys. Oh, well, the car's gone now. Damn you, leaving me alone with your mess. Leaving me again with all your goddamn, gruesome mess t'clean up. Damn, you, wait! You wait! You're not leaving me here like this. You're gonna face me! I won't survive! You cheat! I've got t'have something . . . redemption . . . something. [*She leaves the room, goes down to the parlor and walks in. The coffin is closed. She begins to circle it.*] There you are. Coward. Hiding. Away from me. Hiding. [*Moving in on him*] Look, I know I hurt you something bad, but why did you have to hold her fat, little hand like that? Huh? Treating me like nothing! I'm not . . . nothing. Hey, I'm talking. I'm talking to you. You'd better look at me. I mean it, you bastard! [*She pulls the lid off the coffin.*] Jamey. God, your face. Jamey, I'm scared. I'm so scared. I'm scared not to be loved. I'm scared for our life not to work out. It didn't, did it? Jamey? Damn you, where are you? Are you down in Mobile, baby? Have you taken a spin t'Mobile? I'm asking you—shit—Crystal Springs? How 'bout Scotland? You wanted to go there . . . your grandfather was from there. You shit! You're not . . . I know you're not . . . I love you! God. Stupid thing to say. I love you!! Okay; okay. You're gone. You're gone. You're not laughing. You're not . . . nothing. [*She moves away from the coffin, realizing it contains nothing of value.*] Still I gotta have something. Still something . . . [*as she runs out of the parlor then out the front door*] The trees. Still have the trees. The purple, purple trees—

SISTER MARY IGNATIUS
EXPLAINS IT ALL FOR YOU
by Christopher Durang

The Obie Award-winning *Sister Mary Ignatius Explains It All for You* was first presented by the Ensemble Studio Theater in New York City as part of their annual festival of one-act plays. Jerry Zaks directed and Elizabeth Franz starred. The play was subsequently produced at Playwrights Horizons with a curtain raiser, *The Actor's Nightmare*. It has proved a great, if controversial, success with many regional and college theaters.

Sister Mary Ignatius is speaking to her students at Our Lady of the Perpetual Sorrows School, answering questions on such diverse topics as birth control, why Saint Christopher is not a saint, what is heaven, hell, and purgatory; she covers a galaxy of church dogma with absolute faith in her beliefs, no matter how contradictory they may be. Then she is confronted by four of her grown-up former students; all four are angry, disillusioned, at odds with the Catholic church. Particularly rebellious is Diane, whose faith has been crushed by a series of wrenching experiences that undermines everything Sister Mary taught her to believe.

DIANE: When I was sixteen, my mother got breast cancer, which spread. I prayed to God to let her suffering be small, but her suffering seemed to me quite extreme. She was in bad pain for half a year, and then terrible pain for much of a full year. The ulcerations on her body were horrifying to her and to me. Her last few weeks she slipped into a semi-conscious state, which allowed her, unfortunately, to wake up for a few minutes at a time and to have a full awareness of her pain and her fear of death. She was able to recognize me, and she would try to cry, but she was unable to; and to speak, but she was unable to. I think she wanted me to get her new doctors; she never really accepted that her disease was going to kill her, and she thought in her panic that her doctors must be incompetent and that new ones could magically cure her. Then, thank goodness, she went into a full coma. A nurse who I knew to be Catholic assured me that everything would be done to keep her alive—a dubious comfort. Happily, the doctor was not Catholic, or if he was, not doctrinaire, and they didn't use extraordinary means to keep her alive; and she finally died after several more weeks in her coma. Now there are, I'm sure, far worse deaths—terrible burnings, tortures, plague, pestilence, famine; Christ on the cross even, as Sister likes to say. But I thought my mother's death was bad enough, and I got confused as to why I had been praying and to whom. I mean, if prayer was really this sort of button you pressed—admit you need the Lord, then He stops your suffering—then why didn't it always work? Or ever work? And when it worked, so-called, and our prayers were supposedly answered, wasn't it as likely to be chance as God? God always answers our prayers, you said, He just sometimes says no. But why would He say no to stopping my mother's suffering? I wasn't even asking that she live, just that He end her suffering. And it can't be that He was letting her suffer because she'd been bad, because she hadn't been bad and besides suffering doesn't seem to work that way, considering the suffering of children who've obviously done nothing wrong. So why was He letting her suffer? Spite? Was the Lord God actually malicious? That seemed possible, but farfetched. Maybe He had no control over it, maybe He wasn't omnipotent as you taught us He was. Maybe He created the world sort of by accident by belching one morning or getting the hiccups, and maybe He had no idea how the whole thing worked. In which case, He wouldn't be malicious, just useless. Or, of course, more likely than that, He didn't exist at all, the universe was hiccuped or belched into existence all on its own, and my mother's suffering just existed like rain or wind or humidity. I became angry at myself, and by extension at you, for ever having expected anything beyond randomness from the world. And while I was thinking these things, the day that my mother died, I was raped. Now I know that's really too much, one really loses all sympathy for me because I sound like I'm making it up or something. But bad things sometimes happen all at once, and this particular day on my return from the hospital I was raped by some maniac who broke into the house. He had a knife and cut me up some. Anyway, I don't really want to go on about the experience, but I got very depressed for about five years. Somehow the utter randomness of things—my mother's suffering, my attack by a lunatic who was either born a lunatic or made one by cruel parents or perhaps by an imbalance of hormones or whatever, etc. etc.—*this randomness seemed intolerable.* I found I grew to hate you, Sister, for making me once expect everything to be ordered and to make sense. My psychiatrist said he thought my hatred of you was obsessive, that I just was looking for someone to blame. Then he seduced me, and he was the father of my second abortion. He said I seduced him. And maybe that's so. But he could be lying just to make himself feel better. [*To* SISTER] And of course your idea that I should have had this baby, either baby, is preposterous. Have you any idea what a terrible mother I'd be? I'm a nervous wreck. I suppose it is childish to look for blame, part of the randomness of things is that there is no one to blame; but basically I think everything is your fault, Sister.

FOB
by David Hwang

FOB was first produced by Nancy Takahashi for the Stanford Asian American Theater Project. A draft of the play was then developed at the O'Neill Theater Center's National Playwrights Conference. Joseph Papp produced *FOB* at the New York Shakespeare Festival.

Grace is a Chinese–American college student, currently attending the University of California, Los Angeles. She immigrated to the United States from Taiwan at an early age. In the following monologue, she talks about the difficulty of making that transition.

GRACE: Yeah. It's tough trying to live in Chinatown. But it's tough trying to live in Torrance, too. It's true. I don't like being alone. You know, when Mom could finally bring me to the U.S., I was already ten. But I never studied my English very hard in Taiwan, so I got moved back to the second grade. There were a few Chinese girls in the fourth grade, but they were American-born, so they wouldn't even talk to me. They'd just stay with themselves and compare how much clothes they all had, and make fun of the way we all talked. I figured I had a better chance of getting in with the white kids than with them, so in junior high I started bleaching my hair and hanging out at the beach—you know, Chinese hair looks pretty lousy when you bleach it. After a while, I knew what beach was gonna be good on any given day, and I could tell who was coming just by his van. But the American-born Chinese, it didn't matter to them. They just giggled and went to their own dances. Until my senior year in high school—that's how long it took for me to get over this whole thing. One night I took Dad's car and drove on Hollywood Boulevard, all the way from downtown to Beverly Hills, then back on Sunset. I was looking and listening—all the time with the window down, just so I'd feel like I was part of the city. And that Friday, it was—I guess—I said, "I'm lonely. And I don't like it. I don't like being alone." And that was all. As soon as I said it, I felt all of the breeze—it was really cool on my face—and I heard all of the radio—and the music sounded really good, you know? So I drove home.

PAINTING CHURCHES
by Tina Howe

Painting Churches was initially presented by the Second Stage Theater company in New York. The play subsequently moved to the Lamb's Theater Off-Broadway. The public television series, "Theatre in America," presented a production of the play, which starred Sada Thompson, Donald Moffat, and Roxanne Hart. *Painting Churches* won an Obie Award for distinguished playwriting.

Gardner Church is an eminent New England poet. His wife, Fanny, is a Bostonian from a fine, old family. Their daughter, Margaret (Mags), an up-and-coming painter living in New York, returns to her parents' townhouse in Boston, both to help them move and to try to paint their portrait. Neither parent seems to take Mags or her painting all that seriously—apparently they never have. In the following, Mags confronts her parents with a vengeance as she takes them back to her childhood and her first "masterpiece."

MAGS: That's why I've always wanted to paint you, to see if I'm up to it. It's quite a risk. Remember what I went through as a child with my great masterpiece? . . . Well, it was a masterpiece to me. . . . I didn't paint it. It was something I made! I did it during that winter you sent me away from the dinner table. I was about nine years old. I was banished for six months. Because I played with my food. I used to squirt it out between my front teeth. . . . I couldn't swallow anything. My throat just closed up. I don't know, I must have been afraid of choking or something. I guess I was afraid of making a mess. I don't know; you were awfully strict about table manners. I was always afraid of losing control. What if I started to choke and began spitting up over everything? . . . No, I was really terrified about making a mess; you always got so mad whenever I spilled. If I just got rid of everything in neat little curlicues beforehand, you see . . . *I* thought it was quite ingenious, but you didn't see it that way. You finally sent me from the table with, "When you're ready to eat like a human being, you can come back and join us!" . . . So, it was off to my room with a tray. But I couldn't seem to eat there either. I mean, it was so strange settling down to dinner in my *bedroom*. . . . So I just flushed everything down the toilet and sat on my bed listening to you: clinkity-clink, clatter, clatter, slurp, slurp . . . but that got pretty boring after a while, so I looked around for something to do. It was wintertime, because I noticed I'd left some crayons on top of my radiator and they'd melted down into these beautiful shimmmering globs, like spilled jello, trembling and pulsing. . . . Naturally, I wanted to try it myself, so I grabbed a red one and pressed it down against the hissing lid. It oozed and bubbled like raspberry jam! I mean, that radiator was really hot! It took incredible will power not to let go, but I held on, whispering, "Mags, if you let go of this crayon, you'll be run over by a truck on Newberry Street, so help you God!" . . . So I pressed down harder, my fingers steaming and blistering. . . . Once I'd melted one, I was hooked! I finished off my entire supply in one night, mixing color over color until my head swam! . . . The heat, the smell, the brilliance that

sank and rose . . . I'd never felt such exhilaration!
. . . Every week I spent my allowance on crayons.
I must have cleared out every box of Crayolas in
the city! AFTER THREE MONTHS THAT RA-
DIATOR WAS . . . SPECTACULAR! I MEAN,
IT LOOKED LIKE SOME COLOSSAL FRUIT
CAKE, FIVE FEET TALL! . . . It was a knock-
out; shimmering with pinks and blues, lavenders
and maroons, turquoise and golds, oranges, and
creams. . . . For every color, I imagined a taste
. . . YELLOW: lemon curls dipped in sugar . . .
RED: glazed cherries laced with rum . . . GREEN:
tiny peppermint leaves veined with chocolate . . .
PURPLE: . . . And then the frosting . . . ahhhh,
the frosting! A satiny mix of white and silver . . .
I kept it hidden under blankets during the day . . .
My huge . . . [*She starts laughing.*] looming . . .
teetering sweet . . . I was so . . . *hungry* . . .
losing weight every week. I looked like a scare-
crow what with the bags under my eyes and bits
of crayon wrapper leaking out of my clothes. It's
a wonder you didn't notice. But finally you came
to my rescue . . . if you could call what happened
a rescue. It was more like a rout! The winter was
almost over . . . It was late at night. . . . I must
have been having a nightmare because suddenly
you and Daddy were at my bed, shaking me. . . .
I quickly glanced towards the radiator to see if it
was covered. . . . *It wasn't!* It glittered and tow-
ered in the moonlight like some . . . gigantic Vi-
ennese pastry! You followed my gaze and saw it.
Mummy screamed . . . "WHAT HAVE YOU
GOT IN HERE? . . . MAGS, WHAT HAVE
YOU BEEN DOING?" . . . She crept forward
and touched it, and then jumped back. "IT'S
FOOD!" she cried . . . "IT'S ALL THE FOOD
SHE'S BEEN SPITTING OUT! OH, GARD-
NER, IT'S A MOUNTAIN OF ROTTING GAR-
BAGE!" Daddy exited as usual; left the premises.

He fainted, just keeled over onto the floor. . . .
My heart stopped! I mean, I knew it was all over.
My lovely creation didn't have a chance. Sure
enough . . . out came the blowtorch. Well, it
couldn't have *really* been a blowtorch, I mean,
where would you have ever gotten a blowtorch?
. . . I just have this very strong memory of you
standing over my bed, your hair streaming around
your face, aiming this . . . flame thrower at my
confection . . . my cake . . . my tart . . . my stru-
del. . . . "IT'S GOT TO BE DESTROYED IM-
MEDIATELY! THE THING'S ALIVE WITH
VERMIN! . . . JUST LOOK AT IT! . . . IT'S
PRACTICALLY CRAWLING ACROSS THE
ROOM!" . . . Of course in a sense you were
right. It *was* a monument of my cast-off dinners,
only I hadn't built it with food. . . . I found my
own materials. I was languishing with hunger, but
oh, dear Mother . . . I FOUND MY OWN MA-
TERIALS! . . . I tried to stop you, but you
wouldn't listen. . . . OUT SHOT THE FLAME!
. . . I remember these waves of wax rolling across
the room and Daddy coming to, wondering, what
on earth was going on. . . . Well, what did you
know about my abilities? . . . You see, I had . . .
I mean, I *have* abilities. . . . [*Struggling, to say it*]
I have abilities, I have . . . strong abilities. I have
. . . very strong abilities. They are very strong
. . . very, very strong. . . . [*She rises and runs out
of the room, overcome.*]

THE BRIDES
by Harry Kondoleon

The Brides was first produced in Stockbridge, Massachusetts, by the Lenox Arts Center Music-Theater Performing Group. The play was subsequently seen at the Cubiculo Theater in New York City under the title *Disrobing the Bride*.

Whimsical yet erotic, highly romantic and thoroughly modern, *The Brides* is an eclectic hymn to the relationships of men and women. The entire piece is performed by three to four women. Some of the power of the following monologue comes from the irony of having a woman role-playing the groom. However, this monologue could be very effective performed by a man as well.

Once upon a time a groom—that's me!—came riding on his own horse. Lo! he spotted a fair maiden, her skin a beautiful brown or white or yellow or red or black depending upon what I'm in the mood for that afternoon—I wear what he—the groom—is in the mood for . . . "Oh! fair maiden of multicolored skin, of hair and eyes worthy of the Uffizi, may I stop by this clearing and collect a posy of wild flowers to present to your fair nose?"

"Oh do!" says the bride, already a little wet, a little anxious, already turning the present into the past by mentally describing this happening to her sisters who are less beautiful and stay at home with handicrafts and sketch pads. "Oh do!" says the princess, already sizing up the groom beneath his tight doublet, his tight tunic, his tight tights. Already she is imagining his magic stick, describing it to her sisters who themselves will make quick sketches of the unseen instrument, exaggerating their sister's already exaggerated words. "Oh do!" says the bride, "Oh do! Do!" And the groom picks the sweet things—baby's breath, bachelor buttons and briar roses. "The scent will knock her out," he thinks to himself, already rather horny himself, already mentally unbuttoning the bride, picturing her high firm tits popping from their bondage into the sunlight, furry stingless bees resting on her tall dark nipples, and, unhooking the fuchsia bell—her skirt—finding the honey nest, dipping the spoon, getting hungry.

And when the sun is up over the poplars, over the cypresses, over the maple, the short dogwood and the stubby bush of thorn berries, over whatever is handy in the neighborhood—when it's over that, the bride and groom, their bodies a little damp, a little exhausted, roll away from one another, away from this unhistorical history, away from the morning when everyone feels small and uncounted and into the afternoon where, unnoticed, completely and utterly unnoticed, noon passed, and already everything has been, has been, has been, has been, the crickets shoveling seeds into cracks they won't see in the winter, birds believing in nothing, abandon their twigs and leave town the first signs of snow.

"Oh love me forever!" moans the bride to the groom. This is agony for her, this sudden second sight—this seeing the forest for the trees, this unquenched fire in her heart. "Oh love me forever!" screams the bride, already picturing a white dress a tailor with twelve assistants will slave over, already picturing the tiered cake, the guests milling in petal strewn aisles—already she is picturing all this and—simultaneously—at once with the ecstasy of fulfillment—betrayal—betrayal betrayal betrayal—at once—here—now with the groom inches from her bare hip—she sees his disappearance, the broken promise, the imaginary fouled sheets of his new bride—the Other—the chamber they will retire to when she—if not restrained by her sisters and her I-told-you-so parents would have thrown herself head first down the stone steps leading to the altar. "Is there no sadder story than mine?" weeps the bride, her voice muffled by her gown, her face buried in veils, "Is there no sadder story than mine?—tell it to me—tell it to me!"

BLUES
by Kirk Ristau

Blues was workshopped at the Playwrights Center in Minneapolis and at the Guthrie Theater. The play received its professional premiere at the Cricket Theater in Minneapolis.

Set in a decaying boarding house in the Midwest, *Blues* is a haunting, poetic play, singing the darker, more melancholy side of love. Jessie has fled to the boarding house to escape a love going nowhere. But Arnie, the man Jesse loved (and may still love), follows her. Arnie's arrival affects not only Jessie but the other three women in the boarding house, all of whom are attracted to Arnie in some way—Odie, mysterious, a little crazy, and very bitter about love; Woody, who runs the boarding house, growing old alone, left with only memories of love; and the adolescent Mecca, just learning about love, its pleasures, its pain. Throughout the play Mecca flirts with Arnie; she is coy and outrageous, as much a child as a woman. In her own way, however, she wants Arnie to take her seriously. But in the final moments of the play, when Jessie rejects Arnie once and for all, Arnie takes his rage and frustration out on Mecca, slapping her hard across the face and leaving. Woody comes to comfort Mecca, soothing the girl with her memories, with her hopes for the future.

WOODY: I used to be a dancer, you know that? I liked dancing with men. Used to dance with women during the war when all the men were gone, but I like to dance with men. Women, men, what's the difference as long as you're dancing.

Oh but dancing with men. There's something special in a man's hands. The lines, the veins all blue and pretty. With him holding you there close to him. Swaying to the music. Each little step taking you closer. I feel the strength there and the heat. Smelling his breath and the peppermints when he could afford them. And all the time I kept thinking to myself, "Oh God, don't let it end. Please don't let it end. Tonight, don't let it end." But it'd end and I'd find myself back dancing with a woman the next week. Only I'd remember, and it was nice, nice to remember. The music comes back to you, those clarinets, and it beats here [*points to her heart.*] Soon you find yourself longing for a time when men touched you. Nice young men. And they smelled so clean [*laughs*]. My breasts were firmer then. My hair had a shine. Hmmmm, the days when men touched you and love didn't mean a thing but love. It didn't mean happiness with him, it didn't mean sorrow. All it meant was love. He used to tell me, he used to say, "I like the way your nylons feel slipping down your legs, down your long-stemmed American beauty roses." I'd laugh at that and take him to my breast and hold him close, the moon shining. He smelled like a man and I smelled like a woman, and somewhere there was a war going on but we didn't notice. We were in love and we loved. You can't think of anything else. The bad don't matter 'cause all I got left is the good. And someday you're gonna grow up and the likes of you will never be seen again. Your breasts will be nice and round and your hair pretty. Boys'll line up from here all the way to the Avalon, three blocks away. You're gonna be somethin' special. Don't you believe that? [*Pause*] Well, that's all it takes.

WINGS
by Arthur Kopit

Originally commissioned for National Public Radio's "Earplay," *Wings* was given its first stage performance at the Yale Repertory Theater in New Haven, Connecticut. The play was subsequently produced at the Kennedy Center in Washington D.C., and on Broadway at the Lyceum Theater, in a production featuring Constance Cummings and Mary-Joan Negro, directed by John Madden.

Mrs. Emily Stilson, well into her seventies, a former aviatrix and wing walker, has had a severely damaging stroke. *Wings* traces her recovery in a rehabilitation center, her struggle to put back together her shattered world. Although Mrs. Stilson is still relatively lucid, the part of her brain that controls speech has been damaged, and she is unable to communicate. We watch her learn to speak all over again. We watch her desperate reach for language, which often fails, and she utters only nonsense. This remarkable play, almost a monologue, is like an imperfect prism; we see Mrs.

Stilson both as she perceives herself and as the staff of the rehabilitation center perceives her. The following monologue—part clarity, part confusion, part eloquence, part gibberish—captures the prismatic feeling of the play, as Mrs. Stilson, very early in her convalescence, struggles with her confused notion that she has crashed in a biplane behind enemy lines and that the rehabilitation center is some sort of prison.

MRS. STILSON: Yes no question they have got me I've been what that word was captured is it? No it's— Yes, it's captured how? Near as it can figure. I was in my prane and crashed, not unusual, still in all not too common. Neither is it very grub. Plexit rather or I'd say propopic. Well that's that, jungdaball! Anyhow to resume, what I had for lunch? That's not it, good books I have read, good what, done what? Whaaaaat? Do the busy here! Get inside this, rubbidge all around let the vontul do some yes off or it of above semilacrum pwooosh! what with noddygobbit nip-n-crashing inside outside witsit watchit funnel vortex sucking into backlash watchit get-out caught-in spinning ring-grab grobbit help woooosh! cannot stoppit on its own has me where it wants. [*And suddenly she is in another realm. Lights transformed into weightless blue. Sense of ease and serenity*] Plane! See it thanks, okay, onto back we were and here it is. Slow down easy now. Captured. After crashing, that is what we said or was about to, think it so, cannot tell for sure, slow it slow it, okay here we go . . . [*speaking slower now*] captured after crashing by the enemy and brought here to this farm masquerading as a hospital. Why? For I would say offhand information. Of what sort though hard to tell. For example, questions such as can I raise my fingers, what's an overcoat, how many nickels in a rhyme, questions such as these. To what use can they be to the enemy? Hard to tell from here. Nonetheless, I would say must be certain information I possess that they want well I won't give it I'll escape! Strange things happen to me that they do! Good thing I'm all right! Must be in Rumania. Just a hunch of course. [*The serene blue light starts to fade.*] Ssssh, someone's coming.

SMALLER HEARTACHES
by Frank Pike

Developed at Middlebury College, the comedy-drama *Smaller Heartaches* was workshopped at Playwrights Horizons in New York City and has been performed in Boston and Minneapolis, where it received the Twin Cities Drama Critics Circle Kudos Award.

It's the summer of 1977. Andy, decidedly uncomfortable about his new-found sexuality, returns home to tell his folks and his best friend, Dennis, that he is gay. Andy's family rejects him outright, and Dennis, although supportive, can't really be much help: he has his hands full with Rachel, who, true to the radical politics of the late seventies, has decided "the only true feminist is a lesbian," and is moving out on Dennis to join a radical lesbian commune. The summer is further complicated by the arrival of Lily, Rachel's best friend in college, a quiet, charming Texan, and a lesbian. Rachel, who can deal with the politics but not the realities of lesbianism, is terrified that Lily is going to suggest that the two of them begin a relationship. Lily, carrying around a dark secret she had planned to share with Rachel, is forced to turn to Andy, whom she hardly knows, but in whom she sees a kindred spirit.

LILY: As you might recall, I come from Texas. And my daddy and mama are Jewish. Orthodox, as a matter of fact. And I am gay. As far back as I can recall, my feelings have been my feelings. I can't for the life of me think back to a time when I didn't feel what I feel now. But I never had a relationship with anyone, no less a woman, until I left my family, left Texas, and spent my junior year at Oxford. Where I met Esther. When I got back to Texas, I finished college and found a job teaching in a private school in my hometown. Five weeks or so ago, someone called the school and informed them that I was a lesbian. The school began immediate proceedings to have me dismissed. I eventually resigned. As part of the proceedings, however, they called Daddy and Mama. I remember. I had been invited to supper. I remember Daddy on the phone, pushing back his glasses, his eyes . . . He looked at me the whole time he talked. After supper, we all talked. Daddy and Mama and Sister and I. I tried to lie, but I just couldn't lie anymore. I told them, "Yes, I am a lesbian." Funny when you finally call something something. Daddy just looked at me; Mama just looked away. They went to bed. Rebecca—Rebecca's my sister—just sat there, silent. I finally got up and said good-bye. She didn't say anything. She said nothing. She just came over to me and stroked my hair for a moment or two. Yes. I went back to my apartment. The next day the family sat shiva, the mourning for the dead. My family is Orthodox: When I confessed that I was a lesbian, to them, I was dead. Because, for them, I lived—live an unforgiveable sin. The whole time my family sat shiva, I locked myself up in my apartment. Drew the shades. Rolled myself up in a blanket. Closed my eyes tightly. I tried to picture home. The mirrors covered with black cloth. A white candle burning. Daddy and Mama and Sister and nine strange men, pious men, their eyes averted. Dressed in mourning. Sitting on small wooden stools. I held the blanket tightly around my ears. I didn't want to hear the wailing. For seven days and seven nights, I was afraid to fall asleep. When my daddy and mama and sister awoke on the morning of the seventh day, I was, to them, a memory. To them, I am dead. If I am near them, they don't speak to me, they don't hear me, they don't see me. They don't feel me if I touch them. [*Pause*] A week or so after the family sat shiva, I, I don't know why, I walked into my . . . into the house. The front door was open. Daddy always leaves the front door open . . . for visitors. They were eating supper. I remember. I stood in the middle of the kitchen and watched them. Daddy turned and turned away. Mama paused and continued talking. Rebecca excused herself and ran upstairs. For some reason, I don't know why, I answered a question that Mama had asked Daddy, then I just wouldn't stop talking. I picked up a ladle and started circling the table, shouting, screaming, carrying on like there was no tomorrow. I stood behind Mama and yelled in her ear. I shook Daddy . . . violently. I grabbed his head and tried to make him look at me. I knocked his glasses, I remember, yes, clear across the table. Mama quietly got up and brought the dessert. I stopped screaming. I let go. I picked up Daddy's glasses and put them back on him. Then I ran out. Out the back door. Across the patio. Through the garden. Into the desert. [*Pause*] On impulse—I can be an awfully silly person sometimes—I went back before I left for Philadelphia. The doors were locked.

THE RESURRECTION OF LADY LESTER
by OyamO

An imaginative biography, *The Resurrection of Lady Lester* was originally produced at the Yale Repertory Theatre and later aired on CBS Cable.

The Resurrection of Lady Lester is a nonrealistic, kaleidoscopic look at the life and death of Lester Young, a legendary jazz musician, dying of despair and gin in a midtown hotel room that is directly opposite the Birdland, a famous jazz club in New York City. It's a memory play; time and place are obliterated by Lester's reminisces and regrets, his mind racing back to the music he made, his childhood, his fame, his fall, his friends, his fellow musicians, the women he loved. One of the women his mind conjures up is Lady Day—a.k.a. Billie Holliday—a blues singer. Scalded by life, she finds some solace in drugs. In the following monologue she tells Lester about a reform school experience she had, an experience that helped shape her life.

L.D.: I feel trapped inside of something that ain't real. I need some fresh air. Somehow I don't feel free!

That's what I keep gettin' confused about! Even if I can't see the chains, I know they're there. But I ain't sure who owns them. Some kind of invisible chains. I . . . it's so hard to explain. No wait! I once had a weird dream. I was in the kitchen of this white folks' cabaret eating my dinner. Between bites I was grumbling about how I always had to eat alone in the kitchen. But I remember the food tasted good; I was eating heavy because I was hungry, and my plate kept filling up by itself. And then I heard music, very loud and scratchy; it had a echo like when you shout to God from a mountaintop. I got up to leave and the plate turned into a giant albino roach that sang some funny, high-pitched blues while it shuffled across the table. I got scared and ran for the door, but the door wouldn't open. None of the doors would open. I tried all the windows; they were made of steel. I started hollering, but I couldn't even hear myself. The music was so loud it made my head hurt. I pushed my hands into my ears, but the pain wouldn't stop. I emptied a trash can by the door and started a big fire, and the door started burning, but when I turned away from the fire so I wouldn't get burnt, I saw the freezer door opening and five giant, red-eyed sausages came walking out toward me. They was dressed just like people; they walked like people and they talked like people, but I knew they was sausages. I started to run from them, but there was no place to run; the fire had done spread everywhere. They kept coming toward me; they kept telling me to get in the freezer with them so I wouldn't get burnt, but I couldn't move; I just started crying and screaming and vomiting—and then I woke up . . . This happened in New York, Les, where my dreams wake up with me, and the chains on me ain't got nothin' to do with where I'm at. I mean, I named you the Prez, Les, because you're the best, just like Roosevelt, but you black and no matter how great you blow that tenor, if you don't do what ole marsa "ask" you to do in this place, you liable to be hung out to dry. And no matter how good I sing, I'm still locked up in a hot kitchen, regardless to who marsa is.

CATHOLIC SCHOOL GIRLS
by Casey Kurtti

The life of *Catholic School Girls* began with a production at The Play Factory Off Off-Broadway. The play was subsequently produced at the Douglas Fairbanks Theater in New York City with a summer tryout at Lucille Lortel's White Barn Theater in Westport, Connecticut. *Catholic School Girls*, which won the Villager Award, has been staged in regional theaters and abroad.

The play traces the career of four girls in a parochial school, from grades one through eight. In the following monologue, Elizabeth, a bright, impressionable second-grader, shares her views on Catholicism and life.

LOUD

ELIZABETH: Okay everybody. This is church. This is God's house. If you ever have to talk to him just come right in and kneel down in one of these long chairs and start talking. But not too loud. In here you have to be real quiet. You might wake up the statues and they are praying to Jesus [*bows her*

whisp

head]. Oh, I forgot to tell you something. Whenever you hear the name Jesus you have to bow your head or else you have a sin on your soul. Now, over there is the statue of Jesus' mother. Her name is the Blessed Virgin Mary. She is not as important as Jesus, so you don't have to bow your head when you hear her name. All the girls sit on her side when they go to mass. One time I heard that Margaret Mary O'Donahugue, a sixth grader, was in church saying the rosary, that's the necklace with beads on it for praying, she said that the Blessed Virgin Mary statue started crying right in the middle of mass. I believe it too. Sister says that there are miracles, magic things that happen to people that are real good. Margaret Mary never gets in trouble. In class she always gives the right answers, so I guess she deserves to see a miracle. Well, I'm going to get a miracle someday too. Anyway, the boys sit on the other side of the church, the one with the statue of Saint Joseph. He is Jesus' father [*bows head*]. Hey, you forgot to bow your head. Don't do that 'cause you'll have a black spot on your soul and you'll go straight to hell.

Now in hell it is real hot and you sweat a lot and little devils come and bite you all over. If you are real good you get to go to heaven. In heaven, they have a big refrigerator full of stuff to eat. M and M's, ice cream, little chocolate covered doughnuts, anything you want to eat and it never runs out. But the best thing about heaven is that you get to meet anyone you want. Let's say I wanted to meet Joan of Arc . . . no . . . no . . . Cleopatra. I would go to one of the saints and he would give me a permission slip and I would fill it out and give it to Jesus [*bows head*]. Hey, you didn't bow your head. Okay, I warned you. Then I would fly across heaven, 'cause when you get in they give you wings, and I would have a chat with Cleopatra. The only thing is that I hope everyone I like gets accepted into heaven or else I would never see them again. /

Jewish people can't go to heaven. So if any of you are Jewish I would change into a Catholic or else you have to go straight to hell. Jewish people can't even go to church. If I saw a Jewish person in church I would stand up and tell the priest that there was a Jewish person in church, and he would stop the mass until they left.

One time I heard this story and I know it is true, that a Jewish person went to church for two weeks disguised as a Catholic. He got communion every day except he took them out of his mouth so that they wouldn't melt and he put them in his kitchen cupboard so they would be safe. Then when he had gotten enough, thirteen or so, he put them in a frying pan and he cooked them and blood started dripping from the ceiling and it was Jesus' blood [*bows head*].

You see that crucifix up there. That's how Jesus died. The Jewish people put him up there and they killed Him. If a Jewish person walked in here, that statue would turn bloody. Jesus would start hurting from the nails.

That's all I wanted to say. I just wanted to tell you a few important things. I hope I haven't hurt anyone's feelings but that's just the way it is. Oh one more thing, if you ask Jesus a question, make sure you write the answer down real fast, so you don't mess it up. 'Cause if you mess up an answer from Him it could get you in real bad trouble.

THE WOMEN HERE
ARE NO DIFFERENT
by Nancy Beckett

Originally produced by the Women's Theater Project
in Minneapolis, *The Women Here Are No Different*
has been produced in theaters throughout the country,
including the Missouri Rep in Kansas City, Wisdom
Bridge in Chicago, and the 13th Street Repertory in
New York City. The play won the Twin Cities Drama
Critics Circle Kudos Award.

The Women Here Are No Different takes place in a
battered woman's shelter in the Minneapolis–St. Paul
area. The women in the shelter come from all strata of
society; they are all ages; they are all in pain, at odds
with themselves and the world. The play alternates
between raw, realistic confrontations and introspec-
tive, poetic monologues as it traces the women's coming to terms with what has happened to them and what
they have to do in order to go on with their lives. In
the following monologue, one of the women talks
about the dark underside of what seemed to be the
perfect upper-middle-class marriage, talks about the
events and perceptions that led to her flight to the
shelter.

THERESA: This has not happened to me in my life
    before.

I hear these other ladies talking about their lives.
So I dig deep in my memory,
And come up with nothing. Zero. Ffffftttt.
I try to think back to my mother or my brother
or somebody lettin me have it.
Zilch. I'm not blocking anything, honest.
I can't think of anything like it ever. Never.
It doesn't make sense.

One night he grabbed my arm, hard.
After church on Sunday he threw me down on
the bed.
A month later he slapped me against the screen
door on the patio.
Our neighbors took their drinks inside.
I kept thinking that I was imagining things,
and he kept proving me wrong.
It's like a small zebra or something,
just moves into your rec room one day.
Stands there and chews on the petunias,
looking at you through your sliding glass door.
That's how strange this whole thing is to me.
Strange.

I'm married to a stranger.
He wears a sixteen-and-a-half long,
and his handwriting looks like sharp teeth
and stray bits of wire mushed together.
He's gone so much, he wonders where I am.
I'm in the garden. I'm picking up the kids from
baseball practice.
I make lists, and mark the calendars, to make
sure to answer his
questions, questions, long distance airport inter-
rogations.
I switched to a lady dentist just so he wouldn't
suspect me of that.

And I say to my friends, "Neal is different. Neal
is acting funny.

Neal is making me doubt my ability to go to the dry cleaners."

And they say, "What zebra?"

My mother says, "You married a zebra, now you live with him."

And my priest says, "Pray to the virgin the zebra will go away."

And I think I'm going nuts.

Okay. See it's not that funny, because I have listened to my friends.

I believed my mother.

I have prayed for months.

Who do you trust?

How do you know things weren't really always like this?

Was I always this confused?

So one day last week after school, I packed my three children,

In the car he insisted on buying me after our last fight,

And I didn't go to my mother's.

I didn't go to my best friend's.

I braved the rush hour traffic to come here.

Do you think this is crazy?

5.

Monologues for Men

MA RAINEY'S BLACK BOTTOM
by August Wilson

Ma Rainey's Black Bottom premiered at the Yale Repertory Theater in New Haven, Connecticut; the production, directed by Lloyd Richards, subsequently moved to Broadway's Cort Theater.

In 1927 in a seedy recording studio in Chicago, blues singer Ma Rainey and her band of black musicians are about to cut a new record. As usual, the temperamental Ma Rainey is holding up the recording session. Her musicians wile away the time down in the basement band room, rehearsing blues numbers such as "Ma Rainey's Black Bottom" and "Hear Me Talking to You." Between numbers they joke, taunt each other, argue, harangue, reminisce, swap stories, and dream. Their talk is a kind of blues, singing the hope and hopelessness of trying to make it in a white man's world. Trying particularly hard to make it is the upstart, enterprising trumpet player Levee, whose attempts to climb to the top of the music world the other musicians see as obsequious and demeaning. In the following monologue, Levee defends himself.

LEVEE: Levee got to be Levee! And he don't need nobody messing with him about the white man— 'cause you don't know nothing about me. You don't know Levee. You don't know nothing about what kind of blood I got! What kind of heart I got beating here! [*He pounds his chest.*]

I was eight years old when I watched a gang of white mens come into my daddy's house and have to do with my mama any way they wanted. [*Pause*]

We was living in Jefferson County, about eighty miles outside of Natchez. My daddy's name was Memphis . . . Memphis Lee Green . . . had him near fifty acres of good farming land. I'm talking about good land! Grow anything you want! He done good off of shares and bought this land from Mr. Hallie's widow woman after he done passed on. Folks called him an uppity nigger 'cause he done saved and borrowed to where he could buy this land and be independent. [*Pause*]

It was coming on planting time and my daddy went into Natchez to get him some seed and fertilizer. Called me, say, "Levee you the man of the house now. Take care of your mama while I'm gone." I wasn't but a little boy, eight years old. [*Pause*]

My mama was frying up some chicken when them mens come in that house. Must have been eight or nine of them. She standing there frying that chicken and them mens come and took hold of her just like you take hold of a mule and make him do what you want. [*Pause*]

There was my mama with a gang of white mens. She tried to fight them off, but I could see where it wasn't gonna do her any good, I didn't know what they were doing to her . . . but I figured whatever it was they may as well do to me too. My daddy had a knife that he kept around there for hunting and working and whatnot. I knew where he kept it and I went and got it.

I'm gonna show you how spooked up I was by the white man. I tried my damnedest to cut one of them's throat! I hit him on the shoulder with it. He reached back and grabbed hold of that knife and whacked me across the chest with it. [LEVEE *raises his shirt to show a long ugly scar.*]

That's what made them stop. They was scared I was gonna bleed to death. My mama wrapped a sheet around me and carried me two miles down to the Furlow place and they drove me up to Doc Albans. He was waiting on a calf to be born, and say he ain't had time to see me. They carried me up to Miss Etta, the midwife, and she fixed me up.

My daddy came back and acted like he done accepted the facts of what happened. But he got the names of them mens from mama. He found out who they was and then we announced we was moving out of that county. Said good-bye to everybody . . . all the neighbors. My daddy went and smiled in the face of one of them crackers who had been with my mama. Smiled in his face and sold him our land. We moved over with relations in Caldwell. He got us settled in and then he took off one day. I ain't never seen him since. He sneaked back, hiding up in the woods, laying to get them eight or nine men. [*Pause*]

He got four of them before they got him. They tracked him down in the woods. Caught up with him and hung him and set him afire. [*Pause*]

My daddy wasn't spooked up by the white men. Nosir! And that taught me how to handle them. I seen my daddy go up and grin in this cracker's face . . . smile in his face and sell him his land. All the while he's planning how he's gonna get him and what he's gonna do to him. That taught me how to handle them. So you all just back up and leave Levee alone about the white man. I can smile and say yessir to whoever I please. I got time coming to me. You all just leave Levee alone about the white man.

AS IS
by *William M. Hoffman*

As Is emerged from the Circle Repertory Company's developmental program. Co-produced by Circle Repertory and The Glines, the play opened at the Circle Repertory Theater Off-Broadway, then moved to the Lyceum Theater on Broadway. It won the Drama Desk Award for Best Play, an Obie Award, and a Tony nomination.

As Is focuses on a male homosexual couple dealing with the AIDS crisis: A writer, Rich, has contracted AIDS, and his spurned ex-lover, Saul, a photographer, becomes involved once more, standing by Rich through an endless procession of medical examinations and hospital stays and an endless circle of hope and despair. The play is not a documentary, more an affirmation of love triumphing over death. In the following monologue, Rich talks to Saul about his past—and their relationship—up to the time he discovered he had AIDS.

RICH: I was a good kid, but I was lonely and scared all the time. I was so desperate to find people like myself that I looked for them in the indexes of books—under *h*. I eventually found them—

The next thing you know I moved to the city and was your typical office-worker-slash-writer. I hated my job, so I grew a beard and wore sandals, hoping they would fire me and give me permanent unemployment. I wanted to stay at home in my rent-controlled apartment and drink bourbon and write poems. I did that for a period. I loved it. The apartment got filthy and I did, too, and I'd go out only at night—to pick up guys. And then I found you—in a porno theater—[*he takes* SAUL's *hand*] and we semi-settled down and you took my picture and I started to jog. We bought a loft and loved each other. But that wasn't enough for me. I don't think you ever understood this: you weren't my muse, you were . . . [*he searches for the word*] Saul. [SAUL *rises and looks out the window.*] I loved you but I wanted someone to write poems to. During our marriage I had almost stopped writing, and felt stifled even though our loft had appeared in *New York* magazine.

And then I met Chet and left you in the lurch and lived with him at the Chelsea Hotel. He was shallow, callow, and selfish, and I loved him, too.

We did a lot of coke and I wrote a lot of poetry and the catering was booming and *The New Yorker* published a story of mine and I ran in the marathon. I was on a roll. [*He speaks with mounting excitement as he relives the experience.*] I remember training on the East River Drive for the first time. I didn't realize how narrow and dark the city streets were until I got to the river and all of a sudden there was the fucking river. The sky was the same color as that twilight when I was a kid. I came from the darkness into the light. I'm running downtown and I make this bend and out of nowhere straight up ahead is the Manhattan Bridge and then the Brooklyn Bridge, one after another, and my earphones are playing Handel's *Royal Fireworks Music*. It can't get better than this, I know it. I'm running and crying from gratitude. I came from the darkness into the light. I'm running and telling God I didn't know He was *that* good or *that* big, thank you, Jesus, thanks, thanks . . . [*He slumps back, exhausted from the effort.*]

The next morning I woke up with the flu and stayed in bed for a couple of days and felt much better. But my throat stayed a little sore and my glands were a little swollen . . . [*There is a long silence.* RICH *speaks casually.*] Saul, I want you to do something for me. Will you do something for me, baby?

CURSE OF THE STARVING CLASS
by Sam Shepard

The Obie Award-winning *Curse of the Starving Class* was first produced in England. Since its American premiere in 1978 at the New York Shakespeare Festival at the Public Theater, *Curse of the Starving Class* has gone on to become a frequently produced modern American classic, including a critically acclaimed revival of the play Off-Broadway at the Promenade Theater in 1985.

The Tate family are land-poor farmers: a drunk, violent father, a dotty mother, a fantasy-filled daughter, a stupid, if well-meaning, son. *Curse of the Starving Class* reveals a greedy, materialistic America as exhausted as the soil on the Tate's farm, peopled by those more spiritually than physically starving. In the following monologue, the father, Weston, ruminates on his encounter with a terrifying power.

Kitchen. Fence enclosure with the lamb inside is back, center stage. Pot of fresh coffee heating on the stove. All the laundry has been washed and WESTON *is at the table to stage left folding it and stacking it in neat piles. He's minus his overcoat, baseball cap, and tennis shoes and wears a fresh clean shirt, new pants, and shined shoes, and has had a shave. He seems sober now and in high spirits compared to before. The lamb is heard "baaing" in the dark as the lights slowly come up on* WESTON *at the table.*

WESTON [*to lamb as he folds clothes*]: There's worse things than maggots ya' know. Much worse. Maggots go away if they're properly attended to. If you got someone around who can take the time. Who can recognize the signs. Who brings ya' in out of the cold, wet pasture and sets ya' up in a cushy situation like this. No lamb ever had it better. It's warm. It's free of draft, now that I got the new door up. There's no varmints. No coyotes. No eagles. No— [*Looks over at lamb*] Should I tell ya' something about eagles? This is a true story. This is a true account. One time I was out in the fields doing the castrating, which is a thing that has to be done. It's not my favorite job, but it's something that just has to be done. I'd set myself up right beside the lean-to out there. Just a little roof-shelter thing out there with my best knife, some boiling water, and a hot iron to cauterize with. It's a bloody job on all accounts. Well, I had maybe a dozen spring ram lambs to do out there. I had 'em all gathered up away from the ewes in much the same kinda' set up as you got right there. Similar fence structure like that. It was a crisp, bright type a' morning. Air was real thin and you could see all the way out across the pasture land. Frost was still well bit down on the stems, right close to the ground. Maybe a couple a' crows and the ewes carrying on about their babies, and that was the only sound. Well, I was working away out there when I feel this shadow cross over me. I could feel it even before I saw it take shape on the ground. Felt like the way it does when the clouds move across the sun. Huge and black and cold like. So I look up, half expecting a buzzard or maybe a red-tail, but what hits me across the eyes is this giant eagle. Now I'm a flyer and I'm used to aeronautics, but this sucker was doin' some downright suicidal antics. Real low down like he's coming in for a landing or something, then changing his mind and pulling straight up again and sailing out away from me. So I watch him going small for a while, then turn back to my work. I do a couple more lambs maybe, and the same thing happens. Except this time he's even lower yet. Like I could almost feel his feather on my back. I could hear his sound real clear. A giant bird. His wings made a kind of cracking noise. Then up he went again. I watched him longer this time, trying to figure out his intentions. Then I put the whole thing together. He was after those testes. Those fresh little remnants of manlihood. So I decided to oblige him this time and threw a few a' them on top a' the shed roof. Then I just went back to work again, pretending to be preoccupied. I was waitin' for him this time though. I was listening hard for him, knowing he'd be coming in from behind me. I was watchin' the ground for any sign of blackness. Nothing happened for about three more lambs, when all of a sudden he comes. Just like a thunder clap. Blam! He's down on that shed roof with his talons taking half the tar paper with him, wings whippin' the air, screaming like a bred mare then climbing straight back up into the sky again. I had to stand up on that one. Somethin' brought me straight up off the ground and I started yellin' my head off. I don't know why it was comin' outa' me but I was

standing there with this icy feeling up my back-
bone and just yelling my fool head off. Cheerin'
for that eagle. I'd never felt like that since the
first day I went up in a B-49. After a while I sat
down again and went on workin'. And every time
I cut a lamb I'd throw those balls up on top a' the
shed roof. And every time he'd come down like
the Cannonball Express on that roof. And every
time I got that feeling.

SCOOTER THOMAS MAKES IT TO THE TOP OF THE WORLD
by Peter Parnell

Workshopped at the Eugene O'Neill Playwrights Con-
ference, *Scooter Thomas Makes It to the Top of the
World* has been widely performed in regional theaters,
including the Actors Studio in New York City, the
Denver Center Theater, and the Old Globe Theater in
San Diego.

Dennis has just received news of the death of his
childhood friend, Scooter Thomas, and is packing to
attend the funeral. The play moves back and forth between their childhood and the present as Dennis confronts the ghosts, the guilt over a friendship that went
wrong. Dennis's ruminations set off the memory of
another death, the death of Dennis's grandmother.

DENNIS: Remember when we used to—yeah. Tough
  noogies. [*Beat*] I was alone in the house with her

when it—she died at the kitchen table, while sipping a cup of tea. Lapsang Souchong. Her favorite blend. I haven't been able to look at an old lady or drink a cup of Twinings since. Every time I see someone hunched over asleep on a park bench, in the subway—I have this uncontrollable urge to you know go and—just to make sure they haven't . . . [*laughs*] Isn't that crazy? [*Brief pause*] The doctor asked me to help move the body from the kitchen to the bedroom. I mean, she was beginning to turn blue, and. So I grabbed one end, and he the other—she was incredibly heavy, dead-weight by now—and the doctor had a very bad back, and once or twice he practically—and I remember this terrible thought flashed through my mind that he might have a heart attack also, and then I'd be stuck with two of them there on the living room carpet. "Gott in Himmel, dot vass a heavy voman," he said as we tucked her in. "I vill not forget her for ze rest of my life . . ."

No. [*Beat*] I wanted them to scatter the ashes. To the four winds off Montauk Point. So that parts of her could end up in London, Nantucket, Atlanta, and somewhere past Idaho. She always said she wanted to travel. But they didn't do that. They—packed her in an urn and put her in the earth. Just in case it was what she'd wanted. They hadn't known what she'd—so first they did one thing, and then they did the other. So they wound up doing neither, really. They—I don't know what they did. [*Beat*] The dying wasn't the worst part. It was the sense of obligation I couldn't stand. The dying was just, one minute I was talking to her and the next minute I was still talking to her but she was dead. I found that to be, somehow, very, well, somehow, sort of, funny . . . [*Pause*] Scooter? Hey, Scoots?

No, nothing. It's just, you fell asleep. . . . No. No. It's nothing. Nothing at all.

K2
by Patrick Meyers

K2 was originally produced by Arena Stage in Washington, D.C. The play moved to the Brooks Atkinson Theater on Broadway.

Two American climbers, Taylor, a San Francisco attorney, and Harold, a nuclear physicist, are stuck on the ledge of an ice wall 1,250 feet below the summit of K2, the world's second tallest peak in Pakistan's Karakoram Range. Harold has broken his leg badly and cannot be moved. Taylor won't leave until Harold convinces him to go. Harold is left alone on the ledge, waiting for the signal that Taylor may be on his way back home, then waiting for the night, the intensifying cold, and his death from exposure.

HAROLD: I love you too . . . Go. [TAYLOR *slips over the ledge in one easy motion and is gone.* HAROLD *sits for a long moment looking down the cliff after him.* HAROLD *is breathing more and more spasmodically, his chest rising and falling rapidly. He leans back and closes his eyes and eventually his breathing slows, calms.*] Oh Baby. Sweet Baby . . . hey. Hey. I was gonna write you a letter. Yeah . . . you know me Al. Better late than never . . . right? I heard something real sad but I knew you'd wanna hear it . . . There's this little guy called the Japanese glacier fox . . . this little guy is really pretty . . . really special . . . long fine silky hair . . . the purest white . . . you can spot him for miles when he's below timber line . . . You look so nice. You look so warm. I got you now. [HAROLD *feels the rope.*] Tension. Great. Go Taylor . . . go, go, go . . . SO apparently Darling . . . some of these little nippers are born albinos, but it's in the summer so that's all right cause the snows are melted and they spend a lot of time in their burrows when they're young and in the fall and winter they kind of quasi-hibernate . . . but when the spring comes, the young albino foxes go out with the other foxes to romp and run and play . . . the glare of the sun off the spring glacier snow . . . burns their albino retinas to a crisp within a couple of days . . . and they are blind . . . sad baby. I know . . . I know. It's all right . . . [HAROLD *strokes the rope.*] . . . and for a while they live in the burrow and the other foxes feed them . . . bring back food for them . . . that's nice . . . that's real nice . . . but a day comes when they feel their way out of the burrow, into the light . . . and start down, letting the earth pull them, just going down, to where they have to go. [HAROLD *feels the rope again.*] Go home Taylor, go home . . . and if nothing takes advantage of them, stops them and kills them, they make it to the base of those purple Japanese mountains—out—onto a brown sandy Japanese beach. I love you. I love you . . . And they sit there and curl their plume white tails around their feet and wait, staring blindly at the rolling Japanese sea . . . and they never move a muscle—not a muscle—once they face the sea . . . they sit . . . and let the waves rise around them . . . till they're gone, till they're gone. . . . the Japanese fishermen see one sometimes—once in a great while . . . at dawn . . . sitting . . . waiting . . . on the beach. [*The rope snaps sharply twice.*] Taylor found a crack. Taylor's got a crack baby . . . I love you. [HAROLD *unties the rope and holds it closely to him.*] Taylor's goin' home . . . Taylor's gonna see your pretty smile. Taylor's gonna be warm again. [HAROLD's *breathing starts to become violent again. He closes his eyes. It calms.*] Hold on . . . hold on . . . I have to hold on. Help me hold on honey. I want to stay with you now. I want to be calm like the little fox . . . and stay with you . . . I love you forever . . . forever. [*The rope snaps sharply in* HAROLD's *hands.*] . . . You know what I know? I know why the little fox sits so still . . . My One . . . It's because he knows he'll be back . . . and he'll have eyes next time. [HAROLD *throws the rope into space and it disappears.*] . . . He knows he'll have eyes next time. [*We hear* HAROLD *softly, very softly, as the lights dim out in blues.*] Hold on . . . hold on . . . hold on . . . hold on . . .

STILL LIFE
by Emily Mann

Emily Mann wrote and directed *Still Life*, which premiered in the Goodman Studio Theater in Chicago and moved Off-Broadway to the American Place Theater. The New York production, starring Mary McDonnell, John Spencer, and Timothy Near, won Obie Awards for best production, playwriting, direction, and for the three actors. The play has gone on to become an international success.

Still Life is subtitled "a documentary," and with good reason; it is based on transcripts of a series of tape-recorded conversations the playwright had with a

Vietnam veteran, his wife, and his mistress. In the intertwining monologues, spoken directly to the audience, we can see lives shattered by war. For instance, in the following monologue, Mark, the Vietnam veteran, confesses the horrible guilt he can't shake about his killing a Vietnamese family.

MARK: I . . . I killed three children, a mother and father in cold blood. [*Crying.*] I killed three children, a mother and father . . . [*Long pause*] I killed them with a pistol in front of a lot of people. I demanded something from the parents and then systematically destroyed them. And that's . . . that's the heaviest part of what I'm carrying around. You know about it now, a few other people know about it, my wife knows about it, Nadine knows about it, and nobody else knows about it. For the rest of my life . . . I have a son . . . He's going to die for what I've done. This is what I'm carrying around; that's what this logic is about with my children. A friend hit a booby-trap. And these people knew about it. I knew they knew. I knew that they were working with the VC infrastructure. I demanded that they tell me. They wouldn't say anything. I just wanted them to confess before I killed them. And they wouldn't. So I killed their children and then I killed them. I was angry. I was angry with all the power I had. I couldn't beat them. They beat me. [*Crying.*] I lost friends in my unit . . . I did wrong. People in the unit watched me kill them. Some of them tried to stop me. I don't know. I can't . . . oh, God . . . a certain amount of stink went all the way back to the rear. I almost got into a certain amount of trouble. It was all rationalized, that there was a logic behind it. But they knew. And everybody who knew had a part in it. There was enough evidence, but it wasn't a very good image to put out in terms of . . . the Marines overseas, so nothing happened. I have a child . . . a child who passed through the age that the little child was. My son . . . my son wouldn't know the difference between a VC and a Marine. The children were so little. I suppose I could find a rationalization. All that a person can do is try and find words to try and excuse me, but I know it's the same damn thing as lining Jews up. It's no different than what the Nazis did. It's the same thing. I know that I'm not alone. I know that other people did it, too. More people went through more hell than I did . . . but they didn't do this. I don't know . . . I don't know . . . if it's a terrible flaw of *mine*, then I guess deep down I'm just everything that's bad. I guess there is a rationale that says anyone who wants to live that bad and gets in that situation . . . [*long pause*] but I should have done better. I mean, I really strove to be good. I had a whole set of values. I had 'em and I didn't. I don't know. I want to come to the point where I tell myself that I've punished myself enough. In spite of it all, I don't want to punish myself anymore. I knew I would want to censor myself for you. I didn't want you to say: what kind of nut, what kind of a bad person is he? And yet, it's all right. I'm not gonna lie. My wife tries to censor me . . . from people, from certain things. I can't watch war shows. I can't drive. Certain things I can't deal with. She has to deal with the situation, us sitting around, a car backfires, and I hit the deck. She knows about the graveyards, and R.J. and the woman. She lives with all this still hanging out. I'm shell-shocked.

RUM AND COKE
by Keith Reddin

First presented at the Yale Repertory Theater's Winterfest, *Rum and Coke* was subsequently produced by Joseph Papp at the Public Theater in New York City.

Rum and Coke is a political satire about the Bay of Pigs invasion. Jake, a naive Yale graduate, gets involved with the CIA just before the ill-fated invasion of Cuba and ends up torn between what he feels is right and what he sees as folly. Jake has been assigned to Guatemala—his assignment: to coach the anti-Castro Cuban rebels to speak out against the Castro regime. During a radio broadcast, one of the rebels, Miguel, naively reveals that America is secretly behind the rebel forces.

MIGUEL *at table.*

MIGUEL: Lovers of freedom. Now is the hour of liberation. Now is the moment of decision. Today is the day when the clouds break and the sun of glory shines on us all. Take up your positions in the fields, in the roads, in the cities, in your homes. Down with the Soviet puppet Fidel Castro and his Soviet puppet regime. Down with oppression and mass arrest, down with censorship, and down with poverty, let us together take up arms and end the puppet government of Fidel Castro. Control roads and factories, make prisoners and shoot those who refuse your orders. Jesus Christ and his saints look on this holy mission of liberation. The Virgin Mary and the angels shine on our efforts to free Cuba. *Cuba Libra*, friends. America is with you on this holy holy quest. The virgin prays for your success. One day soon, troops of rebels, rebels in the hills, rebels from the skies, rebels from the sea, will liberate you. They will ask for your holy support to crush the rule of the devil Fidel. They need your help. Mother and child look to you for help, Jesus in his infinite power and glory needs your help. Fighting beside him you cannot fail. America will give you guns. America will give you guns to fight. Pray that the day will be soon, and it shall dawn. Praise Jesus. Praise the holy mother. Praise our father for this day of reckoning that will not be long. Holy, holy, holy day. It will not be long. It will not be long. I will talk to you again tomorrow.

THE WONDERFUL TOWER OF HUMBERT LAVOIGNET
by Lynne Alvarez

Workshopped at the Midwest Playlabs, *The Wonderful Tower of Humbert Lavoignet* in its production at the Capital Repertory Theatre in Albany was co-winner of the 1985 Foundation for the Dramatists Guild/CBS New Play Award.

After awakening from a six-month catatonic state,

Humbert Lavoignet—an unemployed postal worker, a dreamer of unmanageable dreams—begins to build a tower made of trash. Early in the play, just moments before Humbert comes out of his catatonic state, Humbert's teenage son, Mike, talks to his father about his loneliness, his estrangement from other kids his age.

MIKE: You know, this really isn't a great time in my
    life,
    I don't know why . . .
    I grew two inches this month—that should make
    me feel good—
    guess I'm about as tall as you now—
    probably won't grow much more . . .
    School's out—that's okay—not a lot
    of kids around though,
    but runners in my bracket don't have time
    to hang out
    anyways.
    I'm up to ten miles a day—they say
    that's about as much as you
    should train . . . [Pause]
    But I don't know, maybe I could push it.
    I never trust those experts anyways—
    one year they tell you ten miles' the limit, the
    next year
    they're swearing twelve is better, or two.
    I hear it all the time on the radio
    the final ultimate word
    "Take this drug and save your life."
    Six months later they're back with
    emergency bulletins tell you
    "This drug is a hazard to your health."
    I don't know what to think, Dad . . . things are
    getting to me . . .
    Even running.

I like to be out there all alone, but then sometimes it gets lonely.
I miss people, you know?
Dad?

HOME FRONT
by James Duff

Home Front, previously titled *The War at Home*, premiered at the Hampstead Theater in London before opening on Broadway in a production starring Carroll O'Connor, Frances Sternhagen, Christopher Fields, and Linda Cook, directed by Michael Attenborough. The play has had international success, playing in such countries as Israel, Germany, Sweden, and Norway.

In the guise of a family drama *Home Front* is a strong indictment of America's involvement in the Vietnam conflict. The play takes place on Thanksgiving 1973 in the Collier home in suburban Dallas–Fort Worth. Jeremy Collier is a Vietnam veteran who returns home psychologically paralyzed. He hangs out at home, unable to bring himself to look for a job or deal with people outside his immediate family. In the following monologue, he expresses his immense bitterness toward America's indifference towards the returning soldiers when he tells his sister about his good friend, Brady.

JEREMY: I wouldn't hit you. I wouldn't give you the satisfaction. I listened to you, now you're going to listen to me. You have friends, don't you?

Well, I have some too.

Yes, I do. One of them was named Brady. Brady was my friend. From Mobile, Alabama. We were a lot alike, Brady and me. He was drafted, just like I was. Came from the same kind of family, I think, nice people. We were both getting ready to come home about the same time. And a month before we were supposed to get out, Brady got wounded. And when he left the hospital, this was in California, when he got out of the hospital, he called his parents, you know, to say he was on his way and would they mind if he brought a friend home with him. He had met him in the hospital or something, I don't know. And his mother said fine. Then Brady, he said, this guy's gonna need a little help because he doesn't move around very well yet, and his mother asked what was wrong with him, and Brady said he's lost an arm and a leg, he's probably going to need a little help. Well. His mother just lost it. I mean, she couldn't handle that at all. So she put his father on the phone and his father really gave it to him. How could you do something like this to us? That's what he said. His father. Don't you know how much we've been looking forward to this? Why are you trying to ruin everything for us? Brady apologized and when he got off the phone, he went and checked into a Holiday Inn and hung himself in the bathroom. They shipped the body to Mobile. I've tried to picture the expression on his parents' faces when they went to pick up Brady at the airport. The expression on their faces when they saw their little soldier boy was missing an arm and a leg. So. I don't go along. I don't care about any of it anymore. And you can take your social responsibility and your traditional values and shove them up your ass. I'm a survivor. And I got that way by not giving a shit over things that are not worth giving a shit over. And if that's too much for you to handle, then too fucking bad.

A WEEKEND NEAR MADISON
by Kathleen Tolan

A Weekend Near Madison premiered at the Actors Theater of Louisville as part of the Humana Festival of New American Plays. The play was subsequently presented Off-Broadway at the Astor Place Theater.

The time is early autumn, 1979; the place, rural Wisconsin. Four friends who went to college together in the sixties gather at David and Doe's house. Living somewhere between their youthful idealism and the realities of growing older, they share a nostalgia for their college days, especially David's brother Jim, who feels isolated and confused, a victim of the sexual revolution of his generation, whose identity has been undermined by radical feminism.

JIM: Well . . . I . . . I guess I'm kind of overwhelmed by . . . well, you know. Modern life. And all this talk about women. I mean, it just makes me feel, well, not being a woman . . .

I have this memory of this one day when we were all living together? It was a Saturday afternoon in October. Everyone else had gone into Boston for the weekend, so it was just Nessa and you and David and me. Chad Jackson had gotten a big load of wood earlier in the week, and we'd agreed to divide it between the two houses and help each other split the logs on Saturday.

I'd been inside all week, bent over some overdue research paper . . . That afternoon David retrieved me from my little cell and we walked down the road to Chad's. It was this incredible day—bright and windy and it smelled like snow—in fact they were forecasting the first storm, so Chad and David and I got into this kind of frenzy to beat the snow. We were splitting and stacking and yelling and cursing and telling stories, and then the work itself—the physical labor—together with being out in that day—kind of overtook us. And we just kept going, lifting and splitting and lifting and splitting, in silence. Just our breath and the chopping and throwing and the sounds of the woods . . . And when we'd done half of it, we hopped into the truck and drove the rest up to our place and went at it there. And I was panting and aching and soaked with sweat—I had no idea where the strength was coming from to lift the ax. At one point I straightened up and just stood there. The light was fading, the sky was a pale yellow, cut with a thin string of charcoal clouds. A patch of the yard was washed with a golden light from the kitchen window. I looked up, and you and Nessa were standing there, looking out at us. And I waved. And you both waved. And, I felt this fullness . . . I've never felt so full . . . of life . . . as I did at that moment. [*Pause*] And I felt like a man. A man. In some deep, ancient sense. [*Pause*] I don't know. I mean, if I were honest, I guess I'd say that's all I really want. That kind of romantic, traditional thing. I mean, it did feel like we were continuing something . . . the men outside, splitting wood for the long winter, the women in the kitchen cooking dinner. I mean, I mean, everything else seems so insignificant when I think of that moment.

APPENDIX A
The Playwrights

Below is a brief biography and listing of the representative work of each of the playwrights represented in this book.

Lynne Alvarez was born in Mexico and raised in the United States. Her plays include *Graciela, Latinos, Mundo* (which won honorable mention in the 1982 *Playbill* Award), *The Guittaron*, and *Hidden Parts* (which won the Kesserling Award). Her poetry and translations of South American women poets have been published in journals and anthologies in the United States and abroad, including *Review, Nuestro*, and *South & West Literary Quarterly*. Alvarez has received CAPS, NEA, and Arthur grants. She is a member of New Dramatists.

Nancy Beckett has written such plays and performance pieces as *Rotunda, Labor Relations, Holding Patterns, Locker Room Play, Tacit Agreements, Clothes Conscious*, and an adaptation of *Spring Awakening*. She has also written screenplays and a music–theater work, *Religious Figures*, with composer Kim Sherman, which has been performed at St. John the Divine. She is the recipient of Jerome, Shubert, and Lemist–Eisler fellowships, a grant from the Lower Manhattan Cultural Council, as well as a Twin Cities Drama Critics Circle Kudos Award.

Lee Blessing has had numerous productions in regional theaters, including three plays produced in the Humana

New Play Festival of the Actors Theater of Louisville: *Independence, Oldtimers Game*, and *War of the Roses*. His play *A Walk in the Woods* has been produced on Broadway. His one-act play, *Nice People Dancing to Good Country Music*, is included in the anthology *Best Short Plays of 1984*. He has received NEA, McKnight, Jerome, Schubert, and Wurlitzer playwriting grants. He lives in Minneapolis, where he is a member of the MidWest Playwrights' Center.

Marisha Chamberlain's plays, which have been produced in such regional theaters as the Victory Gardens Theater in Chicago, the Cricket Theater in Minneapolis, and the Theater of the Open Eye in New York City, include *The Angels of Warsaw, Slumming, The Snow in the Virgin Islands*, and *Miracle Gardening*. Chamberlain is currently an associate playwright at the Playwrights' Center in Minneapolis and resident playwright at the Cricket Theater. She has received McKnight, Bush, Rockefeller, NEA, and Jerome playwriting grants.

James Duff, a native of Texas, is both a playwright and an actor. He has written plays for Dallas's Theater Three's children's theater program under the auspices of grants from Mobil and Gulf.

Christopher Durang has the rare distinction of being born in New Jersey. His always controversial plays include: *Sister Mary Ignatius Explains It All for You, Beyond Therapy, The Baby with the Bathwater, The History of the American Film*, and *The Marriage of Bette and Boo*, in which he also acted and for which he received an Obie Award. Durang wrote *The Idiots Karamozov* with Albert Innaurato, and co-wrote and co-acted in *The Lusitania Songspiel* with Sigourney Weaver.

Charles Fuller won the Pulitzer Prize for *A Soldier's Play*, which was originally produced by The Negro Ensemble Company. His screen adaptation of this play, *A Soldier's Story*, received an Oscar nomination. Other plays include *Zooman and the Sign, Sparrow in Flight, The Brownsville Raid, A Perfect Party,* and *In the*

Deepest Part of Sleep. Fuller has received Obie, New York Drama Critics Circle, Outer Critics Circle, and Theater Club Awards, and Guggenheim, NEA, and CAPS grants. He was born and continues to live part-time in Philadelphia.

Mary Gallagher is an actress and director as well as a writer. Her plays, such as *Little Bird, Father Dreams, Chocolate Cake, Buddies,* and *Dog Eat Dog*, have been produced in theaters throughout the country as well as in Canada and Ireland, and have been published by Dramatists Play Service. Gallagher has collaborated with writer Ara Watson on the play, *Special Family Things*, and a CBS Movie-of-the-Week. She has written two novels: *Spend It Foolishly* and *Quicksilver*. She is a member of New Dramatists.

Elan Garonzik was born and raised in Lancaster, Pennsylvania. His plays, including *Scenes and Revelations, The Communist*, and *The Blue Mercedes*, have been produced extensively both in the United States and Europe. Garonzik was the co-editor of *An Introduction to the American Musical Theater*, a project sponsored by the National Endowment for the Humanities. He graduated from the American College in Paris, France, and completed his masters at Carnegie–Mellon's drama department, where he was the recipient of a Shubert Foundation Fellowship.

Amlin Gray has been a resident playwright at the Milwaukee Repertory Theater and dramaturg at the Berkeley Repertory Theater. He has written plays on commission for Milwaukee's Theater X, Actors Theater of St. Paul, the Odyssey Theater, Actors Theater of Louisville, and New York's Theater for the New City. His plays include *The Fantod, Zones of the Spirit, How I Got That Story, Pirates, Founding Father*, and *Kingdom Come*.

John Guare's plays include *House of Blue Leaves, Rich and Famous, Landscape of the Body, Lydie Breeze, Women and Water, Gardenia, Muzeeka, Marco Polo Sings a Solo, Bullfinch's Mythology*, and the musical,

Two Gentlemen of Verona. His plays have won New York Drama Critics Circle, Obie, and Tony Awards. Guare has received the Award of Merit from the American Academy of Arts and Letters and he has been a fellow of the New York Institute for the Humanities. His screenplay for the film *Atlantic City* won the New York Film Critics, Los Angeles Film Critics, and National Film Critics Award, and was nominated for an Academy Award.

A. R. "Pete" Gurney, Jr. was born in Buffalo, New York, and currently divides his time between New York and Massachusetts, where he teaches literature at M.I.T. *The Dining Room*, originally produced at Playwrights Horizons in New York City, has become a staple of regional and community theaters. He has had over thirty plays produced, including *Scenes from American Life*, *The Middle Ages*, *The Golden Age*, *The Perfect Party*, and *Children*. Gurney is also a novelist.

Beth Henley won a Pulitzer Prize for *Crimes of the Heart*, which was subsequently produced for film, starring Diane Keaton, Jessica Lange, and Sissy Spacek. Born in Mississippi, her plays—*The Wake of Jamey Foster*, *The Miss Firecracker Contest*, *The Debutante Ball*, and *Am I Blue?*—continue to reflect her Southern upbringing.

William M. Hoffman is a member of the Circle Repertory Company, but has also worked at La Mama, the Manhattan Theater Club, and Playwrights Horizons. His plays include *As Is*, *Spring Play*, *Good Night, I Love You*, *Cornbury*, *Shoe Palace Murray*, and *The Cherry Orchard, Part Two*. The Metropolitan Opera commissioned him to write the libretto for *A Figaro for Antonia*. He has received Guggenheim, NEA, and New York Foundation for the Arts grants. Hoffman has written for television and film, and is the editor of four play anthologies.

Tina Howe began writing plays when she was teaching high school in Maine and Wisconsin. Her best known work, *Painting Churches*, produced by New York City's

Second Stage theater company, won an Obie Award and has been televised as part of PBS-TV's "Theater in America" series. Her other plays include *Coastal Disturbances*, produced by Second Stage, *The Art of Dining*, co-produced by the Kennedy Center and the New York Shakespeare Festival, and *Museum*, which premiered at the Los Angeles Actors Theater.

David Hwang is the recipient of an Obie Award, a Drama Desk nomination, a Chinese-American Arts Council Award, and Rockefeller, Guggenheim, and NEA fellowships. His plays, which for the most part explore Asian–American society, include *The Dance and the Railroad*, *FOB*, *The House of Seven Beauties*, and *Family Devotions*. Hwang also directs plays, has been published as a poet, and has worked as a jazz musician.

Harry Kondoleon received the Molly Kazan Playwriting Award twice as a student at the Yale School of Drama. His plays include *The Cote D'Azur Triangle*, *Self Torture and Strenuous Exercise*, *Rococo*, *Vampires*, *Anteroom*, and *Christmas on Mars*, the last two plays receiving their premiere at Playwrights Horizons in New York City. Kondoleon has received an NEA grant for playwriting and won the Obie and Newsday Awards.

Arthur Kopit has written such plays as *Oh, Dad, Poor Dad, Mama's Hung You in the Closet and I'm Feeling So Sad*, *The Day the Whores Came Out to Play Tennis*, *Indians*, *Chamber Music*, *Sing to Me Through Open Windows*, *Christmas with the Cannibals*, as well as an adaptation of Ibsen's *Ghosts* and the book to the Broadway musical, *Nine*. He is the recipient of the Vernon Rice and Outer Circle Awards, a Guggenheim fellowship, a Rockefeller grant, and an Award in Literature from the American Academy of Arts and Letters.

Casey Kurtti's plays, *An Injury to One, Marry Ramon, Mary Pat McHugh's Sister*, and *Catholic School Girls*, have been performed in the United States and abroad. Kurtti has directed at the Playwright's and Director's Unit of the Actor's Studio in New York, as well as the Theater of the Open Eye and Theater Genesis.

Shirley Lauro is a member of Ensemble Studio Theater. Her plays include *Margaret and Kit* (based on the life of Elizabeth Bowen), *I Don't Know Where You're Coming From At All*, *The Contest*, *The Coal Diamond*, *In the Garden of Eden*, and *Nothing Immediate*. She has won the Heidmann Prize at the Actors Theater of Louisville and her work has been cited by the National Foundation for Jewish Culture. She is also a novelist, whose work includes *The Edge*.

Romulus Linney is both a novelist and a playwright, whose plays, which have been produced throughout the world, include *The Love Suicide at Schofield Barracks*, *The Sorrows of Frederick*, *Holy Ghosts*, *Old Man Joseph and His Family*, *The Captivity of Pixie Shedman*, *Childe Byron*, *Goodbye Howard*, *El Hermano*, *Laughing Stock*, and *Tennessee*, which received an Obie Award in 1980. Linney is the recipient of NEA, Guggenheim, and Rockefeller grants, the Mishima Prize for fiction, and the Award in Literature from the American Academy and Institute of Arts and Letters. He is a member of New Dramatists.

David Mamet has been a playwright-in-residence and associate artistic director at both the Goodman Theater and the St. Nicholas Theater in Chicago. He currently splits his time between Manhattan and Vermont. His plays includes *The Duck Variations*, *Sexual Perversity in Chicago*, *American Buffalo*, *A Life in the Theater*, *Lakeboat*, *The Water Engine*, *Edmond*, and an adaptation of Chekhov's *The Cherry Orchard*. His screenplays include *The Verdict*, *The Untouchables*, and *The Postman Always Rings Twice*. Mamet has won Obie and New York Drama Critics Circle Awards.

Frank Manley is a professor of Renaissance literature in Atlanta. *Rain of Terror* was his first play.

Emily Mann won Obie Awards for writing and directing *Still Life*. Her other plays include *Execution of Justice* and *Annulla Allen: Autobiography of a Survivor*, which premiered at the Guthrie II in Minneapolis and was subsequently aired on National Public Radio's "Earplay."

Mann has directed in theaters across the country, including the Guthrie Theater, the Mark Taper Forum, the Goodman Theater, and The Brooklyn Academy of Music Theater Company. Mann has received Guggenheim, McKnight, NEA, and CAPS grants.

Tim Mason spent the first ten years of his playwriting career in residence with the Children's Theater in Minneapolis. Since moving to New York, his plays, such as *In a Northern Landscape, A Room in Paradise*, and his adaptation of *500 Hats of Bartholomew Cubbins*, have been seen at such Off-Broadway and regional theaters as Circle Repertory, Actors' Theater of Louisville, and the South Coast Repertory Theater in California. Mason is the recipient of the Twin Cities Drama Critics Circle Kudos Award, the National Society of Arts and Letters Award, and a NEA writing fellowship. He has written articles on the arts for *Saturday Review* and *Observer Magazine*.

James McLure is both an actor and a playwright. His plays, which include *Laundry and Bourbon, Lone Star, Pvt. Wars, Hyde and Stream*, and *The Very Last Lover of the River Cane*, have been popular in regional theaters across the country.

Dennis McIntyre, a graduate of Carnegie–Mellon University, has written over thirty plays, including *Modigliani, National Anthems*, and *Split Second*. He is also a novelist, whose work includes *The Divine Child*. He has received MCA, Shubert, Rockefeller, and NEA grants for playwriting. McIntyre is a member of New Dramatists.

Stephen Metcalfe was commissioned by the Manhattan Theater Club to write *Vikings* and *Strange Snow*. His other works include *Half a Lifetime, The Incredibly Famous Willy Rivers, White Linen*, and *Emily*. He has received NEA and CAPS grants.

Patrick Meyers has been a resident writer with the Circle Repertory Company in New York City. He has also acted for the Circle Repertory and Roundabout repertory companies in New York, as well as in regional theaters across the country.

Dallas Murphy's plays include *The Terrorists, Explorers*, and *Fade the Game* (which premiered at the Circle Repertory Company in New York City). His adaptation of *Frankenstein* was performed by the American Conservatory Theater in San Francisco. Murphy's mystery novel, *Lover Man*, is published by Scribners.

Marsha Norman was a book critic and children's page editor of the *Louisville Times* when she was encouraged by John Jory, artistic director of the Actors Theater of Louisville, to write plays. Her Pulitzer Prize-winning play, *'night, Mother*, premiered at the American Repertory Theater in Cambridge, Massachusetts, and moved to Broadway. Norman's film adaptation of *'night, Mother* stars Anne Bancroft and Sissy Spacek. Her other plays include *Getting Out, Circus Valentine, Traveler in the Dark*, and *The Laundromat*, which has been televised in a production starring Carol Burnett and Amy Madigan, directed by Robert Altman.

Mark O'Donnell's plays include *Caught in the Act, The Nice and the Nasty, That's All, Folks!*, and *Fables for Friends*, the last three plays produced at Playwrights Horizons in New York City. O'Donnell has written for *Esquire, The New York Times, Saturday Review*, "Saturday Night Live," as well as various journals and anthologies. He is the recipient of the Lecomte du Nuoy prize and a Guggenheim fellowship.

John Olive is company playwright with Circle Repertory Company and has been a long-time associate with the Playwrights Center in Minneapolis. His plays, produced in New York and major repertory theaters throughout the country, include *Standing on my Knees, Clara's Play*, and *Careless Love*. Olive has written the book for a musical based on *The Gift of the Magi*. He has written a half dozen plays for the radio, both for National Public Radio's "Earplay" and the BBC. In 1986 he became Artistic Associate of the Wisdom Bridge Theater in Chicago.

John Orlock was born in New York City and educated at Pennsylvania State University, but has been living in Minnesota where he has been the resident playwright at the Cricket Theater. *Indulgences in a Louisville Harem* was co-winner of the Actors Theater of Louisville's first Great American Play contest (an honor shared with D. L. Coburn's *The Gin Game*). Other plays include *The Fleece, Orlando, Orlando, Glasswork, The D. B. Cooper Project*, and *Revolution of the Heavenly Orbs.* Orlock has been a resident playwright with Minnesota's Playwrights' Center and has served as literary manager of the Cricket. He has received an NEA grant for playwriting.

OyamO's plays include *The Resurrection of Lady Lester, The Juice Problem, Mary Goldstein and the Author, Fried Chicken and Invisibility*, and *A Hopeful Interview with Satan.* He holds an MFA from the Yale School of Drama, where he won the Molly Kazan Award in Playwriting. He has served as playwright-in-residence at Emory University in Atlanta, where he developed his musical, *Distraughter and the Great Panda Scanda.* He has received the McKnight, Guggenheim, and NEA fellowships. He is a member of New Dramatists.

Peter Parnell lives in New York and has written such plays as *The Sorrows of Stephen*, originally produced by Joseph Papp's Public Theater, and *Romance Language* and *Hyde in Hollywood*, both produced at Playwrights Horizons. His play, *The Rise and Rise of Daniel Rocket*, was televised on Public Television's "Theater in America" series in a production starring Tom Hulce and Valerie Mahaffey. Parnell is a member of the Artistic Board of Playwrights Horizons, and a recipient of commissions from Playwrights Horizons, the Denver Center Theater, the New York Theater Workshop, and an NEA grant.

Sybille Pearson studied playwriting with Arthur Kopit. She has been in residence at Circle Repertory in New York City and has been a member of The Women's Project at the American Place Theater, also in New

York City. She has served as playwright-in-residence at Virginia Polytechnic Institute. Her plays include *Sally and Marsha* and *A Little Going Away Party*. She wrote the book to the Broadway musical, *Baby*. Pearson is the recipient of a Rockefeller grant.

Keith Reddin is an actor as well as a playwright. His plays include *Life and Limb, Rum and Coke, Desperadoes*, and *Highest Standard of Living*.

Kirk Ristau was born in Iowa. His plays include *Better Days, Dancing, Small Affections*, and *Blues*. He served as a resident playwright at the Playwrights' Center in Minneapolis, where he was the recipient of a Jerome grant.

Sam Shepard, born in Illinois in 1943, has over sixty plays to his credit, all doggedly non-traditional in their structure and language, all distinctly American in their subject matter. The plays include *Chicago, Fool for Love* (which he also directed), *The Tooth of the Crime*, the Pulitzer Prize-winning *Buried Child, Forensic and the Navigator*, and *La Turista*. Shepard's work has won more than a dozen Obie Awards. He has written short stories and screenplays for such films as *Zabriskie Point* and *Paris, Texas*. He has acted in plays and such films as *The Right Stuff, Resurrection, Days of Heaven, Frances, Country, Raggedy Man*, and his own *Fool for Love*.

Ted Tally was born in North Carolina. After completing his MFA in playwriting at the Yale School of Drama, he became a resident writer of Playwrights Horizons. His play, *Terra Nova*, has become one of the most produced plays in the country. Other plays include *Little Footsteps, Coming Attractions*, and *Hooters*. Tally has received NEA, CAPS, Guggenheim, and CBS Foundation grants.

Kathleen Tolan is an actress as well as a playwright.

Wendy Wasserstein is a resident writer of and on the artistic board of Playwrights Horizons. Her first success, produced at the Phoenix Theater, was *Uncom-*

mon Women and Others, which was successfully televised with Meryl Streep and Swoosie Kurtz. Her play, *Isn't It Romantic*, has had great popular success throughout the country. Other plays include *Tender Offer* and a musical, *Miami*. She collaborated with Christopher Durang on a play, *When Dinah Shore Ruled the Earth*, and a screenplay, *A House of Husbands*. For PBS-TV's "Great Performances" series, she adapted her own *Uncommon Women and Others* and John Cheever's short story, *The Sorrows of Gin*. Wasserstein is the recipient of a Guggenheim fellowship.

Michael Weller's plays include *Moonchildren, 23 Years Later, More Than You Deserve, Dwarfman, Master of a Million Shapes, Split*, and *Fishing*. He has written the screenplays for the films *Hair* and *Ragtime*. Weller has received a Rockefeller grant.

August Wilson was born in Pittsburgh, Pennsylvania, and now lives in St. Paul, Minnesota. His plays include *Ma Rainey's Black Bottom, Fences, Joe Turners' Come and Gone, Jitney, Fullerton Street*, and *The Coldest Day of the Year*. Wilson has received playwriting grants from the Bush and Rockefeller Foundations. Wilson is also a poet, whose work has appeared in numerous magazines and periodicals, and Harper & Row's anthology, *Black Poets of the 20th Century*. He is a member of New Dramatists.

Lanford Wilson was born in Lebanon, Missouri, the setting of his evolving cycle of Talley plays, including *Fifth of July*, the Pulitzer Prize-winning *Talley's Folly*, and *Talley and Son*. Other works include *The Hot l Baltimore, Lemon Sky, Angels Fall, Serenading Louie, The Mound Builders, Balm in Gilead*, and *The Rimers of Eldritch*. He is co-founder of Circle Repertory, an Off-Broadway theater dedicated to creating new plays through the efforts of an ensemble of playwrights, directors, actors, and designers. His numerous awards include the New York Drama Critics Circle Award, the Outer Critics Circle Award, the Obie, the Brandeis

University Creative Arts Award in Theatre, and the Institute of Arts and Letter Award.

Donald Wollner is the author of *Kid Purple*, *Badgers*, and *Losers*. He is the recipient of a CAPS grant and has been a member of New Dramatists.

James Yoshimura is a native Chicagoan. He holds a M.F.A. in playwriting from the Yale School of Drama. His plays include *Mercenaries* (which was awarded an HBO/TCG Award as one of the five best plays in non-profit regional theater), *Lion Dancers*, *Ohio Tip-Off*, and *Stunts*, and he has written two teleplays, *Reel Room* and *My Elvis*. Yoshimura has received John Golden and Shubert fellowships. He is a member of New Dramatists and a writer-in-residence of the Illinois Arts Council.

APPENDIX B
Where to Find New Plays

This piece first appeared as an article in the March 1985 issue of *Dramatics* magazine. It has been revised and updated for this book.

How do you go about finding the entire text of a play excerpted in *Scenes and Monologues from the New American Theater*? (Perhaps you're interested in reading the play, doing further scene work, or—as the playwrights represented in this book undoubtedly hope—producing it at your theater.) Where do you find other plays by writers whose work you liked in this book? Plays by writers whose work, because of space limitations, not included in this book? A tremendous number of exciting new American plays "hit the boards" each year, more than we possibly could have excerpted. What follows is how to find new plays, not just the plays we were able to include in this book, but the whole flood of incisive, rich plays being produced at America's theaters today.

(First, a word of warning for those seeking a complete copy of a play that has been excerpted in this book: The copyright notice for each play, on pages 294–301 of this book, will tell you who should be contacted for information regarding production rights to the plays from which we have excerpted material. Occasionally the playwright or publisher will take enquiries, but in most cases you must contact the playwright's agent. Quite frankly, if you simply want a complete copy of the play to read, or even if you are considering the play for production at an academic, community, or even a semi-professional theater, an agent most likely will not be eager to help you. Most agents simply do not have the time to handle every request for material that comes across their desk. Don't discount contacting an agent, however: if the play is still in manuscript form, not published by one of the publishers listed below, an agent may be the only person who can help you.)

The easiest way to find a new play that, like many of the plays in this anthology, is written by a playwright who is not yet a household name is to try the play publishers. There are two major publishers of new plays in this country, as well as a good number of smaller specialty publishers. For nearly a century Samuel French has been the undisputed leader of these publishers, with Dramatists Play Service the only serious competitor.

The play publishing business is in a bit of a turmoil directly related to changing trends of producing new plays in the United States. It used to be that a new play rehearsed in New York City was polished in an out-of-town tryout run in one or more cities, then came back to New York City for a highly publicized Broadway opening. If the Broadway run was at all successful, then the playwright's agent sold the rights for amateur and "stock"— summer stock usually—production to one of a handful of publishers who bid for the play. The publisher then published an acting edition of the play that they would sell for a nominal fee to school drama groups and community theaters.

These days, Broadway hits are no longer the only source for acting editions of plays. If Samuel French and Dramatists Play Service had to depend on Broadway for plays over the last few seasons, they would have published four or five plays a year at most. Instead they have turned to the new seedbed of new American plays: Off-Broadway, Off Off-Broadway, and regional theaters.

The best place to start looking for new American plays is in the Samuel French and Dramatists Play Service catalogues. Many of the plays excerpted in this book have been published by one of these two publishers. Their catalogues are available by writing or calling:

Samuel French
45 West 25th Street
New York, New York 10010
(212) 206-8990

Dramatists Play Service
440 Park Avenue South
New York, New York 10016
(212) 683-8960.

Other smaller publishers work with a specific portion
of the market or are just getting started. These, like the
theaters that produce new plays, can be found all over
the country. If you're serious about reading new plays
(and if you're an actor, director, teacher, writer, or de-
signer you ought to be), you should get on the mailing
list for all of these publishers so that you can start discov-
ering what a rich variety of plays are presently available.
Some of the smaller play publishers include:

Broadway Play Publishing
357 West 20th Street
New York, New York 10011

Sergel Publishing
5706 South University Avenue
Chicago, Illinois 60637

Baker's Plays
100 Chauncy Street
Boston, Massachusetts 02111

Dramatic Publishing Company
4150 North Milwaukee Avenue
Chicago, Illinois 60641

West Coast Plays
P.O. Box 48320
Los Angeles, California 90048

Aran Press
1320 South 3rd Street
Louisville, Kentucky 40208.

If you've gone through the catalogues of the publishers listed above and still can't find a play you're interested in, try one of the non-profit playwriting workshops and service organizations that work with many of our country's playwrights. These organizations vary widely in the services they offer. The three biggest, The O'Neill National Playwrights' Conference, the Theater Communications Group (TCG), and New Dramatists, have facilities set up to get the new work they are involved with out to interested individuals and theaters. New Dramatists has a national New Plays Library that includes scripts not only from New Dramatists' playwrights but from workshops around the country. Programs and workshops set up to work with writers include:

The O'Neill National Playwrights' Conference
305 Great Neck Road
Waterford, Connecticut 06385

Theatre Communications Group
355 Lexington Avenue
New York, New York 10017

New Dramatists
424 West 44th Street
New York, New York 10017

Playwrights' Center and MidWest Playlabs
2301 Franklin Avenue East
Minneapolis, Minnesota 55406

Bloomington Playwrights' Project
409 South Walnut
Bloomington, Indiana 47401

The Sundance Center Playwrights Laboratory
19 Exchange Place
Salt Lake City, Utah 84111

Bay Area Playwrights' Festival
Box 1191
Mill Valley, California 94942

Padua Hills Playwrights' Workshop Festival
c/o L.A. Theater Works
681 Venice Boulevard
Venice, California 90291

American College Theater Festival New Plays
John F. Kennedy Center for the Performing Arts
Washington, D.C. 20566

Atlanta New Play Festival
Box 14252
Atlanta, Georgia 30324.

Another possibility for finding the latest plays are the various theater journals and magazines, which often excerpt or publish in full compelling work by America's most avant-garde playwrights. These publications include: *American Theater* and *Theater*.

Bookstores specializing in theater books often have play catalogues. Below are addresses of two of America's most comprehensive theater bookstores, both of which offer complete and formative catalogues:

Applause Bookstore
211 West 71st Street
New York, New York 10023

(Their annotated play catalogue is available for $3.00, including postage and handling.)

Drama Book Shop
723 7th Avenue
New York, New York 10019

(The price of their new annotated play catalogue was still to be determined as this book was going to press.

Being on the Drama Book Shop mailing list includes monthly notification of recently published theater books and plays.)

Another possibility is to contact the playwrights' union, The Dramatists Guild. The Dramatists Guild not only provides services to playwrights but is the only real advocacy organization playwrights in the United States have. Almost all the writers represented in this book are Dramatists Guild members and can be contacted through The Dramatists Guild's office:

The Dramatists Guild
234 West 44th Street
New York, New York 10036.

If you try to contact a producer or theater organization mentioned in the introduction to the various scenes and monologues in this book, remember that these people usually are busy producing more new plays, so don't expect an immediate response to your inquiry. Most of them will get back to you. TCG publishes a directory of addresses and phone numbers for many of the not-for-profit theater organizations in the country. New American Library has recently published *The Playwright's Handbook*, which has detailed lists of commercial and not-for-profit producers and theater organizations.

And speaking of New American Library: A minor revolution is taking place in the publishing world; more and more new plays are being published not only in acting editions but in quality reader's editions. In Europe reader's editions have been a tradition for years. Often European theatergoers will buy a copy of a new play in the lobby of the theater where they have just seen a performance of it. They'll take the play home, read it, contemplate its impact, its resonances, discuss its ideas with friends over coffee, all of which makes for a much richer theater experience. It's wonderful to see that New American Library, Bantam, Grove Press, Random House, Fireside Books, Putnam, and Scribner's, among other publishers, are getting involved in printing quality editions of the latest plays from the American theater. (Yes, some are even available in the lobby of the theater after the performance.) As an example, below are a sampling of New American Library's recent play offerings:

Agnes of God, by John Pielmeier (Plume)

Biloxi Blues, by Neil Simon (Plume)

The Collected Plays of Neil Simon, Volume I: Come Blow Your Horn; Barefoot in the Park; The Odd Couple; Plaza Suite; The Star-Spangled Girl; Promises, Promises; Last of the Red Hot Lovers, by Neil Simon (Plume)

The Collected Plays of Neil Simon, Volume II: Little Me; The Gingerbread Lady; The Prisoner of Second Avenue; The Sunshine Boys; The Good Doctor; God's Favorite; California Suite; Chapter Two, by Neil Simon (Plume)

Fences by August Wilson (Plume)

The House of Blue Leaves and Two Other Plays: Bosoms and Neglect, Landscape of the Body, by John Guare (Plume)

A Lie of the Mind, by Sam Shepard (Plume)

Ma Rainey's Black Bottom, by August Wilson (Plume)

The Normal Heart, by Larry Kramer (Plume)

Nuts, by Tom Topor (Plume)

Plenty, by David Hare (Plume)

A Raisin in the Sun/The Sign in Sidney Brustein's Window, by Lorraine Hansberry (Plume)

Wild Honey, by Anton Chekhov, translated and adapted by Michael Frayn (Signet Classic)